Praise for Gloria Murphy's previous novels of suspense . . .

The Playroom

"ENGROSSING." —*Publishers Weekly*

"MURPHY HAS A WAY OF CREATING CHAR-
ACTERS AND SITUATIONS THAT BUILD SUS-
PENSE IN THE READER . . . It takes talent to do
that and Murphy has all the talent needed for the
job." —*Houston Home Journal*

Bloodties

"A REMARKABLE, FAST-PACED STORY . . .
POWERFUL." —*The Bookwatch*

"AN INGENIOUS PLOT FUELED BY SKILLFUL
WRITING . . . Murphy neatly directs her narra-
tive to its satisfying resolution."
—*Publishers Weekly*

Nightshade

"A TERRIFYING JOURNEY of murder, abuse,
and betrayal. An exciting read." —*Rave Reviews*

"A PAGE TURNER . . . GALLOPS ALONG AT
A FRENZIED PACE." —*Vancouver Sun*

DOWN WILL COME BABY

Gloria Murphy

JOVE BOOKS, NEW YORK

This novel is a work of fiction. Names, characters, places and incidents are either the product of the author's imagination or are used fictitiously. Any resemblance to actual events, locales, organizations or persons, living or dead, is entirely coincidental and beyond the intent of either the author or publisher.

This Jove Book contains the complete text of the original hardcover edition. It has been completely reset in a typeface designed for easy reading and was printed from new film.

DOWN WILL COME BABY

A Jove Book / published by arrangement with Donald I. Fine, Inc.

PRINTING HISTORY
Donald I. Fine edition published February 1991
Jove edition / May 1993

All rights reserved.
Copyright © 1991 by Gloria Murphy.
This book may not be reproduced in whole or in part, by mimeograph or any other means, without permission.
For information address: Donald I. Fine, Inc.,
19 West 21st Street, New York, New York 10010.

ISBN: 0-515-11098-1

Jove Books are published by The Berkley Publishing Group,
200 Madison Avenue, New York, New York 10016.
The name "JOVE" and the "J" logo
are trademarks belonging to Jove Publications, Inc.

PRINTED IN THE UNITED STATES OF AMERICA

10 9 8 7 6 5 4 3 2 1

Dedicated with love to:
Alexandra Leigh and Camden Frank

Thank you:
Laurie Gitelman,
Rennie Browne and Dave King

DOWN WILL COME BABY

PROLOGUE

Robin spread her purple and black striped comforter over the mattress, kicked her foot locker underneath the bunk, climbed onto the cot and waited. Judging by the slow progress of the unpacking and bed-making, she'd give it maybe twenty more minutes until they'd all be told to form a circle and take turns introducing themselves.

Having gone through the same corny routine since the age of eight, five summers in a row, Robin had no wish to go through it again. It was Daddy who had made the decision that she spend another summer at Camp Raintree in Maine. She looked around the cabin—not one familiar face. Maybe the other old-timers had hated camp as much as she did. But they hadn't had to come back.

The girl at the next bunk chewed on her bottom lip as she adjusted, readjusted, tucked and retucked a crisp white bed sheet on her mattress. She was short and super thin—two thirds the size of Robin—with silky yellow-blond hair that barely reached her earlobes.

"You don't have to be so fussy, you know," Robin said. "They never check."

The girl looked up at her, blinking.

Robin pulled down a corner of her comforter. "See, no sheet."

The girl gave her a thin smile, smoothed away a nonexistent wrinkle, then folded a pink knitted afghan dotted with tiny yarn rosebuds onto the foot of her bed. Robin studied the girl's open foot locker: a yellow slicker raincoat, a pair of boots and a foldup umbrella were lined up in one side pocket; a sealed plastic bag of toiletries, a tall bottle of multivitamins, a red diary with a gold-leaf emblem, and a white leather-covered book in the other. Every item of clothing between the two pockets was pressed, sectioned and stacked.

"Did you pack yourself?"

The girl nodded.

Robin got off the bunk, pulled out her foot locker and opened it.

"Me too."

The girl stared at the shorts, shirts, sneakers, and underwear all jumbled together, then put her hand to her mouth and giggled.

"Don't you get *killed* for being so messy?" she asked when she finally stopped.

Robin shook her head. "Uh-uh. Eunice mostly lets me do what I want."

"Who's Eunice?"

"My mother. I call her Eunice."

"And she doesn't get mad that you call her that?"

"She likes it. It makes her feel like we're girlfriends."

After a few minutes of silence, the girl said, "I love your hair, it's so long and beautiful. I wish mine were that long."

"Easy to fix," Robin said. "Just let it grow. Anyway, you have a way better body than me. I'm fat."

"No you're not, I'm just too skinny."

"Who's says?"

"Mama. She's always trying to fatten me up."

Robin stood up on her bunk, stretched her arms in a slow flowing motion and raised her voice.

"Skinny is in, don't you know, mo . . . thah dahling?"

"You're strange," the girl said.

Robin jumped down. "I know, I come from Eunice. And she's just about the strangest person I've ever known."

"What happens now?" Amelia whispered as she squeezed into the circle next to Robin.

"They go clockwise. When they get to you, just say something dumb about yourself."

"Like what?"

"I don't know, anything."

"Oh God, I'm so nervous."

"Why?"

She shrugged. "I don't know, I just am. Whenever I'm called on in school, I choke up so I think I'm gonna pass out. And I never raise my hand, even if I know the answer. Look at my hands." Amelia held out her damp palms. "They're already all yucky and sweaty."

"Just don't think about it," Robin said.

When her turn came, she said, "I'm Robin Garr, I hate this cornball camp, but my father made me come back another year." Then she turned to Amelia. "And this is my good friend, Amelia Lucas. She's so neat and organized you could die. Watch out that she doesn't try to alphabetize your underwear."

It was the fourth night in camp when Robin finally convinced Amelia to sneak away from the cabin after lights out. With her duffel bag slung over her shoulder and a flashlight in her hand, Robin led the way out of the cabin and into the night.

"What about bed check?" Amelia whispered. "Suppose they see we're gone?"

"I told you, they don't check again till midnight."

When they came to the path leading into the woods, Amelia stopped.

"Uh-uh, no way am I going in there."

Robin reached out, took her hand and tugged on it.

"Come on, trust me, there's nothing to be scared of. Wait'll you see where we end up. It's neat."

Amelia allowed Robin to lead her into the woods. When they finally came out in the open again, they were at the opposite end of the half-mile lake. Beyond the large sandy clearing were miles of thick mountainous forest.

"A few summers ago, we had an overnighter here," Robin said as she kicked off her sandals, sank onto the sand and stretched her long legs so that her feet reached the water. Then, in a whispered voice to Amelia, "Behind us, way deep in the woods, there are hundreds of dead bodies buried."

Amelia, who had just gotten down beside Robin, pushed up onto her knees.

"You're lying, right?"

"Uh-uh, it's for real. And they say when it gets real dark at night you can hear—"

"Stop it, Robin!" She glanced behind them. "You know, I wouldn't mind going back now. This place is really giving me the creeps."

"Relax, will you?"

"Are you kidding? If my heart were beating any harder, you'd hear it."

"Okay, no more talk about dead bodies—I promise."

"Thanks." Amelia sank down on the sand.

"I sure wouldn't want to ask you to a sleepover party," Robin said. "I once went to a party where we had this weird séance and one girl—"

Amelia started up again.

"Sorry, I forgot."

Amelia screwed up her face, her eyes blinking.

"Go on, you might as well say it. I'm a world-class wimp . . . and everyone at camp already knows it."

"Well, maybe we can do something about it."

"Like what?"

Robin stuck her hand in her duffel bag and pulled out a fifth of vodka.

Amelia sucked in her breath. "Ohmygosh! Where did you ever get that?"

"Eunice."

"She gave it to you?"

"Well, not exactly. But she always leaves her bottles laying around the house."

"And you drink them?"

"Actually I only tried it a few times. But once you get used to the taste, it's not half bad." Robin put the bottle to her lips and took a swallow. Then she wiped the nozzle with her sweatshirt sleeve and handed the bottle to Amelia.

"Oh, no, Robin, I couldn't."

"Come on, just try a little bit."

Amelia looked at Robin, then at the bottle, then back to Robin.

"Okay," she said. "Only a little, though."

Within an hour, with their jeans legs rolled to their knees, they were dancing around, splashing each other and shooting pebbles at a boulder jutting out of the deep water.

"Why do you suppose some people get real nuts when they drink?" Amelia asked.

"I think the trick is not to drink beyond a certain point,"

Robin said as she washed the grit off her palms, splashed Amelia one last time, then made an escape onto the sand. "Of course, Eunice usually loses that point."

They both started to giggle, then Amelia ran up to Robin and dropped into the sand. She reached up, grabbed Robin's arm and tugged her down beside her.

"Tell me some more about Eunice, she sounds so wild."

"She is. You should see her outrageous get-ups, flowing silk pants outfits, braided silk ropes banded around her forehead, huge clunky earrings, things like that. She's even got a big rose tattoo on her butt."

"No way! Is she pretty?"

"Gorgeous with a super body. And she says and does anything she wants."

"God, do I envy her, I'd love to be just like that. Your father must be crazy about her."

"I guess he is. He forgives her for a lot of things. Like she practically never cooks or cleans or sews or does anything boring like that."

"Then who does it?"

"When it gets to the point where you need a shovel, Daddy calls someone in to clean. And we eat a lot of takeout. I practically grew up with a Burger King mashed in my baby bottle."

Amelia let out a shriek and let her head fall into the sand.

"Oh, I love it, I absolutely love it!" They both went into a fit of giggles.

"Don't you ever get sick eating like that?" Amelia asked later.

"Get serious." Robin swung out her arms and threw out her chest. "Does this body look sickly to you?"

Amelia looked at her, and they again burst into laughter.

"I could only dream of having takeout every night,"

Amelia said finally. "But still, what about your father? It must drive him nuts."

"Oh, he complains sometimes."

"Why do you suppose he puts up with it?"

" 'Cause he loves her, I guess. Lots of guys go nuts over Eunice."

"Does your father get jealous?"

"Mostly he doesn't know about the other guys."

"You mean, she really does mess around with them?"

"If I tell you, swear you'll never breathe a word."

Amelia sat up and crossed herself. "Swear to God, hope to die."

"Well, once when I came home early from school, I walked into her bedroom and found her and a man, both of them naked as jaybirds."

Amelia's mouth dropped. "Ohmygosh! And you didn't tell your father?"

Robin shrugged. "I thought about telling, but then I decided I couldn't."

"Why?"

"Lots of reasons. Eunice starts blubbering all over the place whenever I threaten to squeal about some bad thing she does. I know it's retarded of me, but I always end up feeling sorry for her."

"What's another reason?"

"I guess I just don't want to hurt Daddy." She checked her watch, then jumped to her feet.

"Uh-oh, bed check's in thirty minutes. Better get going."

Amelia stood up, stumbled, then giggled as she caught her balance. "Let's come back tomorrow night, okay?" she said.

"If we do, I get to ask stuff about your folks."

Amelia hesitated a moment, then said, "I guess, if you really want to. But they're boring next to yours." She watched Robin cap the vodka bottle and stuff it back in her duffel bag.

"Is there enough left for next time?" she asked.

"Don't worry, when this runs out we've got two more."

Just before they got back to the cabin, Amelia turned to Robin and laid her hand on her arm.

"I really had the best time tonight," she said. "I know what we did was no big deal for you—you've probably done things like that hundreds of times. But it was for me. All of it . . . the sneaking away, the talking, then getting so silly I thought we'd for sure bust. It was like I suddenly felt so free . . . And I'm not sure what I owe it to—you, Eunice or the vodka."

It was something Amelia never would have done three weeks earlier, but after a few nips from the vodka bottle, she stripped off her shorts and underpants, flung them onto the sand, then raced into the water wearing only her blue camp T-shirt.

"Come on, swim time!" she called back to Robin.

Robin just danced around on the sand . . .

She hadn't drunk as much as Amelia, but still she felt buzzed. So it took a moment for her to connect the screams in her ears with the thought of someone in trouble . . . Amelia was in trouble!

Robin fumbled on the ground for the flashlight, then scanned the beam of light across the lake. She spotted Amelia about forty feet off shore, arms flailing against the water, mouth screaming Robin's name. *Oh my God, how long had she been calling her?*

Robin dropped the flashlight, raced to the water and dived in. As soon as she hit the water, her mind began to clear, and she swam the distance in two minutes. But when she went to scissor Amelia's neck from the back like they had taught her in junior lifesaving, Amelia whirled around and swung her arms out, slamming Robin's face and head as her hands searched to find something to hold.

"Stop it!" Robin screamed, but Amelia was too terrified to hear her. She pounced on Robin's back, her arms clasped tightly around her neck, and dragged her down. Robin fought to free herself, but it was as though strong tentacles were pulling her deeper and deeper.

It wasn't until she swallowed the second mouthful of water that Robin stopped the struggle. Then slowly, slowly, wrapped together like sleeping Siamese twins, they began to drift upward. When they finally broke the surface, Robin took a gasp of air, turned, swung her arm out and bashed Amelia in the face.

Amelia let go.

CHAPTER 1

UNPACKING . . . Robin hated it. It reminded her of camp and death and Amelia. Besides which, as much as she couldn't stomach being around Eunice these days, she hadn't really wanted to move. It was Daddy who'd insisted on leaving Eunice and their big house in Andover and moving into this five-room apartment in Boston.

Daddy said the main reason for the move was to get him closer to his downtown law practice. Eunice said the reason was to keep her from seeing her kid, and though Robin seldom agreed anymore with her mother, she thought Eunice was probably right.

No one mentioned the other reason: the nightmares and screaming fits that would tunnel unexpectedly out of some dark, diseased place in Robin's head. According to what she'd overheard her pediatrician tell Daddy, the best shrinks available were in Boston.

Robin balanced the heavy carton of toiletries on the bathroom sink and examined the narrow bathroom: faded pink tiles, high arched ceilings, a four-legged tub with a circular plastic-curtained section for the shower and, behind

the toilet, a tall window that faced the next apartment
building. It was still pouring, had been since early that
morning when the moving van showed up.

She went to the window and looked down at the dark wet
street. Except for a few Sunday travelers in slow-moving
cars and one woman—her face hidden by a blue umbrella—
walking briskly toward the building's back entrance, the
street was deserted. Robin felt a chill go through her. It was
gloomy in Boston in the rain, gloomier, she supposed, than
out in the suburbs. But who knew for sure, maybe the gloom
was really coming from inside her head.

Looking up, she spotted a boy peering at her through
binoculars from a window of the apartment building next
door. She yanked together the grungy brown plaid curtains
left behind by the former tenants, then went back to the sink
and opened the medicine cabinet. She sniffed. The aroma of
Eunice's jasmine cologne still clung to the bottles and cans
and tubes she took out of the cardboard carton. The same
smell that had soothed Robin when she was little, assuring
her that Mommy was nearby. But those were the days when
Robin believed in Eunice—now all that was changed.

The box finally unpacked, Robin shut the cabinet door
and stared in the soap-streaked mirror, still not at all friendly
with the strange, thin, twelve-year-old girl who stared back:
the sooty circles underscoring her dark eyes now more
noticeable than ever, thanks to the grotesque haircut . . .
Probably it was when she hacked off all that long, lovely
hair that Daddy decided she had totally flipped.

But she hadn't—at least, she didn't think she had at the
time. It was just a gesture for Amelia. And though Robin
wasn't at all sure Amelia even knew about the grand
gesture, if by chance she did, she would understand.

Robin felt her back begin to tingle again—like dozens of
tiny bugs crawling across her skin. She turned, raised the

bottom of her shirt, looked over her shoulder and studied her back carefully in the mirror. How many times had she looked in the past few months? Fifty?

Still nothing there.

With all the chaos of moving day, Marcus Garr still managed to pick up a few bags of groceries. Now that he had finally made the break from Eunice, eating habits would be the first order of change: no more sandwiches or pizza eaten in front of MTV, no more foam containers and plastic forks, no more microwaved mozzarella sticks.

He wasn't naive enough to think that a couple of home-cooked meals would take care of his daughter's emotional problems, but structure, normalcy and some positive role modeling would certainly be a good place to start. Of course, he'd have to be careful not to pressure Robin too much at this point either—if he could only hit on that right balance. These days—more often than not—he had the uneasy feeling of trying to edge a Buick into a parking spot sized for a Volkswagen.

He opened a box of spaghetti, rummaged through the packed carton for a pot, into which he emptied the box's contents, then after filling the pot with water, set it on the gas burner.

"Daddy, what about school?"

He turned. Robin was leaning against the refrigerator, watching him. Since August she had dropped considerable weight, so much so that her once sturdy build now bordered on frailty. He had thought she would be back to her old self by now—time was the universal wonder drug, wasn't it? But her old self seemed as far away as ever.

"What about school, baby?"

"When do I start?"

He began to unpack the new stoneware dishes, stacking them alongside the glasses in the bottom cupboard.

"We'll take care of that on Tuesday. Meanwhile, what about those linen boxes? I spotted a closet in the hall—"

"It's done. Daddy, did you see the bathtub? It has legs."

"Those relics are collector items, you know."

"I like my bathtubs without legs."

"No big deal . . . we'll hack 'em off."

"That sounds like something Eunice would say."

"And more than likely she'd do it, too."

A few moments of silence, then, "You miss her, Daddy?"

He paused, setting a stack of bowls on the counter. "Well, if you mean am I having second thoughts, the answer is no." He gestured to the remaining cartons on the kitchen floor. "Hey, why is it I'm the only one busting my butt in this operation?"

"I *hate* unpacking."

The telephone rang, and Marcus reached for it.

"Hello?"

"Well, well, my sweet, only the first day at the new place and already a phone installed. I *am* impressed."

Marcus sighed. "How'd you get the number here, Eunice?"

"I called your old line and got referred. Why, didn't you intend to give it to me?"

"In time. Well, what do you want?"

"Oh, nothing. I just peeked out the front window and thought to myself, what a dreary day for a move. So I said, go ahead, Eunice, call Marc and Birdie and give them a little cheer-up."

"Thanks, but no thanks."

"Did you know you left your umbrella behind? That big ol' ratty black one you like so much."

"Look, I'm busy, Eunice. I'm not up for this."

"For what, sweetie?"

"The amenities, the 'let's talk about nothing' routine."

"Okay, so let's talk about something. Remember how I used to lie in bed and listen to you prepare those elegant summations of yours? God, your voice would wire me so, I'd reach over and—"

"Stop it, Eunice."

"Or those camping trips in the woods? Make love till we couldn't move, then lie under—"

"Dammit, enough!"

"Okay, press the button . . . there you go, I've stopped. I'll get right to the point. I want you and Birdie back here."

"Nice chatting with you, Eunice , but as I said I'm busy and—"

"Wait!" she cried. "Listen, Marc, a twelve-year-old girl needs a mother, think about that, why don't you."

"I have. Too bad you've never managed to cut it as one."

"And what parenting award did you suddenly swoop up? In any event, while you're basking in your newfound fatherhood, don't count mother out."

"Do what you have to do. And be sure to tell the judge that it wasn't my vodka your daughter had stashed away in her duffel bag."

"Piss on you and your dreary court system. If I want to get to Birdie, I'll find myself a more scenic route!"

Marcus hung up. He turned toward Robin, but she was no longer there. The phone rang again, and he grabbed it up.

"Oops, seems I forgot to hang up," Eunice sang. The phone slammed in his ear.

He took a deep breath, then headed into Robin's room. She was lying belly down on the bare mattress.

"You okay, baby?"

Silence.

"I let her suck me in. I'm sorry."

Robin shrugged, then swiped away a tear with her shirtsleeve. Tears came easily these days, and the worst part was, he never knew what the tears were about.

"Did you want to talk to her?" Marcus said. "I didn't think to ask, but if you do . . ."

"Uh-uh. Not tonight."

"Well, if you change your mind—"

"Sure." She turned to her father, then took a deep breath. "Sometimes she gets stuck in my head, Daddy. Right inside my head and she won't get out."

"Eunice?"

"No. Amelia."

A pause, then, "Sometimes it's just a matter of will-power, baby. Refusing to give in to thoughts like that. You know what I'm trying to say?"

"I guess."

"Look, there's a doctor here in Boston who might be able to help."

"A head doctor?"

"A psychologist. Her name's Mollie Striker. We have an appointment to see her tomorrow."

"Why'd you wait so long to tell me about it?"

"I figured the less time you had to worry about it, the better."

Silence, then, "What will she do to me?"

"Nothing, just talk to you."

"About what?"

"It's up to you, whatever you want to talk about."

"Suppose she wants to lock me away?"

"Come on, why would she want to do that?"

"I don't know, but let's suppose she does?"

"I wouldn't let her. Look, baby, it doesn't work that way. She's just going to try to help you figure out what's bothering you, why those bad thoughts won't go away.

That's it, I promise.'' After a few moments of silence, he said, "Hey, you hungry? I've got spa—" He stood up, sniffed, then raced toward the kitchen with Robin watching him disappear out of the room.

A matter of willpower?

Yep, just like a diet. Don't eat it, and you won't get fat. Don't think it, and you won't get crazy . . .

Hardy, har, har har . . .

By the time Robin walked into the kitchen, Marcus had given up on the blackened pot and had tossed it along with a massive gluey chunk of pasta into the trash. Now, with a dull knife, he was scraping off the sticky white foam that covered the top of the stove and burner.

"Interesting," she said. "What do you call it?"

"Beginner's luck."

"Guess you'd better get a cookbook."

"I've got a better idea. How about you signing up for a home economics class as one of your electives?"

"I hate home ec. They make you eat everything you make. I once saw a girl run out of class and barf all over her notebook."

Marcus tossed the knife into the sink. "Not exactly a sterling testimonial for the teacher. Well, look, if you don't like the idea, forget it, okay?"

The phone rang again and Robin moved toward it, but Marcus put out his hand to stop her.

"Don't. Let it ring."

Robin stared at it.

"Nine times," Marcus said. "I say she'll let it ring nine times. What's your pick?"

"I'll say eleven."

Twenty-two rings later, it stopped. "You'd think by now we'd know not to try to second-guess Eunice," Marcus said. "So what do you say, first night at the new apartment, we go out to dinner?"

"It's still raining."

"Okay, your call. Get wet or we're stuck with eggs."

Marcus had just put on his trench coat when there was a knock at the door. Robin opened it. The woman standing there had pale skin and heavy-lidded dark blue eyes that made her other features fade into the background. Beneath the bangs of her short straight brown hair was a small raised beauty mark. She was taller than average, slim, and wore a crisp pink paisley print dress. In her hands she was carrying a foil-wrapped casserole dish that she held out to Robin.

"Just a little something for dinner," she said. "I know how hectic things can get on moving day."

Robin backed away, then stared, one hand over her shoulder scratching her back.

The woman lifted up the foil, three sprigs of parsley at each edge.

"All fresh ingredients, no preservatives, excellent reviews," she said.

Was Robin just going to stand there all night? Marcus came forward, took the dish and handed it to Robin.

"Why don't you put it in the kitchen," he said; then, to the woman, "That's very kind of you."

"It's lasagne. I hope you like Italian."

"One of my favorites." He put out his hand. "Marcus Garr," he said, then nodded toward Robin, on her way to the kitchen, "And my daughter, Robin. I take it we're neighbors?"

The woman smiled, the dimple that appeared in her cheek giving her the fresh look of a college coed rather than a woman he'd guess to be at least thirty.

"Dorothy Cotton. Second floor, apartment twenty-two. I

couldn't help noticing the moving van out front. I hope you won't think I'm a snoop.''

Marcus smiled. ''On the contrary, I think you're a godsend. I just dumped out some peculiar-looking stuff that by all rights should have been spaghetti. In fact, we were about to go out.'' He waved an arm toward the kitchen. ''It looks like there's plenty there, why don't you come in and join us?''

''Oh, no, I'm one of those cooks who samples the progress along the way. I assure you, I've had my fair share. Just enjoy it—and welcome to the neighborhood.''

She turned and hurried across the hall to the elevator. Marcus closed the door, smiling, then turned to Robin whose attention was absorbed by the closed door.

''Robin?''

Silence.

''Earth to Robin—are you there?''

Robin looked at him.

''Something significant I missed in that conversation?''

She shook her head.

''Then what?''

''Just wondering—is that what they call a Welcome Lady?''

''I guess so.'' Then, looking toward the casserole dish, ''It smells terrific.''

''Better watch out, it might have arsenic sprinkled in with the grated cheese.''

Marcus looked to see if she was serious—he couldn't always tell these days. Deciding she wasn't, he said, ''I tell you what, you get the plates and forks on the table, and I'll be the guinea pig.''

He was right—the lasagne *was* terrific—but Robin ate very little of it, saying she was sick to her stomach. Maybe he should have waited till tomorrow to tell her about the doctor.

The telephone rang four times after dinner. Marcus finally took it off the hook, hoping no one from the office would try to reach him. At about nine o'clock after Robin went off to her bedroom, Marcus did some more unpacking. And some remembering.

Both of them inside one sleeping bag, no tent. "No silly ol' tent to block out that glorious full moon," Eunice had said. What about rain—or worse, animals? Christ, there were bears and wildcats in these woods. "Now, now, sweetie, be big and brave. If a bear dares to show his face, buy him off with the cheddar and Oreos. But not the pistachios, Marc, save those for us." Right, Marcus—keep the food close, within reach.

Silence in the night, except for the wind rustling the tree branches and little animal feet scurrying through the woods . . . and her breathing beside him, her chest moving in synch with his. Her dark, dark eyes looking into his, turning him inside out and any which way she wanted . . .

Right—like a shitload of putty. Better to think about the more recent times when the scent of the jasmine couldn't cover up the stink of the whiskey and those clever remarks had suddenly become little more than a drunk's ramblings.

The doorbell rang; he reached over and pressed the intercom.

"Who is it?"

"Special delivery for Marcus Garr."

He pressed the buzzer, then went to the door and waited.

"You Mr. Garr?" the boy said, stepping off the elevator.

"Right." He took a long, thin box from the boy's arms. Flowers? The box was the right size for long-stemmed roses, but heavier. He closed the door, then opened the box:

his ratty black umbrella . . . and a note. "Give my Birdie a kiss."

As he tossed the umbrella and Eunice's note on his bedroom dresser, a sound like a distant siren came from the other bedroom, then suddenly the siren was screeching right through the room! The cries became words, rushed and garbled and unintelligible, except for one word clearing through the others: *Amelia!* Marcus raced to Robin's bedroom, sat her up and shook her.

"It's me, baby . . . It's Daddy!"

And as suddenly as they had begun, the screams stopped, her body going limp. Marcus held her against him, rocking her and running his fingers across her short uneven hair until her breathing quieted. He looked down at her: she had fallen asleep in her jeans, on a mattress with no sheet or blanket.

He gently lowered his daughter to the pillow, then hunted her striped comforter out of a box and spread it over her. Finally he leaned down and kissed her forehead: she twitched, her arm jerking forward and striking him on the side of his head.

Dear God, this doctor had better know what she's doing.

CHAPTER 2

ROBIN swallowed hard, then not daring to move anything but her eyes, scanned the alien environment where she had awakened. Had Amelia crawled inside her head in the darkness and mashed all her brain cells? Finally she remembered where she was and let out a deep sigh.

She swung her feet to the floor, then went to the tall, bare bedroom window that looked out on Commonwealth Avenue. Though the pavement was still wet, the rain had stopped, leaving the air thick, steamy and gray. She saw people, lots of people, walking down the sidewalk on both sides of the street. No kids, they were probably already in school. She did pick out a woman in a khaki trench coat and brown shoulder bag walking briskly down the block: the Welcome Lady.

"Robin, breakfast!" Marcus called out.

Today was the doctor's appointment.

"Robin?"

Robin watched the Welcome Lady until she rounded the corner, then turned briefly to the mirror, lifted her shirt and glanced at her back. Finally, dropping the shirt, she headed into the kitchen.

Barefoot, hands stuffed into her jeans pockets, she stood in the doorway. Both breakfast plates had two pieces of toast, cut into triangles and oozing butter. Her father dumped some crispy-looking scrambled eggs in the center of each plate, then poured some orange juice into short glasses.

"Not bad for a first try, huh?" he said.

"I don't eat breakfast, Daddy."

"I know, but there's always a first time. Give it a try."

She sat down, picked up her O.J. and took a sip.

"What time's the doctor appointment?"

"Eleven. It's only nine now, so relax."

"When are you going back to work?"

"Tomorrow, once I've registered you in school."

"You know, breakfast wouldn't be so bad if it didn't come first thing in the morning." She began to stand up. "Maybe I'd better go and shower now."

He put a hand on her shoulder and pressed. "Eat first. Come on, give the chef a break. Just try a little."

Come on, just try a little bit.

Oh, no, Robin, I couldn't.

Come on, Amelia, just try a little bit. Just try a little . . . Just try.

She scooped up some egg with her fork.

"I notice you slept in your clothes last night."

She shrugged.

"You do have pajamas, nightgowns—whatever—don't you?"

"Yeah, I guess somewhere in my dresser. Why?"

"How about using them? And when we get back from the doctor's appointment, I'd really like it if you made up your bed. I noticed last night you slept on a bare mattress."

"Why so picky all of a sudden?"

"I'm not trying to pick, baby. I'm just trying to introduce us to a few of the niceties of life. That's all."

"What's the matter, you think I'm uncivilized? I do wash, you know. I even brush my teeth once in a while."

He reached out and put his hand over hers.

"Look, I don't mean to be critical. Honest. It's just that Eunice never got on you about things like this."

"You never did either."

He finished his juice, then set down his glass.

"Maybe we should forget I said anything. If the bed-making is a big deal, I'll do it myself. What I don't want is for you to get upset over this."

"Hey, Daddy, do you think if I wear PJs and make my bed right and learn all those niceties, no one will think I'm crazy?"

He took a deep breath. "Look, if that's meant to be funny, it's not."

"Good, because it wasn't meant to be. *You* think I'm crazy. Maybe you don't say it, but you think it, I can tell by the way you look at me and the way you talk to me. Like you expect any minute I'm suddenly gonna start foaming at the mouth."

"Robin, no. You're way off. What I think is, you went through an awful time this past summer. It's not easy to watch someone die, let alone a friend. But baby, terrible accidents do happen in life, and we have to learn how to go on from there. To leave them in the past where they belong."

Robin watched the tape in her head begin to unwind, then stop at the place it always got stuck: where Robin bashed Amelia in the face, and Amelia slipped underwater for the last time. *Oops, sorry, Amelia, don't you know, accidents do happen. Time to lock you away in a drawer with my pajamas and forget you ever existed.* Robin looked at her eggs now stuck cold on her fork and knew if she ate them, she'd puke.

As Marcus drove, he pointed out their nearest bus stop and told Robin that the doctor's office was only eleven bus stops down Commonwealth Avenue.

"I'll be going there alone?"

"Well, if you have an appointment after school. That okay?"

She nodded.

"Look, if you don't like this lady, we'll find somebody else. I want you to be comfortable with this."

Robin looked down at the skirt he'd asked her to put on. Probably she would have been more comfortable in jeans and a sweatshirt.

The doctor's office was on the first floor of a three-story brownstone.

The gleaming hardwood floor of the high-ceilinged foyer was partially covered by a madras carpet with blue and green tassels at the edges. There were three well-worn easy chairs, none of them matching, and an old mahogany desk piled high with scrap paper, construction paper, and mason jars holding pens, crayons, colored pencils and scissors. A wooden crate served as a cabinet for a tape deck and tapes, and stacks of magazines and paperbacks were piled on the floor against the wall. No receptionist, but a red-lettered sign instructing them to please wait.

Dr. Mollie Striker was as offbeat as her waiting room. Long thick strawberry blond hair pulled back from her freckled face and knotted loosely at the back of her neck. Jeans, sneakers and a baggy blue-striped buttondown shirt. She invited them into an office that looked like a larger version of the waiting room.

"Have a seat," she said, ignoring her cluttered desk and choosing one of the easy chairs herself.

"I thought maybe we could talk alone first," Marcus said, looking around the room.

"Your call, Robin," the doctor said. "Would you rather we do it that way?"

Robin shrugged. "It doesn't matter."

"Okay, then I'll see you when I'm through talking with your father. But if your nose starts itching, if you need to hear what's being said about you, feel free to come back in."

Once Robin was gone, Marcus said, "I don't see any degrees displayed here, but from what I've been told, your credentials are first rate. What was it now . . . Harvard?"

"Masters and doctorate from Harvard, B.U. for undergrad work. I was on staff three years at Mass General, did two years children's psychiatric at Boston City. It's been two years now practicing solo from home."

"You hardly seem old enough."

She smiled, a nice smile showing white, even teeth.

"Don't let the freckles mislead you." Then, gesturing to a file on her desk, "Mr. Garr, I've gone over Robin's file from her pediatrician, but I'd rather hear the story from your perspective, minus the labels and the medical jargon."

"Okay, Miss Stri . . . I mean, Doctor—"

"Mollie is fine."

Marcus talked for about twenty minutes with no interruption.

"Let me see if I picked up the total picture," Mollie said when he stopped. "You've mentioned the home haircut, loss of appetite, the compulsion of looking at or scratching her back, nightmares, melancholia, withdrawal, disinterest in her former friends, morose thoughts, insistence that

Amelia is in her head, invading her thoughts. Have I missed anything?''

"Anger. Directed at her mother.''

"Any at you?''

"If so, she hasn't shown it.'' Marcus went into Eunice's drinking and the consequences he believed—when added to the camp accident—largely responsible for Robin's troubles now. "It's no wonder she's messed up,'' he said. "Though I don't doubt that Eunice loves Robin, she's done a hell of a job showing it. I just don't think she's capable of real mothering.''

"And you, Mr. Garr?''

"As I said, I'm trying my damnedest to get Robin back on track. Give her some structure, some good examples to follow.''

"But you say Eunice has been unstructured and unreliable for years. And Robin, according to you, has been pretty much on her own.''

"That's right.''

"So where were you all that time?''

Daddy didn't say a word about the doctor until they were on the way home.

"Okay, you talked to her,'' he said finally. "So what do you think?''

"I don't know, I guess she's okay.''

"That's it?''

"Well she didn't push me to talk, that was good. She said she'd like to start off seeing me two times a week and asked me to pick the days. I picked Tuesdays and Thursdays. And she said if I wanted to change days later on, like if I get involved in something after school, I could.''

"You know, Robin, if you don't like her, we can find someone else. There's a lot of good doctors in Boston.''

Robin studied his face. "You don't like her, do you?"

He shrugged. "Hey, look, I'm not the one who has to talk to her. It's your decision."

As Daddy drove past their apartment house to enter the back courtyard, Robin looked up to get a glimpse of her bedroom window from the street. But before her eyes made it to the third story, they stopped: sitting, watching out the window from the room directly below Robin's, was the Welcome Lady.

Who's she looking for?

Take your pick—the postman, the trashman, the ice-cream man, Daddy, you?

Don't be dumb, she's just a regular ol' snoop.

Okay, so you tell me—who do snoops look for?

When they got inside the apartment, Robin went to make her bed. A few minutes later, Dorothy Cotton showed up at the door.

"I don't mean to intrude," she said. "I just thought that if you were done with the casserole dish? It's my only one-quart Corning piece. Now I know that might not sound like a crisis situation to you . . ."

"Of course," Marcus said, smiling. "Come on in while I get it for you. By the way, the lasagne was great. Ever considered packaging and marketing it?"

She laughed. "No, but I'll give it some thought."

She stepped inside and looked around the sparsely decorated parlor, then her eyes followed Marcus to the kitchen. He picked her casserole dish and a scouring pad out of a sink full of dirty dishes and turned on the hot water.

"Oh, don't bother with that," she said. "Really, I can do it."

"You were nice enough to bring it. The least I can do is return a clean dish."

Robin called out from the hallway, "Daddy, you used the only fitted sheet we have."

"Take one of the flat ones."

"I don't know how to—"

"Wing it."

"I couldn't help hearing," Dorothy said. "I'd be more than happy to show her."

He turned from the sink, holding the dripping dish. "Sure you don't mind?"

"Not at all. What's to mind?" She walked over to Robin and the linen closet, picked out two clean sheets and a pillowcase, then headed into the bedroom with Robin following slowly behind.

"How old are you?" she asked Robin.

"Twelve. Why?"

"Well, then, I'd say you're old enough to make up a bed properly." She cleared off the mattress, went to the foot of the bed and shook out the sheet so that it snapped in midair. "Now, it's really very simple. First you center the sheet like this, then you go to the right-hand front of the bed to begin the corners." She demonstrated the triangular folds, tucking them once, then twice beneath the mattress. "I always had the silly fear that if I didn't get those corners nice and snug and unwrinkled, I'd surely go flying off the bed some night."

"Did you ever?"

"Fortunately not. A disturbance such as that might get me booted right out of this building."

Robin was studying her. "Do you have kids?" she asked finally.

Dorothy turned to look at her. "No . . . wish I did, but I don't. Why do you ask?"

Robin shrugged. "No reason."

"But when I was a child I had a sister, five years

younger. I often took care of her. She was dark-haired, pretty, but quite the little rascal. She always hated to do chores . . . like tidying up her room and making her bed." She looked around Robin's messy bedroom, then smiled. "Now, why is it I get the feeling you would have had a lot in common with her?"

When Dorothy returned to the kitchen, Marcus had washed the dirty dishes and left them to drain. He handed her the casserole dish, still damp, then nodded toward Robin's bedroom.

"She hasn't had much instruction in that kind of thing. Thanks."

"My pleasure," Dorothy said. "She's a quick study."

"Look, could I interest you in a drink later? Here in the apartment?"

"I'm not much of a drinker."

"I have a bottle of Perrier. Don't misunderstand, this isn't a pass, it's just that you've been so kind, I'd like to reciprocate."

"There's no need." She smiled, then said, "Oh, why not? I think it would be nice. What time should I show up? And should I bring anything?"

"Anytime after nine. And just bring yourself."

And he really wasn't making a pass. Though she wasn't bad to look at, she definitely wasn't his type. Not that he really knew what his type was. Flashy and flamboyant like Eunice? Hopefully he had outgrown that by now. It's just that there was something refreshing and pleasant and comfortable about Dorothy. And maybe, just maybe, Robin would pick up on a few of her homemaking skills.

Robin looked through her dresser drawers for pajamas; finding none, she went to one of the unpacked boxes still sitting in the corner of the room. She knelt next to it, pulled some clothes out—and that's when she spotted the blue and purple striped bikini. She lifted it out, staring at it.

Remember that?

The swimsuit Eunice found in some boutique.

Not just any swimsuit—the one practically every girl in the whole camp would have killed to wear. Remember the time you double-dared Amelia to wear it, to be brave and show some skin?

Uh-uh, don't remember and don't want to hear.

Sure you do . . . Amelia wouldn't even try it, said she was way too skinny. Instead she picked up that dorky suit, the one she always wore—ruffled dark green cotton with high front and back that buttoned at the shoulders—and headed for the lockers. She wouldn't even—

Are you deaf? I said I don't want to hear!

When?

Maybe never!

Robin balled up the bikini, went to the closet and tossed it way back on the shelf. Then she rushed to her bed, pulled the top sheet from her mattress and stuffed it back in the linen cupboard.

She hated top sheets. She also hated to be compared to the Welcome Lady's little rascal sister.

Dorothy came upstairs at exactly nine o'clock, shortly after Robin went to her bedroom.

"Rat cheese and Ritz crackers," Marcus said as he set down a plate and waved her into a seat on the sofa.

"It's fine," she said.

He poured himself a glass of burgundy, Dorothy some Perrier. "How long have you lived in the building, Dorothy?"

"A few years. I moved in right after my husband died. I

still have a place in the country, but I seldom use it. As much as I enjoy country living, gardening, the fresh air and quiet, it's not the same once you're alone.''

Marcus nodded. ''There's something to say for too quiet, I suppose. Are you employed?''

''No, though sometimes I do wish I had a career. I'm afraid my early training prepared me only for marriage—household engineering, I guess they call it these days. I do volunteer at Beth Israel Hospital two mornings a week. Push the library cart or the gift-shop cart, that sort of thing.''

''Any kids?''

''Your daughter asked me that same question. I'm sorry to say, no.''

''Seems to me you would have made an ideal mother.''

''Oh?''

''You just seem the type . . . I meant it as a compliment.''

''Then I'll take it that way. As I mentioned to Robin, I had a baby sister . . . I adored her, played games with her, read to her, taught her to read before she started kindergarten. I guess you could say I mothered *her*. But she died when she was only eight.''

''I'm sorry.''

''Well, it was many years in the past. Robin actually reminds me a bit of her, though of course she's older. But that's enough about me. Tell me about Robin's mother—what is she like, and am I likely to meet her?''

''I hope not. We're split up. Just recently, in fact.''

''I'm sorry,'' Dorothy said. ''I'm intruding.''

''Oh, no, not at all. In fact, it's good to talk to someone about it.''

''Well, if you're sure I'm not intruding . . . I wasn't going to mention it, but apparently my bedroom is right under Robin's . . . Last night I heard her screaming—she sounded just terrified. Has that anything to do with your separation from your wife? And please stop me if I'm overstepping my bounds.''

''No on both counts. Robin's had some other problems. In any event, she's going to be seeing a therapist.''

''Oh, I see. Well, if there's anything I can do to help . . .''

''Thanks for the offer. I go back to work tomorrow—I have a law practice here in town. Robin's able to take care of herself, of course, but it'll be reassuring to know that if anything comes up—''

''Of course, by all means. In fact, why don't you have her give my name as a contact should there by any problem during school? Illness, whatever. They usually ask for a second name and telephone number for their files.''

''You wouldn't mind that?''

Dorothy smiled. ''To be truthful, Mr. Garr—''

''Please, call me Marcus.''

''All right, Marcus. Well, as I started to say, my life is at times a little too leisurely. Oh, I take my daily walks and do my volunteer work, but I'm afraid that doesn't nearly fill all the hours.'' She shook her head. ''It would be lovely to feel useful again.''

The telephone rang and was picked up on the second ring. A few moments later, Robin stuck her head into the parlor.

''Daddy, it's Eunice.''

''What does she want?''

''I don't know. She's drunk. You'd better talk to her.''

Robin went back to her bedroom and flopped down on the bed. Tomorrow was Tuesday . . . her first day at school. Until this year she had always looked forward to it, but now she dreaded the idea of a strange school and new faces. But then lots of things bothered her nowadays, things like moving and this old apartment building—dumb things that never would have fazed her before.

Then, after school, she would see Mollie . . .

Big deal.

What's your problem with Mollie?

Daddy doesn't like her.

So what?

So nothing.

Why do you suppose he asked the Welcome Lady up for a visit?

Maybe because she makes good lasagne.

Or maybe she's chief consultant for the niceties operation Daddy is running.

Not bad . . . I like that.

So glad. Now let's talk about Eunice's phone call.

Why?

Because I want to, that's why. She says she's gonna get you back, right? She cried and pleaded, right?

Right, right, right. Okay, that's it, we've talked.

Whatever Eunice wants, Eunice gets.

Will you stop that! She was just drunk. You know Eunice . . . she's mostly just a lot of crazy talk, no action.

What about that time she locked you in the closet for a solid hour?

That was a long time ago. Besides, she never did it again, did she?

No.

So relax, okay? Jeez, if I didn't know better, I'd think you were trying to scare me . . .

Marcus found it awkward trying to get rid of Eunice with Dorothy sitting in the next room. Finally he hung up the phone, then took the receiver off the hook.

"Sorry about that, Dorothy."

"Oh, please. You mustn't apologize."

Marcus poured some more wine into his glass.

"I couldn't help overhearing Robin call her mother Eunice. Is she a stepmother?"

"No. Eunice encouraged it when Robin was young."

"Forgive me, but it just seems so . . ."

"Does *peculiar* fit the bill?"

Dorothy shook her head. "Well, Mother isn't a title one would give up easily, I'd think. I give you a lot of credit, Marcus Garr."

"For what?"

"Well, a father bringing up a daughter on his own can't be having an easy time of it, particularly in this day and age. And by the sound of things, Eunice isn't doing much to help matters."

"I haven't exactly won any prizes either."

There—he'd finally said it.

Even after Dorothy left, he kept thinking about his admission. That's what Dr. Striker had been fishing for, and not subtly.

So where were you, Marcus . . . when all this was going on, where were you? Busy making a living, building a career . . . And, worse, staying with the piss-poorest excuse for a mother who ever drank on the job.

So now that he had admitted his guilt, would the young doctor feel triumphant? And what did it matter if she did? Despite the funky office, ultra-casual dress and demeanor, despite whatever accusations she might sling at him from time to time, if Robin took to her—and she seemed to like her—that was enough. Less than three months ago, he had driven a happy, vibrant, confident twelve-year-old to camp in Maine.

Was it asking so very much to want her back?

CHAPTER 3

MAYBE Robin didn't fit in with the kids here, or maybe she just didn't have that same old itch to strike up conversations with new people. So when she took her lunch break at the Kennedy Junior High School cafeteria on Tuesday, she found herself sitting alone, looking around the cafeteria, checking out her new environment and comparing it to Andover.

"It sucks, don't it?" a boy said, setting his tray down a few seats away.

Robin looked at him. He had long stringy brown hair, two gold earrings dangling from his left earlobe, and soft, puffy lips that puckered like a bow.

"I know you," Robin said. "You're the weirdo with the binoculars, right?"

"So what if I am?"

"Keep your peeping eyes out of my windows, that's all."

The boy shrugged his bony shoulders, then picked up his fork. "So you're new here, huh?"

"Gee, you're a real whiz, aren't you?"

"And you're a bitch, I can tell that right off."

"Nah, I'm just crazy. I go to a shrink."

"What d'ya do that's so crazy?"

"Kill people, stuff like that."

"I betcha tell lies, too."

"Sometimes, but I'm not now."

The boy mixed his saucer full of mashed potatoes with the lumpy brown gravy until the whole was a uniform light tan, then pushed the saucer aside.

"Don't you eat?" he said, tearing open one of his two milk cartons.

"Don't you have friends to sit with so you don't have to keep bothering me?"

"Nah. I'm like you, I'm crazy. So I sit at the dork table—in case you haven't noticed, this here's the dork table, where people with no friends sit. Guess you'll be eating here a lot this semester, huh?"

Robin didn't answer.

He raised the milk carton to his mouth, tilted his head back and took a swallow, then said, "Hey, my name's Calvin."

"I'm so happy for you."

"So what's yours?"

"None of your business."

"You do any drugs?"

"Why, you a narc or something?"

Calvin smiled, showing a gaping space between his two front teeth. "Hey, no. Just that if you do, I can get you some. That's all."

Robin picked up her untouched tray, brought it up to the front of the cafeteria and deposited it on the steel rack. Then she went out to the courtyard to get some fresh air.

It was nearly three o'clock when she got to Mollie's office. Mollie sat in the easy chair across from Robin, one stockinged foot tucked under her, the other over the armrest. She munched on a peanut-butter-and-saltine-cracker sandwich.

"Want some?" She held out a plateful of them to Robin. Robin took two.

"So how was first day at school?"

Robin shrugged.

"It's not easy changing schools, particularly once the term has already started."

"I don't mind so much."

"My family moved from Vermont to Massachusetts when I was ten," Mollie said. "It was murder making new friends. I was pretty unsure of myself, and kids seem to pick up on feelings like that right away."

Robin nodded.

"But I guess in the long run, they're easier to figure than adults. Kids may pick on you, but at least you know what they're thinking." She waited for a response and got none. "So what do you think of my super analysis?"

"If I don't like what you say, I'll tell you."

"Okay, I can live with that. You know, Robin, I don't know about you, but it seems to me that I spent a major part of my childhood trying to figure out what adults were thinking. I thought if I could just get a handle on that, I'd solve all the problems in my world. Know your adults so you can please 'em. Not that you'd necessarily do what they wanted, but at least you'd know what to say to keep things cool."

"Do you still do that? I mean, with people?"

"No. The fact is, I don't care much what people think. Somewhere along the line, I realized that it's really not important to impress anyone but yourself. Of course, a lot of people might disagree with me about that, might even consider it a bit egocentric. Know that word?"

Robin nodded.

"Good. Anyway, Robin, I bet your mind is busy right now trying to read me so you can keep things cool between us. So I want to tell you up front, things don't have to be cool with us, they just have to be real."

"Suppose it's real, and you don't like me?"

She shrugged. "Take the risk, it's not such a big one. And where's the tragedy if I didn't like you? I'm only one person out of thousands you'll meet in your lifetime."

Robin studied Mollie for a few minutes, then sat forward in her chair.

"My father doesn't think much of you," she said.

Mollie laughed.

"What's funny?"

"Guess I didn't expect a test this soon."

"It doesn't bother you that he doesn't like you?"

"Only if it bothers you, Robin."

On the bus ride home, Robin thought about that conversation. The most important part of it wasn't Mollie's answer but the way she admitted to Robin that she knew it was a test. Of course, Robin hadn't been quite so up front herself. It did bother her that Daddy didn't like Mollie. But she decided to do what Mollie would do: not worry about it.

The bus let her off at the corner, and she walked the two blocks to her apartment building. Just as she reached the front entrance, Calvin ran up.

"Hey, where'd you go?"

"How'd you know I went anywhere? Spying on me again?"

He shrugged. "I looked for you after school."

"Why?"

"I thought maybe we'd walk home together."

"Find another dork to walk home with."

She opened the door into the lobby, then she used her key to unlock the inside door. She took the stairs and when she reached the second-floor landing, the Welcome Lady was standing there.

"Hi, Robin, how was school?"

"Okay."

"Could I interest you in a slice of apple pie and milk? Tuesday is my pie-baking day. I have a very unusual operation running in my kitchen . . . identify the dessert and you'll know the day of the week."

Robin stared at her, not smiling though she knew a smile was what Dorothy wanted.

"Well, how about it, would you like to sample some?"

"Uh-uh, no thanks."

A few moments of awkward silence, then, "I was a little concerned when I didn't see you come home after school."

"I had someplace to go."

"Oh, of course, your therapy session." Seeing the expression on Robin's face, she added, "I'm sorry, maybe I shouldn't have said anything." She stopped, waiting for Robin to bail her out, but Robin was silent. "I noticed you outdoors with that boy," Dorothy said finally.

"What boy?"

"The one who lives next door."

"Oh. You must mean Calvin. What about him?"

"It's just that . . . Well, that long dirty hair, then those silly-looking earrings . . . He just doesn't look the right type to take up with. But then, it is only your first day of school, I'm sure before long you'll meet lots—"

"I like *him* fine."

With her fingers, Dorothy brushed her bangs aside, then smiling, "Even if you don't want any pie, why don't you come inside my apartment for a minute—there's something special I'd like to show you. Something I think you'd—"

Robin turned and raced up the next flight of stairs, feeling Dorothy's eyes on her back all the way. When she got inside her apartment, she slammed the door shut, then threw the bolt. She didn't like Calvin much, but he was a lot easier to take than the Welcome Lady. She was glad she hadn't written Dorothy's name on the school form like Daddy told her to. And why had he opened his mouth and told Dorothy about therapy? What business was it of hers?

The phone rang.

"Birdie-coo," the voice purred when she picked up the receiver. "Birdie-coo."

Uh-oh, drunk again.

"How's my lil' Birdie doing?"

Silence.

"Not gonna answer me, huh? S'okay by me, I was just sitting here thinking how much I miss you. So thought, why not ring Birdie up and tell her."

Robin could feel her eyes begin to water, so she took a deep breath. When she let it out, her voice came out all whispery.

"What do you want, Eunice?"

"I want you, Birdie. I can't just let mean ol' Daddy take you away from me. What kind a Mommy would I be if I did that? You need me and you belong here with me. Even big twelve-year-old girls need their mommies once in a while, don't they?"

Robin let the phone receiver drop into the cradle, then rushed to her bedroom and slammed the door. She slid down to the floor with her back against the door, her entire body trembling. She had always hated it when Eunice talked in that slow drunken voice and said all those lovey-dovey things. But it had never scared her like this.

The phone rang again—fifteen times, she counted—then

again, twenty times. She sat there, not budging an inch,
waiting for it to stop.

It'll stop soon, Robin.

When?

When the fat lady stands up and sings.

Uh-uh, wrong saying.

It'll do for now. Why am I so scared?

How am I supposed to know that?

Marcus let the number ring for five minutes, and still there
was no answer. It was four-thirty, Robin should be home by
now. He picked up the phone again, dialed the information
operator and got Dorothy Cotton's number.

"Dorothy, this is Marcus Garr. Listen, I hate to put you
out, but I'm a little worried about Robin. It's the first day of
school, and she's not home yet. By any chance have you
seen her?"

"Well, yes, about ten minutes ago. I was a little concerned myself when she was so late."

"She had a doctor's appointment after school."

"I finally figured that out. The thing is, when I did see
her, she was with a boy from school."

"What boy is that?"

A brief pause, then, "Oh, just some youngster who lives
in the next building. Long dirty hair, earrings, that type of
thing. Not a very nice boy, though that's just the impression
I've gotten from seeing him hang around the neighborhood."

"And Robin was with him?"

"I saw them talking in front of the building. I mentioned
it to her, but she seemed a bit upset at my interference. She
also made it abundantly clear that she liked him. Apparently
his name is Calvin."

"I see. Well, where is Robin now?"

"When I left her she was on her way upstairs to the apartment."

"Really? I just called there but got no answer. Listen, Dorothy, could you do me a huge favor and go up and check? I'm probably being silly, it's just that I worry about her a lot lately."

"I'd be happy to. But you know it will make her angry, and I—"

"Please do it anyway. And could you get back to me?"

He hung up, wondering if he should have warned Robin about bad kids and drugs and the usual things parents warn their kids about. From what Robin had told him, alcohol was the only drug she'd ever tried—and surely, after the disaster at camp, she wouldn't mess with it again.

Or was he being naive?

Dorothy knocked a dozen times before she heard Robin's footsteps come slowly to the door.

"Who is it?" Robin asked.

"It's me, Dorothy Cotton."

"Go away, I don't want to talk."

"Your father asked me to come up. Please let me in, Robin."

Slowly the door opened.

"What do you want?" she asked.

"Just to see if you're all right."

"I am."

Dorothy looked at Robin's hand, the hand that lifted to push her hair back from her face.

"Robin, you're trembling. What is it?"

"Nothing. I said I'm okay!"

"Won't you talk to me. I just want to help—"

"Leave me alone!" Robin pushed the door closed.

Dorothy rushed back downstairs, called Marcus and

explained what had transpired, then—accepting that there was nothing more she could do—went back to her portable sewing machine to continue the project she had begun earlier. Having had already basted the tissue-paper pattern to the crisp pink and white polka dot cotton cloth, she lifted her sewing shears and cut out the first sleeve. The blouse would have a round peter pan collar and three-quarter-length puffy sleeves with square pink buttons cinching below the banded elbow—a style that would be perfect for Robin.

And wouldn't it make a snappy outfit with pink corduroy pants and jacket?

Robin picked up the telephone receiver, then put it down; she picked it up again, then again put it down. Finally, the third time, she pressed in the number she had looked up in the directory earlier and now had down to memory.

It was answered with a simple hello.

Robin's breathing was labored. It was hard to talk.

"This is Robin," she said finally.

"What's wrong, Robin?"

"I'm not sure."

"You sound short of breath. Are you hurt?"

"No."

"Are you afraid, is that it?"

"Yes!"

"Of what?"

"Nothing. I don't know."

"Robin, it sounds to me like you're hyperventilating. Now, there's an easy way to fix that. Do you have a paper bag around the house, maybe one of those brown grocery bags?"

"Yeah."

"All right, go get it."

Robin went to the refrigerator, reached up and pulled a bag off the top, went back to the phone. "I've got one," she said.

"Sit down on the floor and put the receiver nearby so you can still hear me."

Robin did. "Okay."

"Good. Now breathe into the bag, Robin. Just hold the bag over your mouth as if you were trying to blow it up, then breathe as naturally as you can. Keep doing it till you feel better, and I'll wait right here."

Robin began to breathe into the bag, and Mollie explained more.

"You see, instead of taking in so much oxygen as you were doing, you're now taking in carbon dioxide, and that will normalize the oxygen in your blood."

About two minutes later Robin put down the bag and picked up the telephone, her hand still trembling.

"It's better now," she said. "But I'm still shaking a lot."

"Robin, try to think back to what made you feel this way."

"I can't, I don't know."

"Is it being alone in a new house?"

"No, I don't think so."

"What were you doing before you started to feel afraid?"

"I was on the phone . . . talking to Eunice."

"Did she say something to upset you?"

"I guess . . ."

"But you're not really sure?"

"No, not really. She said stuff about wanting me back with her. How she needed me and I needed her."

"And how did you feel when she said that?"

"I guess, scared."

"Why would that scare you?"

"Maybe because I don't want to go back."

"Robin, according to your father, you didn't really want to move to Boston."

Silence, then, "I didn't. But I want to be with Daddy."

"I see. Do you think Eunice would try to force you to go back with her?"

"I don't know."

"Did she say anything that would lead you to believe she would?"

"Not really."

"Robin, what you're having is called an anxiety attack. It will run its course, then pass. Have you ever had one of these before?"

"Uh-uh."

"Would you like me to call your father at his office, tell him to go home to be with you?"

Robin looked at the kitchen clock: almost five. "No, don't bother him. He'll be leaving in about an hour anyway."

"Okay. Listen, Robin, I know we're not scheduled to meet again till Thursday, but I'd like to see you again tomorrow. Then maybe we can talk more about these feelings you're having."

Silence.

"Would you like that, Robin?"

"I guess."

"For now, I want you to do something for me. As soon as we hang up, go get a pen and piece of paper and write down what you're feeling. Write anything that comes to mind, no matter how silly it seems to you. And bring it along with you tomorrow."

More silence.

"Will you do that?"

"I don't know if I can."

"Try?"

A deep sigh, then, "Okay."

"Robin, I know it's no fun feeling this scared but what you're going through now could turn out to be very useful to us."

"How?"

"Your feelings are already starting to surface. And once they do that, we'll be able to find out what they are and deal with them. Some people go through their whole lives and never really find out much at all about themselves."

"Like Eunice?"

"Well, I don't know Eunice, but from what I've heard, probably. Perhaps even your father."

"You don't think I'm crazy?"

"Absolutely not. Where did you ever get that idea?"

"I don't know."

"Robin, I promise you you're not crazy. And I don't say things I don't mean."

Robin nodded; she could feel her tremors lessening.

"Maybe I'm not crazy, maybe I'm just plain dumb," she said.

Molly laughed. "Maybe, but I doubt it. Listen, you get busy writing before you feel too good to remember all those juicy feelings. And if you need to, you call back."

No response.

"Promise?" Mollie said.

"Okay."

Forty-five minutes later, Robin was sitting at the kitchen table looking over what she had written. If Mollie didn't think she was crazy after she read all of this, she never would.

Suddenly the door opened.

"Robin!"

"Yes, Daddy?" She looked at the clock. "You're early."

He came next to her and stooped down. "You okay, baby?"

She nodded.

"What's this I hear about you being so upset?"

"Oh, it was nothing."

"Not according to Dorothy."

"Don't pay attention to what she says. She's a busybody."

"Listen, Robin, I asked her to come upstairs and check on you. I was worried. I called here—I must have let it ring two dozen times, and there was no answer. Why didn't you pick up?"

"I thought it was Eunice."

"Why? What made you think that?"

Robin shrugged.

"Come on, what's going on? Has she been bothering you?"

"Well, she did call earlier."

"What did she want?"

"Just to tell me she misses me, wants me to come home. Stuff like that."

Marcus knelt down beside Robin and put his arm on her shoulder. "What is it, are you afraid she's going to make you go live with her?"

"I guess."

"Listen to me, you know what a court order is, don't you?"

Robin nodded.

"Well, I've got one giving me temporary custody of you. And even Eunice isn't about to risk going against a court order—the Commonwealth has pretty stiff penalties for that sort of thing. Sure, she may say so, but you know Eunice—she'll say anything. Anyway, I'm not about to let anything like that happen. Try to have a little more faith in me, okay?''

Robin nodded, then suddenly wrapped her arms around Marcus's neck. He hugged her back, then gestured to the paper on the table in front of her.

''What's this, baby?''

Robin pulled away, scooping up the paper.

''It's nothing.''

''Looks like something to me. Want to show me?''

She folded the paper, then started backing up toward her bedroom.

''It's nothing you'd be much interested in. Just boring old school stuff.''

The telephone rang; Marcus went to pick it up, and Robin disappeared into her room.

Though Marcus considered talking to Robin about that neighbor kid, Calvin, he decided against it. When he was a kid, he'd resented the hell out of his folks trying to tell him who to hang out with. Not that he wouldn't put his foot down if he had to, but one conversation didn't make a friendship. Why risk upsetting Robin when he might only be creating a situation where one didn't exist?

He went into her room, happy to see she was doing homework. Not that he'd ever been concerned about her on that account.

''What do you say we eat out tonight?'' he said.

She looked up. ''What happened to all that talk about home-cooked meals?''

''Ah-hah. The thing is, we're going to have one, and I suspect a good one.''

Robin tilted her head.

''That was Dorothy on the phone earlier. She invited us down to her apartment for dinner.''

She turned back to her book. "I don't want to go."

"Come on, baby, I've already accepted."

"Don't I even get a say?"

"Sure you do. But would you do it for me this one time?"

Robin sighed, rolled her eyes, then nodded.

"And it wouldn't hurt for you to apologize to her for being so rude this afternoon. Keep in mind, she was concerned for you."

"She doesn't even know me, what right does she have to be concerned?"

"Robin, she's a lonely woman, her husband's dead, she's got no kids of her own. I don't find it so strange that she takes an interest in her neighbors." He headed out of the room. "Half an hour? And could you do us the honor of dressing for the occasion?"

"Oh, is it formal?" she said. "Maybe I ought to wear my black satin strapless with the slits up the sides."

"Okay by me. But if you can't find it, a skirt will do fine."

Robin unfolded the paper from the zipper compartment of her purse and read it over again, wondering if she shouldn't put something mean in it about the Welcome Lady. Dorothy Cotton could have found a stray cat to mess with, but no such luck—it had to be her and Daddy. She supposed she could understand the part about Daddy: he was dark, with a strong jaw and one of those big beak noses that would have looked wicked bad on a lady but not on a man. Definitely the type ladies looked at.

But why her, what did Dorothy want with her?

CHAPTER 4

THE minute Robin stepped into Dorothy's apartment, her back started to itch and her stomach—assaulted by combined smells of disinfectant, pine room freshener and food—went queasy. Dorothy, of course, was the perfect hostess, greeting them at the door with a cheery smile, then showing them to the sofa in the living room. The coffee table was set with cocktail napkins, a pitcher of tomato juice, a bottle of wine, glasses, coasters, carrot and celery sticks, and a dish of round, puffy pastries with some mysterious filling sealed inside.

Daddy tasted a pastry while Dorothy stood by, waiting for a verdict. Meanwhile Robin studied the room: lots of books and pictures and plaques embroidered with fortune-cookie sayings. Dining-room cabinet shelves lined with little china statues and flowery dishes. Light blue drapes sashed back at their middles to show lacy white curtains underneath. Chairs covered with small printed blue, white and yellow squares. And a vase holding silk flowers—handmade, probably—on a little table under a cuckoo clock.

"You'd never guess it was the same apartment as upstairs," Daddy said. "It looks so . . . homey."

Dorothy sat in the chair opposite them and folded her white hands with the short, smoothly trimmed nails in her lap.

"Actually, most of the furniture itself I picked up at second-hand stores. It's the trimmings that spiff it up and pull it together to make it work. You'd be surprised at the difference a few little touches can make."

Uh-oh, is she going to offer a course on interior decorating?

"I'm glad to see you're feeling better, Robin," she said.

Though Robin had no intention of apologizing, she did manage to fake a smile.

"I never got to ask you about school," Daddy said. "How was it, baby?"

"Okay."

"What about the classwork, how does it compare to Andover?"

"Mostly it's easier, I guess."

Daddy put his arm around her shoulder. "Robin likes to play it down, but the truth is she's a straight-A student."

"Now really?" Dorothy said. "That's quite wonderful. You must be proud of her."

"Very proud."

"When I was a youngster, I used to be very good at mathematics—I like things that have neat, precise answers. The social sciences had so many confusing possibilities, it would make my head spin. Not to brag, but when I graduated from high school I had the second highest math average in my class."

Do we applaud now, or can we save it till after dinner? And, oh yes, where do I go to barf?

"Did you ever think of pursuing it further?" Daddy said.

"Well, there wasn't much money for college. Besides, like most girls in those days, I was eager to get married and settle down. My husband used to say the only real advantage I got from my math ability was being able to negotiate a nifty bargain. It comes in handy when I'm buying antiques."

"So you're one of those people who drives all over town on weekends, looking for flea markets and garage sales," Marcus said, smiling.

"Now, don't you start poking fun at me, too."

Now, Daddy, why would you want to do that?

"You mean, others do?"

"I'll admit there have been some. If you've never been bitten by the bug, you tend to put collectors into the same category as pack rats. We're not like that at all."

No, Dorothy, all this junk couldn't really fill up six moving vans, could it?

"Hey, if I was thinking that, I take it back."

"The truth is, I haven't been to a flea market or a garage sale in ages—but you'd be surprised at some of the things people discard, not even knowing what they're worth. At one house, I picked up a music box sitting in a pile of children's toys that dated back to the mid-seventeen-hundreds. I had the mechanism repaired to get it to play but basically it was in excellent shape."

"What's the tune?"

" 'Ring Around the Rosy.' "

"Really? The nursery rhyme dates back that far?"

"That it does. In fact, the song was made up by children in fourteenth-century Europe—the words are actually a description of what happened to the population during the plague. The Black Death."

Daddy sat forward. "Ashes, ashes, all fall down," he said. "The people falling down dead in the streets?"

"Exactly. And since pleasant smells were supposed to ward off the plague, people took to carrying flowers around in their pockets. A pocket full of posies."

"Where did you ever come up with all of this?"

"Once I found the music box, I got interested enough to do some research. Since then, I picked up a number of other music boxes that play nursery rhymes and dug into their origins as well. All quite interesting." She looked at Robin. "If you hadn't run off this afternoon, that's what I was about to show you. But if you'd like to see them now, I'd be glad to—"

"No. I mean, thank you, but I don't think so."

"Why not?" Daddy asked.

"It's all right," Dorothy said. "They'll be here another time. Dinner won't be for another twenty minutes, Robin. Why don't you have a broccoli-cheese puff?"

Broccoli and cheese . . . mystery solved.

"Uh-uh, I'll wait."

"I think we need to fatten you up some—what do you say to that, Daddy?"

"Doesn't sound like a bad idea."

Robin's stomach lurched. She jumped up from her seat and cupped her hand over her mouth.

"Where's the bathroom?"

"Is she all right?" Dorothy asked Marcus when he returned to the living room.

"She was feeling sick to her stomach but she says it's passing. She just wants to stay put for a while."

"Do you think she's ill? We could call a doctor."

"No, I don't think it's physical. Some people get headaches when they're upset, Robin gets stomachaches."

Dorothy put her palm to her chest. "I hope she didn't find all that talk about the nursery rhyme too depressing."

"I doubt it. The thing is, you never know what's going to set her off these days." Marcus sighed. "It always seems to go back to what happened this summer."

"You mean the separation from Eunice?"

Marcus shook his head, then sat forward on the sofa, shoulders hunched, elbows resting on his knees.

"Well, you know Robin's in therapy . . . maybe I ought to give you a clearer picture of the problem."

"Please."

"You see, I sent Robin to camp this summer. It was a good camp, she'd gone there before . . ."

Dorothy nodded.

"Well, this time she didn't want to go. Maybe I should have listened to her, but I was determined to get her away from Eunice— even if only for the summer."

"From what I gather," Dorothy said, "it certainly seems like a reasonable decision."

"Not as things turned out. When Robin went off to camp, she had several bottles of vodka stashed in her duffel bag."

"Where in the world did she—oh, no!"

"Oh, yes. Eunice. As you probably figured out from her phone call last night, she has a drinking problem. She's had it for quite some time, and it's been getting worse in the last year . . ."

Dorothy waited.

"It's not like she was drunk full time, nothing like that. It was just something she did occasionally. At least, it was occasional in the beginning." He looked up at Dorothy. "Believe me, I'm not trying to make excuses for her or me. It's just that it never dawned on me that Robin would get hold of the booze, much less decide to try it out herself."

"At twelve years old. It's mind-boggling, Marcus."

Marcus paused. He had started it, so he might as well keep going.

"It seems she and this Amelia had been sneaking away from their cabin after lights out and nipping at the vodka. Well, this time, the other kid decided to go for a swim in the lake. I guess she'd drunk more than she realized. In any event, she couldn't make it back to shore. And though Robin tried—desperately—she wasn't able to save her. She drowned that night."

"Oh, dear God," Dorothy whispered.

"An accident, of course. It was Robin who brought the vodka, but most kids experiment with alcohol at one time or another. What she doesn't seem to understand is that she was as much a victim as her friend."

"Except the other child died."

"Right. And Robin's killing herself with the guilt."

Dorothy was quiet for a few moments.

"It's tragic," she said finally. "To bear so heavy a burden at so young an age. What does her therapist say about all this?"

"So far, not much. Robin went into treatment only this week. At this point, I'm just hoping I picked the right doctor."

"Tell me, Marcus—what was it that upset her earlier today?"

"Oh, that. It was Eunice harassing her by phone. From what I was able to get out of Robin, Eunice's determination to get her back scared the wits out of her."

"Eunice can't make her come back, can she? I mean, legally?"

"No way. With Eunice's track record, she's not about to get custody. But she's clever, she knows how to intimidate, just what buttons to push. All of which is the last thing Robin needs now."

"Can you stop her?"

"I intend to try, but Eunice is a fighter—at least she is when she's sober."

Dorothy reached out, hesitated, then laid her hand on Marcus's hand. "What can I do? I mean to help Robin get through all this."

He shook his head. "You know, Dorothy, you're really something."

"Why do you say that?"

"You don't know either me or my daughter that well, I just told you a story that clearly shocked you, and your response is simply, 'What can I do to help?'"

"Am I overstepping my bounds? If I am—"

"Not at all. It's just kind of rare nowadays to find people who want to put themselves out. And to answer your question, I don't really know what you can do. I'm not sure what *I* can do—I've been sort of treating Robin with kid gloves for the last couple of months. Sure, I'd like to see you two be friends, I think my daughter could learn a lot from a woman like you. But she's not exactly open to friendships these days . . ."

"Never you mind. If I have to, I'll work at it. I'm one of those eternal optimists—a thing may be difficult, but never impossible. You know, Marcus, I'm glad you told me all of this. At least I understand now why Robin is so sullen and standoffish. And here I was beginning to think it was personal."

"Good—because it *is* personal!"

Marcus and Dorothy turned to find Robin standing in the hallway. Marcus stood up.

"Robin, that was uncalled for. I'd like you to apologize to Dorothy. Right now."

"Why should I when it's the truth?" With that she ran past them, out the apartment door and up the stairs.

Marcus looked at Dorothy.

"Please, Marcus, it's all right. Go to her."

• • •

Her face burning, her heart hammering, Robin sat on the bed waiting for what she knew was about to come. Her bedroom door was closed, but when Daddy got there, he pushed it right open. Robin backed up against the headboard, hugging her pillow to her chest.

"Robin, how could you do that to her?"

"What about what *you* did? You had no right to tell her all about me as if I were some kind of freak!"

"Robin, nobody thinks you're a freak. I don't, Dorothy certainly doesn't—"

"Then she's either stupid or she's a liar!"

"Or just a kind neighbor who wants to be your friend."

"Well, I don't want to be *hers*."

"Why?"

"Because I don't like her. If you like her so much, *you* be her friend."

"I am her friend. That's why I was talking to her."

"Yeah, about me!"

"So who do I talk to about you, about what happened at camp? Eunice? My clients? My parking attendant, maybe my barber? You know, you're not the only one going through this shit!"

Tears started down Robin's cheeks.

"What about me, Daddy?" she said, her voice cracking. "Did you ever think of talking about it to me?"

That's when the telephone rang and Daddy went to answer it. Though Robin held her pillow snugly over her ears, she could still hear him shouting at Eunice before he slammed down the phone and retreated into his own bedroom. So what that he didn't come back to her room? He didn't know what she was talking about anyway.

You ought to tell him to dump weird ol' Dorothy.

Can't, won't . . .

Why not?

You heard him, he needs someone to be his friend.

So call Rent-a-Friend.

Not funny.

Okay, so what're you gonna do—hop on the Welcome Wagon?

No. But I suppose I could be nicer to her.

Oh, give me a break.

I don't have to like her, just be nice. It won't kill me.

Yeah, says who?

It happened at the dork table the next day, when Robin again refused to tell Calvin her name.

"I told you mine," he said.

"So what, did I ask you?"

"What's the big deal?"

"No big deal. I just don't give out my name to everyone who asks. That's all."

Suddenly he grabbed her purse off the table.

"Hey, give that back!" She stood up and snatched at it.

"Who's gonna make me?" He swung the purse away from her and dug his hand inside.

"Calvin, I'm serious, give it back!"

He pulled out Robin's Feelings paper. "Sure, but first I'm gonna find out your name."

"All right, I'll tell you, okay? It's Robin, Robin Garr. Now give that back to me!"

He dropped the purse on the table but kept the folded paper.

"I dunno, Robin Garr. Maybe I got myself somethin' real good here. All kinds of secret stuff, maybe."

"Don't be dumb, it's a homework assignment."

"Then you won't mind me lookin' at it, will ya?"

As he unfolded the paper, Robin sprang for it. Laughing,

Calvin spun away from her and ran. She chased after him, but his legs were longer. He ran around the tables, through the cafeteria, out into the courtyard. He was backed up to the chain link fence when Robin pounced, dragging him down, punching at his face.

"Okay, okay, you can have it back."

She raked her stubby nails down his cheeks, then grabbed a handful of his long hair and yanked.

"Ouch—shit! Hey, you're crazy. I said you could have it!"

"What's going on here?" a voice shouted over Calvin's. Robin could feel firm hands pulling at her but she whacked them away.

"Young lady!"

Another pair of hands joined in, pulling Robin off Calvin. Calvin, panting, a hand pressed against his bleeding face, got up off the ground.

"Now suppose you tell me what's going on here."

Robin stared past the angry woman to the giggling students who had formed a circle around them.

"Are you going to answer me?" The teacher looked at Calvin. "You're hurt, go to the nurse."

"Naw, I'm okay." He wiped blood from his face with his shirtsleeve and pushed back his hair.

"To the nurse, I said. Now!"

"Hey, it was my—"

"If I have to say it again, it'll be two weeks' detention. Your choice."

Calvin looked at Robin, then turned and pushed his way through the crowd.

"Now you," the teacher said, taking hold of Robin's arm, "come with me."

Robin pulled away to scoop up the crumpled paper and stuff it into her purse.

"Give that to me!" the teacher said.

Silence.

"Are you deaf or are you simply defiant? I said, give it to me!"

Robin refused to surrender the paper, even when she was marched to the principal's office, to the bald, pig-eyed principal who now stood over her blowing his garlic breath in her face.

"If you don't give up that paper, I'll have no choice but to suspend you."

"I told you, it's private."

"I looked through your record, Robin. I must say, top honor students do not normally get into this kind of trouble. Now, I'm trying to take into consideration that you're a new student here, but you're making it difficult for me. Apparently the boy you assaulted was not only willing to return your paper but never once struck you back."

Silence.

The principal turned away from her, went to his desk and pressed the intercom.

"Have you reached the father yet?"

"According to his office, he's at court, in trial. They're not certain what time he'll be back."

"I see. Do we have another contact?"

"Yes, we do. A neighbor, Dorothy Cotton."

"No!" Robin said. "I don't know anyone by that name. That must be a mistake."

The principal looked at Robin, then pressed the intercom again. "What exactly is going on here, Muriel?"

"I don't know. When I made up the file on this girl yesterday morning, I saw we didn't have a second contact listed so I called Mr. Garr at his office. He's the one who gave me this name and number."

"Call Mrs. Cotton," the principal said. He glared at

Robin with his beady eyes. "Lying, fighting, rudeness, and defiance don't go over well in this school, Miss Garr. I suggest that you use this two-week suspension period to think seriously about your future here."

The Welcome Lady was at the school office within fifteen minutes. While Robin sat in the lobby, Dorothy went into the principal's office. When she came out, she led Robin through the parking lot to her dark blue station wagon, then stood by the passenger door until Robin climbed in and buckled her seat belt. It wasn't until she got into the driver's seat herself that she spoke.

"I'm sure you know it's wrong to fight like that, Robin."

Robin looked down at her sneakers.

"I know you've had your problems, serious problems. But violence is no way to solve them. If you stand your ground, speak firmly without raising your voice, you'll get the respect you deserve."

As Dorothy drove toward home, Robin clung to the promise she had made to herself the night before. She wouldn't be rude to Dorothy, she wouldn't even answer her back. Besides, it wasn't Dorothy's fault that the school had called her in, was it? And what she was saying right now wasn't so bad. If Daddy were here, he'd probably be saying a lot worse.

But the more Dorothy talked, the more Robin had to fight down the urge to scream and never stop. Maybe Daddy's first impression of Mollie was right, and she didn't know so much after all.

Maybe Robin really was crazy.

Noting Robin's pallor and silence on the drive home, Dorothy ended her gentle reprimand well before they pulled into the courtyard parking lot. Though it was Dorothy's intention only to walk Robin to her apartment, then leave her to digest the wisdom of her words, at the doorway she detected a hesitancy in the child's step and a look in her eyes that told Dorothy she didn't want to be left alone.

So Dorothy came inside to sit in the parlor, and Robin seemed secretly relieved to have her there. She mumbled something about being tired, went first to the bathroom, then headed into her bedroom for some much-needed rest.

It was only a small step at best—in fact, she doubted the child even realized it herself—but Dorothy could sense that she and Robin had finally begun to make a connection.

When Robin got to her bedroom, she crawled under the covers and shut her eyes.

What?

I don't know what. Just bad feelings, I guess.

Because of the fight?

I doubt it.

Then what? Because of her?

I told you, I don't know!

Scared? Mad? Both?

All, nothing, everything, zero. Tired, I think just tired. Now let me sleep, will you?

Dorothy didn't plan it that way, it just happened. She went into the bathroom to relieve herself, then spotted Robin's purse open on the floor next to the sink. Robin had battered that boy to get the crumpled paper back, then refused to hand it over to the principal—obviously, whatever was written on it was important to Robin. Surely something Marcus should know about, perhaps even Robin's therapist.

She leaned over, pulled out the paper and smoothed it on her lap. And read:

My Feelings
by Robin Garr

It would be easier if my feelings were made up of clay because then I could see them and touch them and maybe even twist their shapes to fit what I want them to be. Instead, they're made out of nothing but they count for everything. It figures, doesn't it?

The big thing these days is being scared. Being scared of everything and being scared of nothing at all. I no longer dare to let the sleek black cat rub against my leg because its fur has gotten stiff and wiry and can make me bleed. And the plastic Wizard has steel jaws that can crush my bones to powder.

Want some more, Mollie? Okay. The old, ugly building I live in bolts its doors at dark and traps me deep inside . . . And new people aren't really new people but old people dressed up in new clothes. Amelia knew all about being scared—maybe I did too, but I never let on. Even to myself.

Sometimes I wonder if it isn't Amelia creeping into my head at night, bringing along her bogeyman to see if I can figure out how to get rid of it. Or freakier yet, maybe it was Amelia who won the underwater fight, and Robin who really drowned. A real crazy thought, huh?

Not long after Dorothy had dried her eyes and rinsed her face, the phone rang. She rushed to answer it, hoping it was Marcus.

"Is Robin Garr there?"

"Who is this, please?"

"This is Mollie Striker. Who am I speaking to?"

"Mrs. Dorothy Cotton."

"I see. Do I have the right number?"

"Yes you do, but Robin is resting now. Can I take a message for her?"

"Are you family?"

"No, no, a neighbor. A friend."

"Robin had an appointment with me this afternoon. Thirty minutes ago."

"Is this her therapist?"

A pause, then, "Yes, it is. Look, is something wrong there?"

"Well, there was some trouble in school. Fighting. Robin got punished with a two-week suspension."

"I see. Would you put her on the phone? I'd really like to speak to her."

"Well, she seemed very tired. Perhaps it's not a good time to bother her."

"Why don't you go to her room and ask *her*."

"I really don't think—"

"Please, Mrs. Cotton. I'm just asking you to see if she's awake. If she is, she may want to talk to me."

"Well, if you insist." She put down the phone, tiptoed to Robin's room, and cracked open the door.

Robin immediately shot up to a sitting position, startling even Dorothy.

"Oh dear, I'm sorry to wake you. I tried to tell her you were resting, but—"

"Who . . . what?"

"Your doctor's on the phone. She insisted I come in."

Robin ran her fingers through her hair. "The appointment, I had an appointment."

"It's not important, you can always make another for tomorrow. I'll tell her if you'd like."

Robin shook her head, then got up and went to the kitchen

phone, Dorothy following behind her. She lifted the receiver and turned to face the wall.

"Hi, Mollie. Guess I fell asleep."

"According to your neighbor, school wasn't much of a hit today."

"No, I guess not."

"Want to tell me about it?"

Robin glanced at Dorothy, then turned back to the wall.

"I'm really too tired to talk now."

"Okay, not a problem. But I'll be expecting you tomorrow, right?"

"Yeah, sure."

"Even if you're tired, Robin."

"Okay."

When Robin went back to her bedroom, Dorothy again tried Marcus's office, but he was still unreachable. She looked around the kitchen—she couldn't think of leaving Robin, not when she so clearly wanted company. So as long as she was here, what better way to soothe her nerves than to tidy the kitchen and start dinner?

It all began when she went to put the dishes away—why, everyone knew that china and glassware went in the upper right-hand cabinet, didn't they? Apparently not. When Dorothy opened the china cabinet, she found a clutter of canned goods, jars, pots, pans . . . She had no choice but to clear out the shelves and begin from scratch.

Ninety minutes later, Dorothy stood back and sighed as she examined the fruits of her labor. She had scrubbed the shelves, lined them with heavy-duty foil, stacked and arranged the various contents in order of size, use, and/or food type and washed and polished the appliances.

Of course, she was weary, that went without saying. But work never scared Dorothy—in fact, aside from playing her music boxes, work was her therapy. The cold tension she'd felt earlier over Robin's misery had vanished.

Of course the serenity would go—it always did. But fortunately there were always more tasks, more things that needed doing. She looked at her watch—goodness, didn't time fly? Before she knew it, Marcus would be home, Robin would be awake . . .

And dinner hadn't even been started.

CHAPTER 5

THE first thing that hit Marcus when he came inside the apartment was the incredible smell . . . Pot roast, stew? He stood in the kitchen doorway a moment, watching Dorothy stir the big pot on the burner. He walked closer to sneak a look inside: meatballs—likely made from those pre-packaged hamburgers that were in the freezer—with carrots, potatoes and onion in a tomato gravy. He looked around at the kitchen: none of the usual mess, not even dirty dishes.

"What's going on? The kitchen looks—"

She jumped, then spun around. "Shhh, not so loud."

"I didn't mean to scare—"

"That's okay," she said softly. "But Robin's sleeping. I stayed because . . . well, she seemed not to want to be alone."

"Why? What happened?"

"Don't worry, Robin is fine." She led him to the living room, then handed him a glass of wine as he took off his trench coat. "The school office called me at noon today.

71

Naturally they tried to reach you first, but you were unavailable."

"Reach me about what?"

"Well, it seems Robin got into a fight with a boy. Apparently he'd taken a paper of hers and she was trying to get it back. But by the time the teacher spotted Robin beating the boy up, he was willing to return the paper—in fact, he was pleading for mercy."

Marcus bit back a smile.

"I'm afraid it's not as amusing as it sounds. She scratched up the boy's face, made it bleed, even pulled a chunk of hair from his head. For all of which she was hauled off to the principal's office and told in no uncertain terms to hand over the paper."

"And she wouldn't?"

"Absolutely refused. So the principal saw no alternative but suspension."

"He *suspended* her? For how long?"

"Two weeks."

"That's just ridiculous—it's not like she was harboring drugs or stolen goods. If this paper was simply personal, he really had no right to demand it. A lengthy suspension is way out of line."

"Well, so was Robin."

"Okay, so she gets punished for fighting, but two weeks' suspension, considering she was fighting to get back something that was hers, is pretty severe." He paused. "What the hell was in this paper that she couldn't show it to him, anyway?"

Dorothy considered for a moment, then said, "I think you'll have to ask her that yourself."

Marcus remembered the paper Robin had refused to show him the day before.

"I don't want to push you into anything you'd rather not

do, Marcus, but in view of the problems she's been having, I do think you ought to read it.''

He nodded. ''You're probably right. When she gets up, I'll ask to see it. Then tomorrow I'll call the principal, have a talk with him. How upset is she?''

''Very. She missed her doctor's appointment today. The therapist called here while she was sleeping.''

''What appointment? Her appointment's tomorrow.''

Dorothy pressed her lips together and shook her head.

''Not according to her therapist, and not according to Robin. She came to the phone to apologize to the doctor. Marcus, I think it's important you keep in touch with what's going on with Robin outside the home. These are tough times for her, and the one thing she shouldn't feel is alone.''

He lifted his wine and took a swallow. Dorothy was right. He had left Robin on her own too often in the past, and that was going to have to change. In any event, he was grateful to Dorothy. She not only had a good deal of compassion, she had insight, another rare commodity. And though he hadn't been here for Robin today, at least *she* had been.

After Dorothy left, Marcus took the tray she'd prepared and carried it to Robin's room. He held the plate of stew close to her nose.

She opened her eyes. ''Daddy?''

''How'd you guess?''

She rubbed her eyes, then sat up.

He fluffed her pillow and doubled it up against the headboard. She sat back, and he put the tray on her lap.

''You made this yourself?''

''Do you have to ask?''

Robin studied the plate. ''Look at those meatballs.''

''What's wrong with them?''

"All the exact same size. Looks like they rolled off a conveyor belt."

"That's what they're supposed to look like. Come on, eat some."

Robin stabbed one with her fork and scowled. "Did she tell you what happened in school, too?"

"I think I've got the picture. Who was the victim?"

She shrugged. "Just a kid."

"Apparently a pretty sorry kid."

"I guess. You're not mad about the suspension?"

"I'm not real happy about it. But considering the crime, the punishment seems a bit excessive. I'll call the school tomorrow, have a talk with your principal and see if it can be cut down. Meanwhile, what about this paper?"

"What about it?"

"What was in it?"

"Just some stuff I wrote."

"About what?"

"My feelings."

"Oh. Well, can I see it?"

She shook her head.

"I can't, Daddy, please don't ask me. Besides, some of it's so weird, I don't even know what it means."

"Okay. But if you don't show it to anyone, who's to help you figure it out?"

"Mollie."

So Robin was going to show it to her therapist. Hey, that was good, wasn't it? Still it hurt him to know his daughter trusted a woman she'd met only days ago more than she trusted him.

Not having to get up for school the next morning, Robin slept till after nine, then lazed around on the living-room sofa, watching reruns on cable. At ten-thirty there was a loud rapping at the door.

"Who's there?"

"Birdie, it's me."

She swallowed hard. "Eunice? What're you doing here?"

"Dammit, save the amenities for later. Now open the door and let me in!"

Robin cracked the door, and a wave of jasmine rolled in. Eunice's soft-curled, inky black hair was swept back from her face, showing off her super high cheekbones, baby-smooth skin, and big brown eyes. She was dressed in black tights, a red satin shirt with wing sleeves, a black suede tasseled vest and heavy gold earrings. And on her feet, fluffy red bedroom slippers.

"Well, do I collapse right here in this dark, miserable hallway or do I get asked in?"

Robin's eyes went from the red slippers to the bags in her mother's arms. She opened the door and stepped back.

"Ignore the slippers. I stubbed my big toe against the fridge—you know, the damn bolt that juts out and snags one of us at least once a month. It was barefoot or these."

"How'd you know I wasn't in school, Eunice?"

"I buzzed the school to see when you'd be dismissed, having in mind a grand entrance somewhat later in the day. Can you imagine my delight to learn my Birdie was already a school celebrity? Canned and only the second day of classes—like in kindergarten, when you put the toad in the pitcher of apple juice. You ought to check to see if two days isn't some kind of record."

"I got into a fight."

"I trust you had a reason, so spare me the gory details. Come look." Eunice dug into one of the bags and pulled out a large box. She took off the lid and removed a smaller box, opened that one and pulled out a yellow marbled ball the size of a plum.

"What is it?" Robin asked, keeping her distance.

"You're supposed to hold it." She reached out and dropped the heavy ball into Robin's palm. "Now close your eyes tight, grip it real hard and feel it. Really feel it, deep inside your gut."

Robin didn't close her eyes. "What's it supposed to do?"

"It's supposed to put you in a deep relaxed state. It seeps out all that nasty ol' tension."

"Where'd you get it from, a guru?"

"Now, now, let us not be cynical." She took the ball back and tossed it into Robin's purse, sitting open on the floor. "It'll be there if you need it." She opened another bag and took out a cardboard container and a plastic spoon.

"What's that?"

"What does it look like?"

"A Pistachio Crunch sundae?" Robin sank onto the carpet, removed the cover and poked at the ice cream with the long-handled spoon. "With Reeses' Pieces."

"There you are, at least your mind hasn't gone totally. And you don't have to inspect it, I watched them make it personally—no accidental walnuts."

Robin had taken only a few tiny tastes of the ice cream when Eunice jumped up and headed toward the bathroom. Robin heard a loud bang, left the sundae on the floor and ran. When she reached her bedroom, Eunice was tossing clothes from the dresser into the suitcase open on the floor. Then she headed for the closet.

"What're you *doing*?" Robin shouted, chasing after her.

"Taking you home with me!" One arm swept the room. "God, will you look at the size of this hole—not even enough space to dance."

"I don't dance anymore."

"Well, it's no wonder—the place is a dump!"

"It's my dump, Eunice. I'm not going."

"You'll do what I say, I'm your mother!"

"Daddy has custody—"

"Screw Daddy. Dammit, I should never have let you go off with him to begin with. You're scared of your own shadow. You're skinny, pale as a gravestone, and you look like shit!"

Robin ran to the kitchen phone and started to dial the law office number. Eunice followed her, yanked the receiver out of her hand, then lifted the telephone and smashed it to the floor.

"You're crazy!" Robin shouted, backing into the hallway.

"So are you!" Eunice screamed, tears washing mascara down her face. She rushed toward Robin but Robin backed off further, crouching on the floor against the wall.

"Oh Birdie, I didn't mean it, I swear I didn't mean it. God, don't you know how much I love you?"

"Stay away!" Robin shouted.

"What is it, what in hell is *wrong* with you?"

"Nothing's wrong with me. Just stay away."

"What's going on here?" a voice behind them said.

Both Robin and Eunice turned.

"Who the hell are *you*?"

"I'm Dorothy Cotton, a neighbor and friend. I heard the commotion from my apartment. What are you doing to Robin?"

"None of your fucking business."

"Abuse is everyone's business. I know who you are, and I think you'd better leave."

Eunice walked toward Dorothy. "Oh, do you now?"

Dorothy took a deep breath. "If you don't, I'll go downstairs and telephone Marcus."

Eunice looked at Robin, crouched in the hallway corner, then marched up to Dorothy. Robin's muscles tensed as Eunice raised her hand and smacked Dorothy's face.

"I'll be back, Birdie." She grabbed her purse from the sofa, then spotted the sundae on the floor. She drew back her slippered foot and kicked it, sending the melted green ice cream, Reeses' Pieces, and marshmallow cream all over the carpet.

"See, Birdie, no nuts!"

The door slammed. Robin looked down at the floor; Dorothy looked at Robin not making a sound. But Robin could feel her eyes drilling in. Finally Robin glanced up at Dorothy, trying to unscramble the expression on her face.

Is she scared? Mad? Embarrassed? What?

Uh-uh, none of the above.

Then what?

Hard to tell. Maybe she wants a thank you. Maybe she wants an apology for Eunice.

Whatever it is she wants, don't give it to her.

I did wish for someone to shut up Eunice and get her out of here.

Yeah, but did you really want your wish granted by the ol' Welcome Lady?

Though Robin would rather have stayed in bed, at two o'clock she got dressed and headed out for her appointment with Mollie. When she arrived, she took the paper out of her purse and handed it over.

"Don't read it till I leave," she said.

Mollie glanced at the crumpled paper, then reached over and dropped it on her desk.

"Am I wrong or has that piece of paper been through hell and back?"

A tiny smile broke through, a soft giggle got loud, loud,

louder—then suddenly Robin began to cry, her body wracked and trembling. Mollie sank down to the floor and held out her arms. Robin went right into them, burying her head against Mollie's shoulder.

"That's it, hon, none of that stingy teary stuff goes down around here. If you feel it, make some noise about it."

It was a good ten minutes before Robin caught her breath and pulled back.

"Okay." Mollie took some tissues from her pocket and handed them to her. "It's your call. Where do we start?"

Robin wiped her face, blew her nose, then took a deep breath.

"Amelia. I want to talk about Amelia."

It was the first time Robin had really talked about it to anyone. Just the mention of camp or her friend's name made Daddy uneasy, and the only time Eunice dared bring it up was when she was so drunk, she made no sense. The camp director had even written twice asking Eunice to pick up the box of things Robin had left behind, but she had never done it.

Oh, there were a lot more problems in Robin's life—she knew that—but right at this moment, Amelia was the most important one.

Which might have been true even if she had lived. Though Amelia hadn't told any of her deep dark secrets, Robin felt sure she had plenty of them to tell. She ground her teeth at night, blinked her eyes over and over again, even woke up twice with screaming nightmares. Now Amelia's bogeyman was chasing down Robin, trying to scare her. And doing an excellent job of it.

"It does sound like Amelia was troubled," Mollie said. "But what makes you think she was scared?"

"I just know, some things a kid just knows."

"Well, you got real close to her in those few weeks together—why didn't you ask her about it?"

"I couldn't do that."

"Why not?"

Robin thought about it, then shook her head. "I think I figured that when she was ready to tell me, she would."

"But you're sure she was afraid?"

"Very sure."

Mollie nodded. "Okay, let's take that as a given. How does that affect you now?"

"What was scaring her is scaring me."

"How is that possible?"

Robin shrugged. "Maybe I'm part Amelia now. Or maybe Amelia is asking me to help get rid of her bogey-man."

"Why would she ask you to do something so frightening? She was your friend."

"Yeah, but she trusted me. She thought I was brave."

"And are you?"

"I used to think so."

Mollie sat quietly for a few minutes, waiting to see if Robin would go on with the story herself. But when she didn't, she said, "Robin, do you think Amelia blames you for her death?"

"Sometimes I think that."

"Do *you* blame you?"

She nodded.

"What about the police?"

"They thought it was an accident."

"What about Eunice and your father, what did they think?"

"I guess the same. But I was the one there, not them."

"And you're absolutely convinced it was your fault?"

She nodded. "I could have saved her, and I didn't."

"Okay. Next time, come here prepared with the best arguments you have. Over the course of our therapy sessions, I want you to convince me of that."

"Why?"

"Because if you really are responsible for Amelia's drowning, we should know it for certain. Then we can decide what to do about it."

"You mean whether or not I should be punished?"

"I suppose, if that's what you think you deserve."

Calvin was waiting near the bus stop when Robin stepped off the bus. She tried to ignore him but couldn't help noticing that he had gotten a haircut.

"Robin, wait!"

"Get lost. I said all I had to say to you yesterday."

"Hey, look, I just wanted to say I'm sorry about that."

"Yeah, sure."

"I mean it. I didn't figure you'd be so mad. I mean, it was only a lousy paper."

She stared at him. "How much of it did you read?"

"Just the first line: 'My Feelings by Robin Garr.'"

"And that's all?"

"Yeah, that's all. Honest."

She started to walk, and he walked along beside her.

"I like your haircut," she said finally.

"Yeah, my mom does too. It's not like I had a choice, I looked like a freak with that whole big piece missing. Where'd you ever learn to fight so dirty?"

She shrugged.

"Guess it's a good thing you don't have long nails, you might of ripped my face off."

She winced at the sight of the red scratch running the length of his cheek.

"So when you comin' back to school?"

"I'm supposed to be out for two weeks, but my father said he'd talk to the principal today. To see if he'll lower the time."

They had reached the front of her apartment house.

"Well," she said, "guess I'll be going."

Calvin nodded. "Yeah, sure. Hey, you always do that?"

"Do what?"

He looked down, running the tip of his sneaker along the crack of the sidewalk.

"You know, the feelings thing. Write 'em down like that."

"It was kind of like a homework assignment."

"Yeah, for who?"

"For my shrink."

"Oh. I was thinkin', it's kind of like writing poetry, isn't it?"

"I don't know. Why, you write poetry?"

"A couple of times I got shit-faced and rhymed some stuff onto paper. Nothin' great, mostly a lot of complaints and four-letter words—just somethin' to fill up my trash basket. 'Course, if anybody ever found out, they'd really figure me for a dork."

"Well, don't sweat it. Nobody's going to find it out from me. I might be transferring from this school soon anyway."

"Yeah, where're you going?"

"Who knows, maybe jail."

Though Robin had spotted Dorothy staring at her from the window the moment she started up the walk, she went out of her way to pretend not to notice. Once inside the building, she headed toward the stairs . . .

Stop!

What?

Take the elevator so you'll miss seeing her.

Good idea. Why didn't I think of that?

You did, birdbrain. So how long do you think she'll wait for you?

A minute, an hour, till the janitor mops the stairs, till she suckers someone in to shovel down Thursday's goodies . . .

Robin sat at the kitchen table and watched Daddy reheat last night's stew for dinner. He opened the bottom cabinet to get two clean dishes—and found canned goods.

"What happened? Where are the dishes?"

Robin shrugged. "Don't ask me."

He opened doors overhead until he found the dishes in a cabinet to the right of the sink.

"That's funny, I could have sworn I put them down there, and the food up—"

"Maybe they got up and tippy-toed to another cabinet in the middle of the night."

He glanced at her, then looked away.

"Don't panic, Daddy . . . only kidding."

"Yeah, well, maybe I'm getting prematurely senile. Anyway, it seems to be set up pretty good as it is, so—" He shrugged, then ladled stew onto the plates and set them on the table. "How did your appointment go today?"

Robin took a forkful of stew, removed a carrot, then ate.

"Okay, I guess."

"You can go back to classes tomorrow. You'll have to stay for some after-school detentions, though."

"How many?"

"Two. Tomorrow, then again Monday. I cleared it so you won't have to miss any of your therapy sessions."

Robin looked up. "Did you tell the principal I go to a shrink?"

"I told him you had doctor appointments, that's it . . . I hear Eunice dropped in this morning."

The ice cream! Robin stretched her neck to look in the

living room. But the carpet was clean—cleaner than it had been before.

"Gee, Daddy, I wonder where you heard that?"

"Don't be ungrateful. From what I understand, Eunice gave you a hard time. If it hadn't been for Dorothy, it could have been worse."

"I suppose."

"Next time don't let her in the building."

"I didn't. I mean, she was already at the door."

"Oh. I'll call her tonight, tell her I don't want her showing up without notice."

"You think she'll listen?"

"If she doesn't, I'll go to court and get a damned restraining order to make certain she does. Even Eunice is not above the law."

Robin looked up. "Neither am I, you know."

"What's that supposed to mean? If you mean school, then you're way off base. I just told your principal I thought suspension was too severe. I was right, and he agreed."

"I wasn't talking about that. I was talking about Amelia."

"What about her?"

"Well, if I was responsible for her drowning, I ought to be punished."

Marcus tossed down his fork. "Look, Robin, you're not responsible, it was an accident. The police know it, I know it, the camp directors know it, even Eunice knows it."

"But you *don't* know it. You guys weren't there."

"Christ, I don't have to be there, Robin. I know the facts, I know you. Do you think I need to be at the scene of the crime to know whether or not my client's guilty?"

"I think you choose sides, then fight about who's right. The best fighter wins. But the only one who knows the real truth is the person who was there to begin with."

Marcus sighed. "So what are you saying, Robin?"

"I'm just saying that maybe I ought to be punished, that's all."

"I don't understand, is that what you want?"

Her hands started to tremble. She laid her fork on her plate and clasped her hands together in her lap to steady them.

"No," she said in a small voice.

"Then why are we even discussing it?"

Robin stood up, tears in her eyes.

"Because just in case . . . I wanted to prepare you, that's all."

Marcus went over to her, leaned down and took hold of her shoulders.

"Prepare me for what, baby? For you being hauled away to juvenile detention hall?"

"Well, I don't know. Maybe."

"Why would you even think that might happen?"

"Because Mollie and I are going to decide it."

"Dammit, decide what?"

"If I'm a killer or not. And if I am, then I've gotta be punished."

It was all he could do to wait until Robin went off to bed before calling Dr. Mollie Striker.

"Just what kind of garbage are you feeding my daughter?"

A pause, then, "Would you like to identify yourself? It sometimes helps speed things up."

"Marcus Garr."

"Oh yes, Robin's father. Now if you could tell me what you're upset about . . ."

He took a deep breath, let it out slowly. "Robin tells me

you two are going to decide if she's guilty of killing that girl in camp.''

''Her name's Amelia.''

''I know her name. According to Robin, if she's guilty, she'll need to be punished for the crime.''

''I see. Well, if Robin discussed it with you, I suppose I'm free to do the same.''

''That's decent of you.''

''So what exactly would you like to know?''

''I'd like to know why I'm hearing these things from her! What kind of Mickey Mouse operation are you running there, telling her she might be guilty? What happened this summer was an accident—tragic, but an accident. The police accept it, the camp officials accept it, I accept it.''

''But Robin doesn't.''

''And that's your job, Doctor. To convince her.''

''Fine. That's what I'm trying to do.''

''By setting up a trial on the merits? Just you and she as judge and jury?''

''In a way, except that Robin's the only judge. Don't you get it, Mr. Garr? Robin doesn't give a hoot about majority vote here. She's been denied a fair hearing, and until she has one, she can't possibly be certain she's innocent.''

''Okay. Suppose after this pseudo hearing—''

''Not pseudo. There's nothing phony about it.''

''Look, did it ever dawn on you that she might come up with a guilty verdict?''

''Seems to me she's already done that. Which leaves only one way to go, Mr. Garr. Up.''

''And what if this slick little maneuver backfires, Doctor? What if she decides she deserves this punishment she talks about?''

''Wait a minute, are we talking about the same girl here? I don't know what *you'd* call what she's doing to herself now, but I'd sure call it punishment. The courts wouldn't be half as rough on her as she's being on herself.''

Silence.

"Mr. Garr, is there anything else you want to discuss? Because if not, I really—''

"No, that's it.''

Marcus put down the telephone. She *had* given him pause to consider it further. Dammit, if she just weren't so arrogant . . .

He was still considering when the telephone rang again.

"Marc.''

"Eunice.'' He sighed. "I don't suppose you're calling to apologize for the fiasco this morning.''

"Actually, I thought I'd get the little lady's phone number so I could apologize direct.''

"Which lady is that?''

"Dor-o-thy,'' she said, emphasizing the syllables. "She didn't tell you I smacked her? She must have wanted to spare you the horror.''

"Jesus Christ, Eunice. No, she didn't tell me that.''

"God, you've changed, Marc. Must be the city living. Still, one would think you'd be able to find somebody with a little more zip than that Dorothy thing.''

"What does that mean?''

"I mean she's not your type.''

"She's a neighbor, a friend. That's it.''

"Sure. Well, I didn't call to talk about your wretched taste in bedmates, I called to talk about our kid.''

"Good, I was about to call you. From now on, I want notice before you come up here to visit Robin. I won't have you upsetting her the way you did this morning.''

"I see. And I suppose you want to stand around and

oversee the visit too? Or maybe use your friend-slash-neighbor as a warden?''

"If I think we need a third party present, then we'll have one.''

"Over my dead body.''

"I'll get a restraining order if I have to, Eunice.''

"They don't issue the order that could stop me. Come on, your memory hasn't fogged that much, has it? When I put my mind to something, Marc, I usually get it.''

"Don't count on it this time.''

"Birdie's a disaster—she's stiff, unnatural, moves like she's being stalked. I brought along her favorite sundae, and she tasted it like it was loaded with toxic waste. She was actually scared to come near me. Me,'' Eunice said, her voice suddenly cracking, ''her own mother. Oh, she's been mad at me, plenty of times, but she's never been scared of me. In fact, other than snakes, she's never been scared of a damned thing!''

"Look, Eunice, she's getting therapy. Why don't you leave her alone for a while? Give it time to work.''

"You mean roll over and play dead while she gets screwed up even more than she is now? Not a chance. I *am* going to get her out of that dump you have her in. Away from shrinks plucking away at her brains, away from nosy neighbor weirdos, and away from you. And if you think I can't do it, just watch me!''

The phone slammed in his ear, leaving his insides cold. This conversation was different from the others: she wasn't drunk, not even slightly lit. He'd have to get going on the restraining order tomorrow. And find out how Eunice managed to get past the security system this morning.

Mollie had been reading through Robin's Feelings paper even before Marcus Garr called. It was never easy for a parent to turn over control to a total stranger, but it would have been a lot easier if Robin's father and she had started out on a better footing. It wasn't the first time her directness with a parent had come off as abrasive. Maybe it was time she learned to use some tact.

She read over the paper again, noticing how well Robin had expressed herself, even to the clay figures she had sculpted in her mind. The sleek black cat . . . a symbol of Eunice? The plastic wizard . . . would that be Marcus Garr? At this point it was hard to say. The apartment house perhaps stood for Robin's feelings, locked so tightly away she couldn't get to them. And the old people in new clothing, a sign of her sudden suspicion of people she'd once believed in. Like Eunice, like her father— the ones who hadn't been able to save her from the horrible events of last summer.

The parent, the symbolic protector against all evil. A formidable job by any standards. *Ah, Robin, if only it were that easy.*

CHAPTER 6

A<small>FTER</small> his conversations with Eunice and Mollic, Marcus was in no mood for visiting, but from what Eunice had said, he clearly owed Dorothy an apology. So he left Robin sleeping and went downstairs.

"When you told me about the scene with Eunice, you didn't mention that she attacked you."

"Look at me, Marcus," she said, smiling. "All moving parts still in place. Really, I held together rather well."

"In any event, let me apologize," he said. "You've been an enormous help to me and Robin, and the last thing you deserve is to get caught in the cross fire."

"Well, it wasn't you firing. The worst part of all was seeing Robin cowering in the corner, so vulnerable . . ."

He sighed. "Yeah, well, I'd like to make sure it doesn't happen again. One of the things I wanted to ask—how do you think Eunice got inside the building this morning? According to Robin, there was no ring from the lobby."

"Residents and visitors often don't bother to shut the doors tightly. I once found a German shepherd roaming the hallways. The only way I was able to convince it to leave was by tossing a soup bone onto the front sidewalk.''

''I'll talk to the superintendent tomorrow, see if anything can be done about that problem.''

He sat back on the sofa and took a deep breath; she came around behind him, stood over him and put her cool hands inside his collar, massaging his neck.

''Ah,'' he sighed, ''that feels good.''

''Goodness, Marcus, your muscles are tight as piano wire. But I have something that might help—at least, it always helps to relax me when I'm tense.''

She hurried into her bedroom, came out with a white porcelain music box. She set it on the coffee table, opened the cover and the simple, haunting melody began.

He sat back and listened for a few moments.

''It has an incredibly rich tone. I don't recognize the tune, that's not one of the children's songs, is it?''

''Actually this one isn't. It's an eighteenth-century piece called 'Woman Knows.'''

He smiled. ''Somehow I think I've had enough of knowing women for one day.''

''And why do I suspect Eunice is one of those women? I wish you wouldn't worry so, Marcus. For one thing, I'm around during the day, and I intend to watch out for Robin.''

''I'm grateful. But still, as you've seen today, Eunice isn't easy to handle.''

''Well, I can be pretty tough myself when necessary. Eunice is aggressive and loud, but she doesn't intimidate me. And despite our nasty run-in this morning, I'm not angry at her. Actually I feel rather sorry for her.''

''You do?''

''Because of her inabilities as a mother, she's managed to lose her daughter. That was clear from Robin's reaction to her. And I don't suppose that's an easy thing for any parent to handle."

A few moments of silence, then, "Well, hopefully in time, Robin and Eunice will make their peace."

"Perhaps." Suddenly Dorothy laughed—quietly, then with more exuberance.

"Okay, I give up . . . what's funny?"

"Just that I wonder about any mother who would bring her child an ice cream sundae at ten-thirty in the morning. But to put that in perspective, encouraging Robin in poor eating habits is hardly the worst of Eunice's crimes, is it?"

The music box hadn't helped; neither had Dorothy. In fact, Marcus went back to his apartment more tense than when he came down. Actually, considering what Eunice had put Dorothy through, she had been easy on her, probably given Eunice more compassion than she deserved. And she certainly hadn't said a thing about Eunice that Marcus hadn't thought himself.

But somehow hearing Dorothy laugh about that damned silly sundae rubbed him wrong. Was it inappropriate, or more likely, was he simply in too rotten a mood to see anything as funny?

"Describe how your back feels," Mollie said when at their next session Robin started to scratch.

"Tingly, itchy, like little bugs running over my skin."

"Are you afraid of bugs?"

"No, but I hate the feeling."

"I imagine it's very uncomfortable. Did you fall, hurt yourself any time this summer?"

"Not that I remember."

"Anyone ever touch your back or touch anywhere on your body against your will?"

"Uh-uh."

"When do you usually feel the sensation, Robin—first thing in the morning? At night? When you're feeling upset or tense?"

Robin thought about it. "It just suddenly happens, not really any special time."

"You talked about you and Amelia walking through woods on the way to your private spot at the lake. On the way there, did you get scratched by branches?"

"A few times on my legs, but it was no big deal. And if Amelia did, she never said so."

"What about in the water, Robin—think. Might there have been some thing, some object you rubbed against when you were trying to rescue Amelia?"

She shook her head, then bit down hard on her lip.

"What's wrong, Robin?"

She shrugged. "Tired of the subject, I guess. Do we have to keep talking about this?"

A few days later, Robin was walking home after school when the silver Z-28 pulled up alongside her and beeped. She stopped, looked at the car—the passenger window was open—then slowly walked closer to it.

"What're you doing here, Eunice?"

"Come on, hop in, I'll take you home."

"No, that's okay, I'll walk."

"Open the door and get your tush settled in here. And take a look." She reached behind the seat, held up a pair of lemon and purple striped sneakers, with a row of tiny gold buckles down the sides. "What do you think?"

"They're weird."

"My thought exactly. The moment I spotted them, I knew they'd be just right for my Birdie. You'll start a craze within days of wearing these oddballs—your little peers will be groveling at your feet, begging you to tell them where you picked them up.''

Robin smiled.

''Ah, a smile, an honest-to-God smile? Wait, hold it, let me get the camera!'' She shuffled madly through the papers in the glove compartment.

Robin moved up to the car, reached inside and caught hold of the right hand.

''Stop that. Will you?''

''Only if you let me drive you home. If not, I intend to follow you every step, beeping the horn nonstop as I snap an entire series of pictures which I shall entitle, 'Birdie Walks Home.' And which I will then send on to a teen magazine.''

Robin opened the door and sat down in the passenger seat.

''Okay, but what's the big deal to take me home?''

Eunice tossed the sneakers to Robin.

''Here, put them on. The big deal is, I get the chance to talk to my Birdie.''

Robin kicked off her white sneakers, then began putting on the new ones.

''I'm not such great company these days,'' she said. ''So you're not missing anything so special.''

''Let me be the judge of that. Guess what, Birdie—I've been cutting down on my drinking. I know you've heard this worn-out tale before, but this time it's legit. In the past few days, I can't have had more than—''

Securing the last buckle, Robin sat up—they were about to enter the on-ramp to Storrow Drive. ''Wait! This isn't the way to the apartment. Where're we going?''

''Let me see those sneakers on you. Come on, hold both feet up so I can see.''

''You promised you'd take me home!''

''That's what I'm doing, Birdie. Taking you home, to

Andover with me, where you belong. It'll be totally different, Birdie, you'll see—''

Robin went for the door handle; Eunice reached over, grabbed her short hair with her right hand and yanked her away from the door.

"Don't do that, dammit, you'll get *hurt*!" Eunice shouted.

Robin's hands flew back, grabbed onto her mother's hand, twisting at her fingers till they released their grip. Eunice, trying to keep her eyes on the road as the car zigzagged slowly up the ramp, swung out her arm blindly . . . It was when Robin turned her face to Eunice and screamed at the top of her lungs that Eunice's hand caught her full in the face.

Robin's hands went to her eye; the car swerved.

"Oh God, Birdie, I didn't mean . . . Are you hurt?"

Robin turned, opened the door wide and, as Eunice slammed on the brakes, jumped out. She fell onto the tarred roadway, a band of horns tooting behind her. Before Eunice could get out of the car, Robin had picked herself up and started running.

She was still a block from home when she sank down onto the curbstone and started to cry. Her jeans were torn, her legs and arms were bleeding, her left eye was swollen shut.

"What fight were you in this time?"

She looked up at Calvin, then shook her head.

"Go away, leave me alone."

"Who did it?"

"Me, I did it to myself."

"Come on, I won't tell."

"I said go away! Now!"

"Do as she says," came a low, steady voice.

Calvin backed up. Dorothy hurried over to Robin and

grasped her gently under the arms, lifting her to her feet. She leaned Robin's weight against hers, supporting her, and led her to the building.

Just as they reached the entrance, the Z-28 squealed to a stop at the curbstone. Eunice jumped out of the car.

"No!" Robin pulled in closer to Dorothy.

Eunice stopped. "Please, Birdie, just let me talk to you."

Robin shook her head; Dorothy shielded her with her arm.

"I don't know what happened here," Dorothy said. "But whatever it was, you've clearly done enough damage. I think you'd better leave."

"You stay out of this!"

"I won't, I can't. Now, either you leave or I call the police."

Eunice brushed tears from her eyes. "Birdie."

Robin squeezed her eyes shut and buried her face deep in Dorothy's coat.

Bare to her underpants and shirt, Robin sat on the toilet seat in Dorothy's bathroom while the woman washed the cuts on her arms and legs, then applied peroxide to the wounds. Finally Dorothy had Robin put on her jeans, led her into the kitchen, and sat her down in a kitchen chair while she made up an ice pack. Robin watched her count out the ice cubes.

"I suppose it would be just as cold if I used eleven ice cubes, or maybe even thirteen," Dorothy said, "but don't ask me why, I've always been fond of the number twelve."

Robin knew that Dorothy was trying to make her smile but she couldn't even manage to fake one. Dorothy dropped the ice cubes into the bag, sealed the cover and held the bag over Robin's swollen eye.

"How's that? Better?"

Robin nodded.

"All right, now suppose you tell me what happened."

Robin looked down at her new striped sneakers. But Dorothy lifted Robin's chin so that their eyes met.

"Please answer me, dear," she said, not raising her voice. "And I want the truth."

Robin stifled a sob as a tremor shook her body.

"Eunice," she said finally. "She tried to kidnap me."

Can a mother really kidnap her kid?

I don't know, ask the Commonwealth.

Since when do you care about the Commonwealth?

I guess, since I've been crazy.

You're back's tingling, right?

Mollie says to try to ignore it. So that's what I'm doing. Now would you get off my back?

Yuck, yuck, yuck . . .

The new rules were: Robin was not to get into a car with Eunice under any circumstances—or, for that matter, talk to her on the telephone. Daddy had the super put new springs on the front and back doors of the building so they would slam shut when people went in and out. He had also gotten a court order to keep Eunice from coming near or even talking to Robin, though Robin very much doubted that any restraining order would restrain Eunice.

Eunice, for her part, had gotten herself a Boston lawyer and filed a petition asking that temporary custody be given to her. The court hearing wasn't for another eight weeks, and though Daddy said Eunice hadn't a chance of winning, still the thought of the hearing and all the emotion that would go along with it terrified Robin.

Most days, either on her way home from school or from one of her appointments with Mollie, Robin spotted the Welcome Lady outdoors, watching for her. Of course, Dorothy always acted like she just happened to be out taking a stroll, but though Robin knew it was only some weird game of pretend Dorothy was playing, she found herself going right along with the game.

Besides, these days Robin wasn't so sure that she wanted Dorothy to go away. She didn't like the Welcome Lady any more than she had when they first met, but Dorothy was trying her best to protect her from Eunice. Loyalty, Robin figured, ought to count for something.

The bottom line was, Robin was scared most of the time, more scared than she had ever been in her whole life. The only place she felt really safe was in Mollie's office.

"Tell me something about your neighbor," Mollie said at one of her sessions.

"Dorothy? Why?"

"Well, she seems to be playing a big part in your life lately."

Robin shrugged. "She spies a lot, she watches out that Eunice doesn't come and get me."

"You don't mind that?"

"Sometimes I do, mostly I don't."

"You think she's protecting you?"

"I guess so."

"How long have you and your father known her?"

"Not long, three or four weeks, maybe. Since we moved to Boston."

"Hmmm. You know, the time I called and she answered the phone—what was it, after only your second visit here? She seemed to be kind of taking charge even then."

"That's just her way, she takes over a lot. I guess Daddy lets her because he likes her."

"Do you?"

"No. But Daddy's right, she means well. I mean, she's always around if I need her, and I like that."

"Give me a for instance."

"Well, a couple of days ago when I was leaving school, I started to have one of those attacks."

"An anxiety attack?"

Robin nodded. "I went into a phone booth in the school lobby and tried to call you, but your line was busy. Then I called Dorothy but there was no answer. I sat in the booth about fifteen minutes, scared to come out when all of a sudden I looked up and there was Dorothy. When she didn't see me come home, she came looking for me."

"And that made you feel better?"

"I guess so. Then, on the way home, she showed me how to take big, deep breaths and shake my hands and arms to make my muscles relax. When we got home, she took me upstairs to show me her collection of music boxes."

"Oh?"

"Yeah, she has a bunch of them in her bedroom, she played them for me. Mostly nursery rhymes and baby songs. Did you know the song 'London Bridge' was made up because people were scared to cross bridges?"

"No, I didn't."

"When they built a bridge, they'd kill a kid, then toss the dead body in the cement as a sacrifice. They figured it would keep the bridge from falling down."

"Sounds gruesome."

"Well, Dorothy knows a lot of gruesome things like that. I guess she told me about the nursery rhymes because she goes for that weird kind of stuff, and she wants me to like what she likes."

"Then, I take it, you don't?"

"Not really."

"What about Eunice, has she bothered you since that time she picked you up at school?"

"She still calls on the phone."

"What does she say?"

"Nothing. She just stays on the line for a while, then hangs up."

"So how do you know it's her?"

"Because who else would it be? Besides, it's something she would do. It's her way to get me."

"Why would she want to do that?"

"Maybe she thinks if I'm scared enough, I'll leave Daddy and go home to her. And she won't even have to bother with the court."

"Seems to me it would work just the opposite. I mean, if she really scares you, wouldn't going home with her be the last thing you'd want to do?"

"Yeah, that's the way a normal person's mind would work. But Eunice isn't normal."

"Does it scare you when Eunice calls?"

"Yeah. But mostly I hang up quick and try to ignore it, that's what Dorothy says to do. She says if I ever need to, I can always come downstairs and get her."

"And do you?"

"No, but at least I know if I wanted to, I could."

"Just knowing that Dorothy's there helps?"

Robin was quiet for a few minutes, then took a deep breath. "Yeah, but mostly I'm trying to learn to control things—like Dorothy does. You know, I've never once seen her mad? Anyhow, whenever I get scary thoughts, I concentrate my mind real hard till I blank them out, then I fast-freeze my head so they won't get back in."

"That's not dealing with your feelings, Robin, it's just pushing them away temporarily."

"I know, but it's the best I can do."

"I see. Robin, I called Eunice the other day."

Robin's hands gripped the arms of the chair. "Why?"

"I thought maybe if she'd come down here, we could talk all this through."

"What's there to talk about?"

"Well, for one thing, maybe she could explain what she was trying to do that day in the car."

"She tried to take me away, what's to explain? Are you sticking up for her?"

"Not at all—what she did was wrong. But sometimes it helps to listen to the other person's side. You'd be surprised how differently she might see what happened."

"I don't want to hear her side, I'm not interested."

Mollie held out a bowl of fruit, and Robin hesitantly picked out a banana.

"Not to worry," Mollie said. "Eunice refused my invitation. Seems she doesn't have much use for shrinks."

After Robin left, Mollie phoned Marcus at his office.

"I'd like to see you," she said.

"Oh? I thought what went on between you and your patient was private. Parental involvement not encouraged."

"If I think a parent can help, I'm more than happy to include him. My philosophy is, whatever works."

A pause, then, "When?"

"Tonight, if possible. What time do you leave work?"

"Six."

"What about six-thirty? Will that give you enough time?"

When Robin reached the bus stop at the corner of Mollie's street, Calvin was waiting for her on his bicycle.

"What're you doing here?" she asked.

"Picking you up, giving you a ride home." He patted the bar across his ten speed.

"How'd you know where to come?"

He shrugged. "Promise if I tell, you won't get mad?"

She hesitated a few moments, then nodded.

"I saw you take the bus at school and followed it on my bike."

"Why?"

"Because aside from lunch, where you're in and out in five minutes, I never get much chance to see you."

"What about after school, I don't see you racing to see me then. Not that I'd want to talk to you if you did."

"Maybe you would, maybe you wouldn't. But it doesn't matter, either way, she won't let me near you."

"Who?"

"That fruity busybody neighbor of yours."

Robin smiled at his description of the Welcome Lady. "That's Dorothy Cotton. She tries to watch out for me, that's all."

"Yeah? Who d'ya need protection from, me?"

Robin sighed. "Don't flatter yourself. Who'd ever be scared of you?"

"Well, she doesn't like me, I'll tell ya that."

"How do you know?"

"By the way she looks at me. Like she thinks I'm not good enough for you."

Robin remembered the day in the hallway when Dorothy had just about said as much.

"Well, she doesn't pick out my friends."

"Yeah? There's a Friendly's around the corner and one block over. Ride down there with me for a soda?"

Robin bit down hard on her lip. Dorothy wouldn't like it, but so what? She climbed up onto the bike's crossbar, and Calvin pedaled off down the block.

"Who beat up on you that day?" Calvin asked once they were both seated in a booth with their sodas.

"I told you, no one."

"I may be dumb, but I'm not a total retard."

"Okay, if you must know, it was Eunice."

"Who's she?"

"She's my mother."

"Holy shit, your mother did that? What for?"

"Because I wouldn't go back to live with her."

"Oh. Christ, I betcha learned how to fight from her."

Robin put down her soda. "Maybe you're right. Maybe I did learn from her."

"Then why do you let that fruity lady run your life?"

"I told you, she doesn't."

"Could of fooled me. Every afternoon, right after school or after your doctor appointment, you run straight home like a good little girl."

"What makes you think I do that because of her?"

"Well, she's always around, watchin' your every move—like she leads you around by remote control. Once you're inside the building, it's like you're locked away in your cave for the night."

Robin's argument crumbled before it crossed her lips. Was Calvin right about her? Every day since that big blowup with Eunice, Robin would go right inside after school, and not much later Dorothy would come marching upstairs and offer to help Robin clean the apartment, then start dinner. Robin hated to cook and clean—she hadn't even signed up for home ec in school—but it was the one thing she could do these days to make Daddy happy with her.

Sounds as good a reason as any, I guess.

You're saying you don't think that's why I do it?

Gee, did I say that?

CHAPTER 7

Marcus arrived at Mollie Striker's office at seven that evening. "Sorry I'm late, traffic was impossible." He loosened his tie and settled into a chair across from hers.

"Mr. Garr, I asked you here because I'm not happy with Robin's progress."

"Well, it's only been about six weeks. That's not very long in this kind of thing, right?"

"Right. But—"

"I've noticed she's much less obsessed with her back. I seldom see her scratching."

"Only an illusion. It's still there—at least, the reason behind it is. But not being able to make sense of it, I've asked Robin to try to ignore the itching. To concentrate on other things whenever she feels it."

"Whatever works—as I believe you put it."

"Yes . . . I suppose. Look, aren't we taking the wrong roles here?"

"Come again?"

"I know you don't like me much, Mr. Garr, I know you think I may be the wrong therapist for your daughter. I guess

105

I figured my admission of discouragement about Robin's progress might give you a chance to justify your feelings."

He studied her for a few moments. "*Are* you? The wrong therapist for Robin?"

"No, I don't think so. I really care about her and we have a good rapport. I'm part of that new breed of doctor who thinks those things count. Of course, it's still important that a therapist know what she's doing—which I assure you I do—but mutual caring between doctor and patient can go a long way. You've heard the expression, love heals?"

"I've heard it, and I believe it. I even see that your relationship is helpful to Robin. Still, you're telling me you don't think she's making progress, at least apparently not as much as you had hoped she would at this point."

"That's right. I'm missing something here, passing it over, and I can't figure out what. Tell me, Mr. Garr, do you really think Robin is as frightened of Eunice as she says?"

"If you have this terrific rapport, how can you ask me that?"

"Oh, she *thinks* she's frightened of Eunice. I'm just not so sure that fear is real."

"Look, psychology wasn't my best subject, but if you think an emotion's real, it's real—right?"

Mollie grimaced. "I didn't say that very well. What I meant was, has Eunice done anything to justify such a fear on Robin's part?"

"Wouldn't you be scared of someone who abducted you, then whacked you when you tried to get free? Robin jumped out of a moving car, Doctor. We're just lucky she wasn't hurt seriously."

"Still, it wasn't a stranger, it was her mother."

"I suppose if it were her father, her fear would be more justified?"

"That's not what I'm saying at all. But from what Robin

told me—and she's talked about Eunice a good deal—I get the impression that Eunice might be a lousy mother, but Robin takes a kind of pride in her anyway. Kids tend to admire outrageous behavior in adults.''

''Even when the outrage is directed at them?''

''Look, Robin doesn't trust her mother's judgment—and she's right not to. She also blames you on that count, but let's not get bogged down there. The important thing is, Eunice never physically abused Robin, is that right?''

Marcus nodded. ''As far as I know. There's harassment, of course—I'm sure Robin's told you about the phone calls, and I don't suppose I have to tell you about emotional abuse. Promising to be somewhere, getting drunk and never showing up—Robin can never count on her mother.''

''No, and I'm aware there was plenty of that sort of thing. And anger is a perfectly appropriate reaction to it. Fear isn't.''

''Look, I guess you'd have to know Eunice . . .''

''Can I?''

''Can you what?''

''I tried to get Eunice to come see me. She refused.''

''Does Robin know that?''

''Of course. She was relieved, she hated the idea of my seeing Eunice.''

''Doesn't that tell you something?''

''It tells me that Robin isn't willing to confront her mother or the fear. But that may only be because she'd rather let the fear stick where it's safe, where it can't really do any damage.''

''What exactly does that mean?''

''It means, maybe it isn't Eunice she's afraid of at all.''

''You're saying the fear is related to what happened at camp?''

"And to Amelia. Robin thinks she's ready to face up to what happened, but she's really not."

"So your mock trial didn't pan out as expected?"

"My trial, as you call it, is ongoing. But so far, Robin hasn't let go of her guilt. Which leads me to the next thing I wanted to discuss with you. I should warn you first, what I'm about to suggest is a bit unorthodox."

"Why doesn't that surprise me?"

Mollie leaned forward in her chair.

"I want Robin to confront Amelia's parents."

"That's not unorthodox, it's plain crazy."

"Why?"

"Because . . . because she—"

"Killed Amelia? You said yourself, Mr. Garr, it was an accident."

"I know that. But these are the parents . . . Christ, their kid is dead. How the hell do we know how they view the incident, how they feel about Robin? I mean, if it were me, I might well blame the other kid."

"Again, could they see it any worse than Robin sees it now? And if she's put on the spot, she's likely to defend herself. Think about it, Mr. Garr—this is a twelve-year-old who beat up a boy to get back what was hers, then faced down the principal of her new school. And all when her confidence was at a low."

"I'm not sure what you're getting at—"

"Just that it's one thing to tear yourself down for something you've done, but quite another thing to stand by while someone else tears you down. Gutsy people—into which category I put your daughter—defend themselves. You're an attorney, Mr. Garr, don't the accused usually come up with reasons for what they've done, even the ones with working consciences?"

Silence.

"There's another factor, too."

"What's that?"

"I think Robin is burying something from this summer, something besides the accident. Confronting Amelia's parents might force whatever it is to the surface."

More silence.

"Well, what do you say?"

Marcus thought about it a moment, then nodded.

"Okay, I'll buy it, at least to a point. I'll see the Lucases, check out their attitude, then we'll go from there."

Mollie smiled, jumped up from her seat and took Marcus' hand in hers.

"Do you always act like this when you get your way?"

"My father was a lawyer—he warned me to stay out of law. According to him, I would never wholly get the hang of the straight face and dignified posture."

Calvin didn't drop Robin off at the apartment house until after dark. When she reached the first-floor landing, the Welcome Lady was waiting for her.

"Where were you?" Dorothy asked. "I was worried, I almost called your father."

"I went for a soda at Friendly's. What's the big deal?"

"With whom?"

"Couldn't you see good enough from your spot at the bedroom window?"

Dorothy swallowed so hard Robin could hear the noise that came from deep in her throat, but still Dorothy kept her calm.

"I thought we'd make up a casserole for dinner. I have a new recipe—cheese and tomatoes and peppers and sausages. It's very much like a pizza, only—"

"I don't want to."

"What will you and Daddy eat?"

"I don't know, I don't care."

Robin ran the rest of the way upstairs, hurried into her apartment and locked the door.

The telephone rang.

"Hello . . . hello?" A pause. "Whoever it is, please say something."

She looked around the gloomy apartment, feeling her hands begin to get clammy. This time, even if she wanted to, she couldn't go running downstairs to Dorothy. "I hate you, Eunice, I hate you for doing this!" she screamed. She slammed down the receiver, raced into her bedroom, and turned her radio on full blast. When the phone rang again, she wouldn't hear it.

Suddenly the bedroom door opened: Dorothy. She went directly to the radio on Robin's desk and turned down the volume.

"Goodness, what's going on here?" she asked cheerfully. "The building rattled so hard I thought we'd scored a six on the Richter scale."

Don't answer, don't smile, don't do a single thing . . .

"It's a good thing your father thought to give me a spare key. I could have called and knocked and banged for hours without you even hearing me."

I'm scared, though.

I don't care, don't you dare tell her that!

Dorothy's blue eyes squinted.

"There is something wrong, isn't there, dear?" Without waiting for an answer, she sat down on Robin's bed and took Robin's sweaty hand in her cool hand. "I don't mean to fuss at you, Robin. It's just that when you're late coming home, I immediately think of Eunice . . . Certainly I needn't remind you how irrational she can be.

"And then when you do finally come home, I learn that you've been off with that awful boy doing God knows what.

For once, Robin, try to think of me . . . of *my* feelings."

I ought to think how she feels . . .

Why? I've said it once and I've said it a hundred times . . . what you ought to do is dump her.

Easy for you to say.

You never used to be such an ol' wimp.

And you never used to be such an ol' pain in the butt.

"Robin!"

Robin looked at Dorothy, who was now standing over her, pointing down at her bedsheet.

"Where's your mind, dear? I was asking, when did you last change your sheet?"

Robin looked down at her crumpled sheet. "A few days ago."

She shook her head and reached for Robin's hand.

"Come on, you, off the bed. Let's change this to a clean sheet."

"But it is."

"It doesn't look it to me." She walked to the hall closet and looked over the stack of linens. "Were these done with the other laundry at the cleaners?"

"We had no clean sheets so Daddy took them to the laundromat."

She pulled one out. "Okay, where's the iron?"

"We don't have one. But we don't need it, the labels on them say permanent press."

"Never pay attention to labels, Robin, they're only there to mislead the homemaker. You strip that bed, and I'll go downstairs and get my iron and traveling ironing board."

She hurried out of the apartment; Robin turned toward the bed.

Iron a sheet? Puh-leeze, you've got to be kidding.

That's what normal people do.

Which normal people are those?

The ones that keep a spit-sparkling, shining clean house.

Welcome to the weepin', creepin', wondrous world of homemakers.

Does your mouth ever shut up?

Does a traveling ironing board really travel?

On the drive home, Marcus was still considering Mollie's plan. It was a risk, a big risk. But if it paid off, he would get his little girl back.

As far as he knew, Amelia's people came from southern Connecticut, but except for a condolence card and a wreath sent to the funeral home, he had never actually contacted them. He hadn't thought there'd be any point to it.

If, God forbid, it had been Robin who'd drowned that night, he certainly wouldn't have wanted to face Amelia's parents. Or Amelia. Assuming the Lucases agreed even to meet with Robin, what would they say to her? Would they look at her and hate her as he might have hated Amelia if the situation were reversed? Or would they be big enough people to tell her it wasn't her fault?

First he'd sound them out, then decide where to go from there . . . But when it came to getting Eunice in for a consultation, well, Dr. Mollie Striker was going to have to deal with that one herself.

When Marcus got home, Dorothy was setting the table and some kind of cheese dish was baking in the oven. An iron and small ironing board were leaning against the wall near the doorway.

"Everything okay around here?" he said, suddenly wishing he could skip dinner and go to bed without talking to anybody.

"You're late," Dorothy said.

"I tried calling earlier, but there was no answer. I had an unexpected meeting with Robin's doctor."

"Oh. Nothing wrong, I hope."

He shook his head, not wanting to discuss it until he had thought more about it.

"Well, Robin was late getting home herself. She didn't arrive here until nearly six."

"Oh? Where was she?"

"Having a soda at Friendly's. With that neighbor boy, Calvin."

He shrugged. "Sounds harmless enough."

"For pity's sake—she's only twelve years old, and he's very likely into drugs and who knows what else. My intuition in these things is seldom wrong."

He looked at her for a moment, then whipped off his tie and flung it onto the sofa. "You're right, of course, I'll talk to her about it right now." He went to Robin's room, where he found her bent over her homework. "How's it going, baby?"

She didn't look up. "Okay, I guess."

"So what's this I hear about Calvin?"

"What did *she* tell you?"

"I'm asking you, *you* tell me."

"What's the big deal? We had a soda."

"Does Calvin do drugs?"

"*I* don't."

"I'm asking, does he?"

"I don't know, he might."

"What does that mean?"

"It means he might. Lots of kids do, you know. I don't rush up to them and ask them outright. And so what if he does? Eunice boozed it up for years, and she did it right in front of me, which didn't seem to bother you much at the time!"

He came out of the room with his stomach in knots. And there was Dorothy giving him her so-what-happened? stare. He looked from her to the kitchen table, already set up for dinner, then with a mixture of relief and guilt noticed that the table was set for only two.

CHAPTER 8

THE next day after school, Robin asked Calvin back to the apartment. She could tell by the look Dorothy gave her when they met in the hall that Dorothy wasn't pleased, but Robin walked right past her. After all, what could she really do? Daddy made the decisions, and though he hadn't exactly said Robin could buddy around with Calvin, he hadn't said she couldn't.

After he'd settled in front of the television with his root beer and cookies, Calvin asked her, "So who'd you kill?"

"Is that why you want to be my friend, to find that out?"

"Naw, just curious. Somebody says they killed someone, you want to know who, that's all."

"Well, I don't want to talk about it."

He shrugged. "Hey, okay, no big deal. My dad shot a guy once."

"Really?"

He nodded. "He was robbing a store. When the guy behind the counter pulled out a gun, he shot him dead. He's doing thirty years at Walpole."

"He sounds awful. Are you scared of him?"

"Not really, he never bothered me much. Besides, even if I was, I wouldn't have to worry for another twenty-five years. Hey, maybe you'll get to meet him when you go to jail. Just ask for Frank Shepherd, tell him you're a friend of mine."

"No thanks, he doesn't sound like someone I'd really want to know."

"You're pretty stuck-up for a criminal."

"I'm a different kind, I didn't shoot anybody."

"Did the other guy die?"

"Well, yes."

"Then ain't it the same thing?"

"I didn't—" She took a breath. "Look, I said I don't want to talk about it!"

"Okay, okay, stay cool. Hey, tell me about that Dorothy lady downstairs."

"There's nothing much to tell."

"I bet she does freaky things."

"Yeah, I guess."

"Come on, tell me."

Robin sighed. "Okay. Well, she's got some kind of weird thing about the number twelve."

"What d'ya mean?"

"Well, for instance, if she's stirring a pot, she'll stir it exactly twelve times. If she's washing a plate, she'll circle the sponge around the plate twelve times."

"Wow, that's far out. Does she count out loud?"

"No, but if you watch her when she's doing it, you can tell."

"Did you ever call her on it?"

"Uh-uh. Once she noticed me watching her count twelve ice cubes into an ice bag, though. When she saw me watching, she tried to make it into a joke."

"Did you laugh?"

"I make it a rule never to laugh at her corny jokes."

"What other weird things does she do?"

"Just the regular stuff that most housewives do, I guess."

"Yeah, like what, watch soap operas?"

"Not that. Come to think of it, I don't think she even owns a television."

"Really? I never knew anyone without a TV. What does she do with herself all day, yap on the telephone?"

"I doubt she even has friends."

"So what *does* she do?"

Robin threw up her hands. "Regular old boring housewife things—cleaning, sewing, cooking, baking."

"Any way you put it, it still sounds to me like she sits home all day waiting for you."

From the office, Marcus tried to call Camp Raintree—that was where he had originally gotten the information about Amelia's family. But it was late October, the camp had shut down for the season and there was no winter telephone listing. Unable to remember the name of the funeral home, he got hold of a Connecticut directory and looked through the yellow pages until he recognized the name, Larchmont Chapel, in Bridgeport.

"Lucas?" the funeral director said when he called. "When would you say that was?"

"Early August. A young girl, first name Amelia."

"Hold on while I check my records." He was back in a few minutes. "Okay, I got the parents' name here . . . Mr. and Mrs. Howard Lucas."

"What about an address?"

"Yep. Los Angeles."

"As in California?"

"That's how it reads."

"But they live in Connecticut, I'm pretty sure of that."

"Well, maybe they moved, people do . . . Wait a sec, I do have one other little notation here. Looks like Raintree . . . Bangor, Maine."

"No, that would be where the girl drowned. Where you picked up the body."

"That's it, then. Los Angeles, take it or leave it."

"I'll take it," Marcus said. "What about a telephone number?"

"Sorry."

Information in Los Angeles, Marcus discovered, had no listing for that name and address. He pressed the intercom for his secretary.

"Shari, what's the name of that detective agency we use?"

"Academy, on Charles Street. We deal with the main guy, Craig Oswald."

"Get hold of him for me, will you?"

Meanwhile he called Mollie Striker to fill her in on his progress.

"I'm about to contact a detective agency we use here in the office," he concluded. "Maybe they can line me up with an agency out in L.A."

"Good idea. What about paving a way to Eunice?"

"Sorry, that's off limits."

"Why? Does she still get to you that much?"

A sigh, then, "I don't know . . . The bottom line is, the less I see of her the better."

"I'm only asking that you call her."

"No. Look, it's not like I have a lot of influence with her. In fact, the best way for me to get her there would be to call her and tell her not to come. You've got a certain amount of persuasive power, do it yourself. Oh, and there's something else."

"What's that?"

"Actually it was Eunice who brought it up first, a couple of days before she tried to take off with Robin—and I was thinking about it last night. She said that after the accident, Robin was furious with her, but not scared of her. At least, not until we moved to Boston."

"That's right, it began the day Robin got a call from Eunice, then proceeded to have an anxiety attack. While the conversation might have been painful to Robin, it doesn't really account for the fear. Maybe it was something you said to Robin about Eunice."

"Look, I don't go around twisting Eunice into some kind of monster, if that's what you mean. She is what she is."

"No need to be defensive, I'm just looking for answers."

"Well, maybe you should start to look closer to home."

"What does that mean?"

"Well, Eunice said—and she's right—that Robin started to get worse once she began seeing you. I don't deny that she had serious emotional problems before that point, serious enough for me to get her to a psychologist. But it was right around that time when she became noticeably more fearful."

Silence.

"Hey, come on, Doctor, aren't you going to defend?"

"Not if you're right. Maybe I did say something to release those feelings without being aware . . . Or maybe I *am* missing something that I shouldn't be missing."

Though Dorothy stayed to help Robin make chicken for dinner that night, she was gone by the time Marcus got home. Later, while Robin was doing her homework, Marcus asked Dorothy upstairs for tea and told her that he was looking for Amelia's parents.

"Please don't say anything about this to Robin," he said.

"Oh, no, of course not. But it frightens me, Marcus.

Suppose they blame her—that would only make things harder on Robin.''

"That was my initial reaction. But her therapist seems to think—even if that should be the case—a confrontation might help her. In any event, I want the chance to talk to them first."

Dorothy sighed. "It's never easy to determine the right thing to do, is it? Children have a way of confusing even the purest and surest of us."

Marcus smiled. "Sounds like you might be feeling relieved that you never had any."

"Oh, no. In fact, when you think about it, children are what life is about, don't you think? I mean, would people continue to drive themselves so hard, trying to make the world into a better place if not for children? I seriously doubt it. The truth is, I care about Robin, as though she were my own. Granted, I have absolutely no right to feel that way, but it's not something I can help."

He studied her for a few moments, then said, "You know, in the short time you've known Robin, you've been a good friend to her. Not to mention what you've taught her about homemaking. Oh, she still balks plenty when she cleans up around here—I think to change that I'd need to call in a miracle worker. But I owe you, Dorothy Cotton."

A half-hour after Dorothy left, the telephone rang. Marcus looked at his watch: nearly midnight. Which meant it had to be the last person he wanted to talk to, especially in the condition she'd be in at this hour.

"Well, at least I didn't wake you," a light, clear voice said when he picked up the receiver.

"Dr. Striker?"

"Right, and I am sorry about the hour. I just wanted to toss something out at you."

"Go ahead."

"I was thinking about what you said earlier. That Robin became noticeably more frightened after beginning her therapy. What about your neighbor, Dorothy?"

"What about her?"

"That was when she came into the picture, too. It's at least possible that she may have said things to Robin that frightened her."

"Like what?"

"I don't know, maybe something about Eunice."

"Forget it. She didn't even know her until later, and she's not the vindictive type—she walked away from that blowup in the apartment feeling sorry for Eunice. I'm sure Robin told you that Eunice belted her without provocation."

"Yes, she told me. Though I wouldn't necessarily say there was no provocation."

"What would you have had her do, Doctor? Stand there and watch Eunice drag Robin feet first out of the apartment?"

"Of course not. I'm not even suggesting that her ordering Eunice to leave wasn't justified. But justified or not, interfering in a fight between a mother and her daughter constitutes provocation."

"Look, I've had it with your habit of defending Eunice. Dorothy Cotton has been a godsend to me— and Robin. She watches out to see that Robin's okay while I'm off at work, and if you don't think that's one hell of a major relief to me, then you don't know the first thing about single parenting."

"Can I ask you something without risking an explosion?"

"Go ahead."

"Do you like Dorothy Cotton or do you put up with her because you think she's good for Robin?"

• • •

"Robin, are you uncomfortable with Dorothy?" Mollie asked outright at her next visit.

"What do you mean?"

"I mean does she make you tense, say things that maybe upset you? You mentioned that morbid story she told you about 'London Bridge'—did that bother you?"

"No, not really."

"What about other things?"

"Well, I guess sometimes . . . I mean, she's so . . . well, you know . . ."

Mollie waited.

"She worries about me so much you'd think I was two years old. And she's always trying to get me to be the perfect little homemaker just like she is. I mean, she's weird, I think she really likes to clean house and cook and take care of people."

"And it doesn't bother you that she picked you to take care of?"

"At first it did."

"But?"

"Well, I guess I got used to it. And now, when it does get to me, I try to hide away the feelings. Most times I can."

"Why bother?"

"Mostly because of Daddy, he feels better knowing she's around to watch out for me."

"And not because of you at all?"

"Why're we talking about Dorothy again anyhow? Can't we talk about something else? Something important?"

A week later Robin again asked Calvin up to the apartment after school.

"Want some cookies?" she asked as she tossed her jacket on a chair.

"I got something even better." He reached in his jacket pocket and pulled out a plastic bag with marijuana and some wrapping papers.

"Not here," she said.

"Okay, then where?"

"Anyplace you want to do it, but not here."

"What about you?"

"I don't do drugs."

"Booze?"

"Uh-uh, not any more."

"Yeah, why not?"

"Because I don't. And I don't have to give you any reason why not, either. If you want to go someplace else and do your thing, go ahead, but leave me out of it."

He stuffed the pouch and papers back into his jacket pocket, then tossed the jacket on top of hers.

"Okay, no big deal, I'll take cookies. Got any of those chocolate marshmallow jobs?"

She went into the kitchen, opened a package of Mallowmars, then set napkins, glasses of root beer and a dish of cookies on a tray and lifted it. Suddenly she looked down at the food and she drew in a breath. Her hands began to shake, the tray tipped—she tried to steady it, but it smashed to the counter, the soda spilling everywhere.

Calvin came running in. "Wow, what a klutz!" He stopped. Robin was crouched against the counter, tears in her eyes. "Hey, lighten up, it's not all that bad."

Silence.

He stooped down. "What the hell's wrong? Afraid the old man's gonna beat on you for spilling the stuff?"

She shook her head, then managed a smile. "I told you I was crazy, didn't I? Now, maybe you'll believe me."

"Shit, you don't have to go through all this to prove it—I believed it way back when you first told me."

Robin started to giggle, and Calvin joined in. Calvin finally took her hand and pulled her to her feet. He tossed the soggy cookies and napkins in the trash, dumped the tray in the sink, then mopped up the wet counter with a dish towel.

"You do that like a pro," Robin said, watching him.

"Yeah, well, my mom makes me do dinner dishes."

He refilled the glasses, lifted them, leaned forward and grabbed the cookie package with his teeth. Robin followed him into the living room, where they sat on the floor.

"So what was that all about in there?" he said, biting into a cookie. "You really freaked out."

"You're going to think it's dumb."

"Tell me anyway."

"Well, as I started to carry in the tray, I saw that I was getting to be like her, which is enough to freak anybody out."

"Like who?"

"Dorothy. I mean, I never carried anything in on a tray before. And suddenly there it all was—just like she would have done—folded napkins and all."

"So if you don't want to be like her, stay out of her way."

Robin sighed. "If only it were that simple."

"I don't get it—what's so hard?"

Yeah, I'm with him—what's so hard?

A few minutes after Calvin left, the doorbell rang. Robin pressed the intercom button.

"Who's there?"

"Delivery. Package for Robin Garr."

Silence.

"Miss, you still there?"

"Yeah. Okay."

She pressed the button, then waited at the open door until the messenger stepped off the elevator carrying a big square box wrapped in brown paper.

"You Robin Garr?"

"Yeah."

She took the box, carried it to the coffee table and set it down, then looked back to see the messenger already standing by the elevator. "Hey, wait, come back," she called out. She ran into her bedroom, stuck her hand in her money jar and grabbed up a handful of change, then raced back to the door.

The messenger looked at the coins and laughed.

"What's the matter, don't you want it?"

"Hey, no, I'll take it." He pocketed the change, tipped his hat and left.

Robin closed the door and went over to the package. She looked for a card—there was none—then pulled off the ribbon, then the brown wrapping paper. The box underneath was tin, with a line of tiny holes around the top and bottom rim. Finally she lifted off the cover.

She fell back as if she were thrown by a powerful wind, and started to scream.

Dorothy, who had been about to go help Robin start dinner, raced upstairs the minute she heard the first scream. She burst into the parlor, her eyes following Robin's eyes to the box on the coffee table.

The coiled five-foot brown water snake lifted its head as if to strike. Robin screamed louder. Dorothy slammed the box cover on tight and rushed to her side.

"It's okay, Robin, it can't hurt you now."

Robin screamed.

"Stop it, Robin."

Robin kept screaming. Finally Dorothy lifted her hand

and gave her a light, stinging slap. Robin's hand went to her cheek; Dorothy put her arms around Robin and cradled her.

"Now, how did that get here?"

"A man, a delivery man."

"Who is it from?"

Silence.

"Answer me, Robin."

"Eunice."

"Was there a card?"

She shook her head.

"Then how do you know who—"

"I know, I just know."

"You stay put while I make a phone call."

"No, don't!" Robin clutched at Dorothy's blouse. "Don't leave me here alone."

Dorothy wrapped her arm around Robin's shoulder and led her to the kitchen. As she pressed in the super's number, she held Robin close, gently stroking her neck.

"This is Dorothy Cotton calling from apartment thirty-two. I'm afraid we're the victims of a sick joke here. I have a snake in a box, and I'd like it removed."

Two men were there within five minutes to take the box away. Robin, still shaking, let Dorothy lead her to the living room.

"Come here, dear." Dorothy took Robin's jacket off the chair, folded it onto the end table, then sat down and patted her lap. Robin looked at her gesturing hands, then, swallowing hard, sank down on Dorothy's lap. As Dorothy wrapped her arms around Robin, she pressed her head against the woman's breast. "Now, now, that's my girl . . . Nothing to be afraid of any more. Dorothy's right here with you."

"Why, *why* would she do that?" Robin whispered.

"I can't answer that, Robin. I wish I could."

They had been sitting there for nearly five minutes when Dorothy noticed something sticking up between the chair cushion and the side of the chair. She reached down and pulled out the cellophane marijuana pouch. She jerked forward, pushing Robin to a standing position, then stood up and held out the pouch.

"What is this doing here?"

Robin stared at the marijuana.

"Where did you get this?"

"I . . ."

Dorothy dropped the pouch on the table and started for the door.

"Where're you going?"

"I've had enough, Robin. I've tried my best, but it just doesn't seem to be good enough. Certainly you know how much I care about you. Well, relationships can't be just one-sided—now, can they?"

Robin shook her head, tears welling in her eyes.

"I'm sorry," she said, her voice cracking. "Really, I'm sorry."

"Sorry isn't good enough, Robin. I want you to promise me you'll have nothing more to do with that boy."

"But he didn't smoke it or—"

"That's not the point. The point is, you have no business keeping company with a youngster who takes drugs. Now you give me your word on this or I'll have no other choice but to wash my hands of you completely. I won't sit idly by while you destroy yourself—and tear me apart while you're doing it."

Robin stood there, her head aching so hard she thought it might explode. In a way, she wished it would.

"I'm waiting," Dorothy said.

Robin nodded. "I promise," she whispered, then lurched

forward and vomited up everything she had eaten the entire day.

Mollie was trying to clear the mess from her desk when the phone rang.

"Dr. Striker, it's Marcus Garr."

"Any word yet?"

"That's why I'm calling. The agency in L.A. located Howard Lucas in San Francisco. Apparently he's on the bottle."

"Damn. What about his wife?"

"I don't think they're living together at this point, though he wouldn't open up much to the detective. Meanwhile they're looking for the wife, they have reason to believe she's still in that general area. What I thought I'd do is fly down in the morning to see Howard Lucas. Maybe he'll be more receptive to my questions than to the detective's. In any event, I'm going to try."

"When will you be back?"

"I figure Saturday afternoon, evening at the latest."

"What about Robin?"

"I'll ask Dorothy if she'll watch her overnight. I don't think she'll mind."

"Are you sure? Because if—"

"Hold on a minute. I've got a call on the other line." He was back in about three minutes. "Nothing ever goes right, does it?"

"What's the problem?" Mollie said.

"That was Dorothy calling. And the problem is Eunice, the same lady you keep trying to defend."

"What did she do now?"

"She had a package delivered this afternoon to Robin. Inside it was a good-sized water snake. Robin is absolutely petrified of snakes—always has been—and of course,

Eunice is well aware of that. Anyway, this one scared the shit out of Robin.''

"Then why on earth would she—''

"You figure it, you're the doctor.''

"What about Robin? I could go over there—''

"Thanks for the offer, but apparently Dorothy has things under control. She gave Robin a mild sedative and put her to bed. Maybe you would fit her into your schedule tomorrow or Saturday.''

"Of course, I'll call her tomorrow.''

"Good. Then I'll phone you when I get back.''

Mollie put down the telephone. A *snake?* What mother would do that to her child? It didn't make sense.

Tomorrow morning she would call Robin to see when she could come in. And tomorrow she would clear her afternoon schedule and drive to Andover. If it took camping out the entire afternoon and evening on Eunice's doorstep to get her to talk about Robin, then that's what she'd do.

Dorothy sat on a straight chair beside Robin's bed, holding her soft little hand as she slept. She had given her a warm sponge bath, then some clear bouillon, something light and easy to digest. While Robin ate, Dorothy cleaned up the mess in the parlor. Finally she had flushed the pouch of marijuana down the toilet, with Robin standing by to watch.

She would not tell Marcus about Calvin or the drugs—at this point there was no need. The crisis was over, and she had handled it successfully without outside interference.

"Dorothy?''

She turned; Marcus was whispering from the doorway.

Gently she released Robin's hand, then tucked it beneath the covers. She stood up and followed Marcus to the parlor.

"How's she doing?''

"She hasn't gotten up since I spoke to you.''

"Good. I don't know how to thank you—"

"No need, you know how I feel about Robin."

He nodded. "Listen, I have to ask a favor. I hate to after everything you've done, but I've got a line on Howard Lucas. He's living in San Francisco."

"That's good—at least I hope it's good."

"I don't know for certain. I guess he and the wife broke up, apparently over his drinking. In any event, I want to fly down to San Francisco tomorrow. I figure I'll be back Saturday evening at the latest. What I'd like to know is, could Robin—"

Dorothy put up her hands. "The answer is yes, Marcus. Of course she can stay with me."

After checking in on Robin once again, Dorothy went downstairs to her own apartment. She hated to leave Robin's side for even a minute, but her father was home now and at this point in time it was his place to be with her.

She could feel her heart drum beneath her blouse. She counted twelve beats . . . twelve more beats, then another twelve. As always, it struck her as awesome that anything so positive could result from anything so negative. Despite the terrible crisis with the snake, despite Robin's terror and pain, something quite wonderful had come of it.

The connection between her and Robin that had begun weeks earlier was finally complete.

CHAPTER 9

MARCUS planned to take the ten A.M. flight to San Francisco, which would give him enough time to get Robin settled into Dorothy's apartment before grabbing a taxi to the airport. Though he would have preferred to know that Robin would be going to school the next day, he doubted she would be in any condition to go: she had already woken twice with nightmares.

In any event, he would only be gone two days, one night. Dorothy would take care of Robin, and Robin would more than likely be seeing Mollie while he was gone.

As for Eunice, he'd have to deal with her when he got back—just how, he didn't know. Perhaps he could have the package traced back to her, then get her charged with harassment. A minor criminal charge just might scare her into laying off Robin. At least it would put a quick end to that flimsy change-of-custody petition.

He sat at Robin's bedside in the darkness, the moonlight that filtered through the curtains throwing just enough light for him to see the strange contortions pinching at her features. Bad dreams, even as he sat watching her . . .

• • •

After the fourth nightmare, Marcus fell asleep in the chair beside Robin's bed. When he heard her stir in the morning, he opened his eyes and sat forward.

"Good morning, baby," he said. "Want some breakfast?"

"Uh-uh."

"Eunice really pulled a doozy this time, didn't she? But I'm going to stop her, Robin, I promise."

She nodded.

"Look, baby, I have to fly to San Francisco this morning—only a short trip. I asked Dorothy if you could stay with her while I'm gone. Okay with you?"

"I guess so. Why're you going?"

"Business. Important business that can't wait. I'll be back tomorrow evening at the latest."

She licked her lips and sighed.

He put his hand to her cheek and stroked it.

"I know I'm no good at laying out my feelings . . . But you, Robin Garr, are the most important thing in my life, and that's not going to change—no way, no how. You got that straight in your head?"

She pressed her lips together, squeezing tears out of the corners of her eyes.

He gave her a quick hug and rushed out of the room. That's all she needed now, to see him falling to pieces too.

When Daddy helped her downstairs to Dorothy's apartment, Robin could feel a band of pressure, like an elastic headband wrapped around her head. Dorothy led them into the spare bedroom, where the bed was already made up and waiting. Robin took off her robe and sneakers, then climbed into the bed.

Daddy hadn't been gone five minutes before Dorothy was

back with a breakfast tray. Robin wasn't hungry, but Dorothy pressured her to drink half her orange juice and eat several spoonfuls of the cereal, which tasted exactly like sawdust. Before she took away the tray, she handed Robin a pill, the same kind she'd given her the night before.

"I don't want it," Robin said.

"It's just a mild sedative, dear, nothing more. It's important that you get your rest."

"But—"

"No buts."

Robin looked into her eyes, then took the pill from her hand and swallowed it along with some water.

"Good girl," Dorothy said, finally removing the tray. "I'll be in the kitchen, dear. If you should wake and need me, just call out and I'll come running."

Dorothy headed out of the bedroom. Robin's invisible headband got tighter—so tight that she reached up to yank it off. To her surprise, there was nothing there to pull.

London bridge is falling down, falling down, falling down, London bridge is falling down, my fair lady . . .

Mollie tried to telephone the house several times but got no answer. Of course—Robin would be downstairs in Dorothy's apartment. She checked information for the number.

It was picked up on the second ring.

"Mrs. Cotton, this is Dr. Striker, Robin's therapist."

"Oh, yes."

"How is Robin this morning?"

"Fine, at the moment, she's sleeping."

"I see. I'd like to get her into my office this morning to see me."

"I don't think that's a good idea. What she needs today is rest."

Mollie took a deep breath. "Look, how about if I call back in about an hour?"

"I would prefer that the telephone not ring and disturb her."

"I need to talk to her, Mrs. Cotton."

"If you like, I can have her get back to you this afternoon."

"I won't be here."

"I see. Well, tomorrow, then."

Mollie was about to suggest tonight, but she really had no idea what time she'd be back from Andover.

"Okay. But if Robin should need me, she can call here and leave a message on my machine." She gave Dorothy the number, though Robin probably knew it by heart. "I'll be checking my messages every couple of hours."

"Thank you, Doctor."

Mollie put down the telephone. God, that woman absolutely infuriated her—what gave her the right? She was pushy, presumptuous, overbearing, oppressive, domineering. *Come on now, Mollie, be easy on her. For God's sake, you haven't even met the woman.*

Mollie didn't start for Andover until nearly two o'clock. But traffic was light and she made good time, arriving at the large single-family brick-front colonial at just a little after three.

She found a silver Z-28 parked in the driveway—presumably Eunice was home. She took a deep breath, headed up the flagstone walkway and rang the bell. Waited, then rang it again. She could hear loud rock music coming from inside, but no one came to answer the door.

She banged on the glass insert, then finally tried the doorknob and found it unlocked. Why was she not surprised? From everything Robin had told her about Eunice, she wouldn't be the type to lock her doors.

Mollie followed the music to the paneled den where she found Eunice dancing by herself and sipping from a glass in her hand. Eunice saw Mollie, stopped, went over to the tape deck and turned down the volume.

"Sorry, I'm not buying today," she said. "Besides, that Avon stuff sucks. I've got some marvelous base and coverup you might want to try yourself, though—something to cover those freckles of yours. Men don't take to freckles these days, you know."

"Mrs. Garr, I'm Mollie Striker. Robin's therapist."

Eunice walked over to the bar and refilled her glass with vodka.

"Well, well, won't you have a drink, Dr. Bitch?"

"I need to talk to you about Robin. I need you to help me understand her."

Eunice laughed, a loud fake laugh with an edge of hysteria.

"You shrinks are a fresh kick, aren't you? First you screw up her mind, then you want my help to get it back together again. What is it, you can't figure out what color pins to stick in her head next? Try purple, my Birdie's always had a real thing for purple."

"I need to know why she's scared of you, Mrs. Garr."

Eunice held up a hand showing long fingernails enameled in black and white stripes.

"What'sa matter, I don't look scary enough to you? Maybe Birdie didn't tell you how I snack on sweet little boys and girls. Of course that's only after I'm through sucking on their sweet little ol' daddies." She smacked her lips and took a long swallow of her drink.

Mollie hit the glass out of her hand. It fell to the floor, the vodka soaking into the carpet. Eunice swung out and whacked Mollie's purse from her hands, spilling the contents onto the wet spot. Mollie knelt down and quickly swept the things back into her purse.

"Okay, how about calling it even?" Mollie said.

"What do you want?" Eunice asked. "Isn't it enough you scooped out my Birdie's brains, you need to slice into my head, too?"

Mollie looked up at her. "I just need to understand why she's so scared. You never hit her, did you?"

"Hit my little girl? Never, never, never. Whoops, I did lock her in a closet once, does that count? Kept her there a solid hour."

"When was that?"

"Oh, she was a little thing then. Ran into the street and nearly got run over by a truck. Thought I'd die right there on the spot. So I put her in the closet to make sure she didn't forget the lesson. Naughty, naughty Eunice. I checked later in the child care book under Lessons, and would you believe I couldn't find closets listed anywhere?"

"How did she react to it?"

Eunice shrugged. "Birdie used to have a lot of guts in those days. If she was scared, she wasn't about to admit it to me." She walked over to the sofa and sank down. "Okay, ready to hear more true confessions?"

Mollie nodded.

"Marc was pretty busy setting up his practice . . . You know how men can get, intent on one thing to the exclusion of all else. Well, I was all else. And sweet little all else began to feel sort of discarded. You know the scenario, I'm sure you've had it dumped on you before. So I screwed around a bit on Marc. Always while Birdie was in school, but one time she walked in."

"What happened?"

"Well, I didn't invite her into the bedroom, if that's what you mean. I sent her out, the guy got dressed and left."

"And?"

"Asked her not to tell Marc."

"And she didn't?"

"Birdie's not the squealing kind. Got a lot of character, more than most adults I know."

"I've noticed. Was she upset?"

"Some, I guess. She got over it."

"Tell me about the things she didn't get over."

Eunice shrugged. "I'm sure you've heard it all. Showing up blotto at a parent-teacher's meeting. Spoiling a birthday party—I got so drunk, Birdie had the kids go home before we got to the cake and ice cream. Forgetting to pick her up from a softball game—she had to walk home in the dark . . . Lots of those kind of things.

"Hey, she tell you how she went and chopped off all that hair of hers? Long, glorious hair any girl would have sold her soul for. Birdie was some kind of knockout before all this happened, a real-life miniature Eunice."

"Is there anything else?"

Eunice wiped her eyes, which were now tearing.

"I don't know. Really, I don't know. I mean, I'm pretty weird, I do and say wild things, but Birdie never seemed to mind that much. In a way, we were friends. Then in another way I suppose we were competitors."

"How so?"

"For Marc. Little girl loving her Daddy, but Mommy having Daddy's love all sewed up." Eunice shrugged. "Guess she finally won on that count, didn't she?"

"Is that the rationale for the scare tactics? To get back at Robin for winning?"

"What scare tactics?"

"The anonymous phone calls. The water snake."

"What the hell are you talking about?"

"Mrs. Garr, you must know what I'm talking about. Marcus and Robin were so sure—"

Eunice stood up. "Get out."

Mollie didn't move. "Are you saying it wasn't you?"

Silence.

"For God's sake, if that's so, then say it."

Eunice went to the tape deck and turned the volume to blasting, poured herself another drink and began to shuffle-kick her way across the room.

The interview was over.

The plane was delayed more than two hours on takeoff, so Marcus didn't get to San Francisco until four P.M. Woody Bagen from the King Agency—a small, bespectacled man with thinning hair who looked more like an insurance agent than a detective—was there to meet him.

"Good news and bad news," he said as Marcus climbed into the passenger seat. "Which do you want first?"

"Start with the bad."

"Howard Lucas took off with a suitcase this afternoon."

"You couldn't stop him?"

"Look, I laid it out for you. He was not impressed with our presence, and he really didn't want to talk to you."

"Shit. Well, do we know where?"

"That's the good news. One of our men followed him to Butte City, and surprise, surprise—the house he's staying at is rented to one Georgette Lucas."

"The wife?"

"Bingo. We had it checked out. They've been separated—one of those on-and-off deals—for a couple months now."

"Okay. How long a drive we talking about?"

"Two hours without traffic. But at this hour on a Friday,

if we get there before eight, we'll be lucky. You might want to hold off on the visit till morning. I've already booked us into a hotel a couple of blocks from the wife's place.''

''Suppose he takes off early?''

''We'll have a guy watching.''

''I don't know, the sooner I can talk to him . . .''

''Look, let's play it by ear. See how you feel when we get there.''

Marcus sighed—maybe Woody was right. He was already tired. By the time he got to Butte City, he'd be exhausted. And he would need every ounce of strength he had to deal with those people.

Mollie called her answering machine from a phone booth in a diner. Three messages—a prospective date, a referral from an associate, and a salesman pushing tranquilizers and antidepressants. She called Dorothy Cotton's number.

''Robin is doing just fine,'' Dorothy said.

''Good, can I talk to her?''

''That's not possible, she's still resting.''

''Mrs. Cotton, all this rest is not necessarily good for Robin. People sometimes try to escape from their problems by sleeping.''

''Rest never hurt anyone as far as I know.''

''Look, I don't want to argue theory with you, but right now trust me, it's far more important that Robin talk about her feelings.''

''She was up at lunch, we had a nice talk then.''

''I see. And what did she say?''

''Just that she was feeling better.''

Mollie took a deep breath. ''Look, Mrs. Cotton, Marcus wanted me to see Robin either today or tomorrow. If I'm not going to see her today, I must see her tomorrow.''

"That's no problem," Dorothy said. "In fact, why don't we set a time now?"

"All right. What about nine tomorrow morning?"

Mollie hung up the phone. Finally after all that hassle, it was Dorothy who had suggested they set a definite time. So okay, who was more of a puzzle, Dorothy or Eunice?

Robin, she decided, had painted a fairly accurate picture of her mother. Though she had never mentioned the closet incident—or, for that matter, Eunice's men friends. But even adding all that in, Mollie still had a hard time believing Robin could really be scared of her. Eunice seemed genuinely surprised when Mollie mentioned the phone calls and the snake. But if it wasn't Eunice Robin was scared of, then who?

Amelia? Was it all somehow tied up with her and the guilt Robin still clung to? Yet if that was it, then there were definitely things Robin knew about Amelia and wasn't telling Mollie. Or more likely, there were things that Robin knew but couldn't remember.

It might be a hornet's nest Mollie was asking Marcus to open by contacting Amelia's parents. But it was one that had to be opened.

Robin didn't know anyone was at her side until she felt the sharp teeth of the comb against her scalp, then with it, the whispered counting. She sat up and looked at Dorothy.

"I'm sorry, Robin, did I frighten you?"

She shook her head.

"I was just trying to fix your hair a little. Even when you're ill, it's nice to stay neat and clean. It makes you feel so much better." She took several more strokes with the comb, then set it on the bedside table.

Robin looked around the room. "What time is it?"

"Almost dinnertime."

"Did Daddy call?"

"No, but then I didn't expect he would. Oh, yes, before I forget—you have an appointment with Mollie. For tomorrow morning."

"Oh, good."

"You like her, don't you?"

"Yeah, I like her a lot."

Once Robin had eaten enough dinner to satisfy Dorothy, Dorothy took the tray away. Then she handed Robin another pill and waited till Robin swallowed it.

"Now, while you rest, I'm going to be in and out of the apartment for a while."

"You're leaving me alone?"

"For a while, dear. Just a while."

"Where are you going?"

"I have errands, Robin. Things I've put off doing so I could care for you. Understand, I'm not complaining, it's just that I do need to get some of these things taken care of."

"When will you be back?"

Dorothy looked at her watch. "It's five now, I should be finished with what I need to do within an hour. And, oh yes, I'll take the phone off the hook so it won't disturb you. We wouldn't want Eunice bothering you with her phone calls."

Robin's eyes widened. "She knows I'm here?"

"No, she doesn't. Still, I wouldn't put it past her to phone here if she didn't get an answer at your apartment."

"Suppose Daddy tries to call?"

"If he does, he'll call back. Now, don't worry. You lie down and go to sleep like a good girl, and by the time you wake, I'll be sitting right here beside you."

As soon as Dorothy shut the front door, Robin walked barefoot into the living room, her legs so weak that she had to hold on to the walls for support. Why had Dorothy made her take those sleeping pills? She felt sleepy enough without them. Oh well, this one would be the last—tomorrow she'd get up and dressed and out of the house to go see Mollie.

She looked at the telephone receiver lying on the coffee table. Dorothy had said not to answer it, but she hadn't said a word about not calling out. She picked up the receiver, pressed in Mollie's number, then waited while the recorded message played out.

"Hi, Mollie, it's me, Robin," she said after the tone. Pause. "I'm not feelin' so hot." Pause. "I'm so tired I can barely stand up straight, and my head hurts real bad when I try to think." Pause. "Well . . . see you tomorrow."

She put down the receiver, careful to leave it off the hook, and went back to bed. For a moment she thought of Calvin, of how she had promised she'd never see him again. She hadn't wanted to make that promise, yet she had done it anyhow. For Dorothy.

The band gripped tighter and tighter around her head. She lay down on the bed, closing her eyes and trying with all her might to draw a blank. Instead she heard music—it was silly, she knew Dorothy's music boxes were way down the hall in the other bedroom. Could the music be coming from her head?

Rock-a-bye baby on the tree top, when the wind blows, the cradle will rock. When the bough breaks the cradle will fall, and down will come baby, cradle and all.

Eunice didn't take her last drink of the day until the anger was pretty much gone. She had thrown herself on the mercy of the shrink, told her everything—at least everything she could remember. But telephone calls? Snakes? What was that about? Were those the kind of spooks Birdie's mind was drumming up now? And, of course, sweet Daddy-o backing her to the limit.

It was a bitch being a mother, especially for someone as unprepared as Eunice had been. Growing up in that silent house, just her and her folks, she hadn't known the first thing about raising kids—only how not to raise them. And despite all those damn how-to books she'd read, nothing ever seemed to mesh with her personality. But she did love her daughter. Oh, yes, yes, yes. From the moment Birdie stretched open that mouth, revved up those heavy-duty lungs and screamed at her.

Eunice stepped out of her robe and kicked it across the bathroom floor into a pile of dirty clothes. She'd have to get to that laundry one of these days. She reached into the stall shower, turned on the faucet, adjusting the water. Hot . . . scalding hot, that's how she liked it. Finally she stepped inside, lifted her head up and closed her eyes, letting the powerful spray beat away at her face.

No matter how much she played it over in her head, she still couldn't understand the fear factor. Hey, it wasn't like they had never had fun together, played dumb games, acted silly like two crazy-assed kids . . . And you could always see it on her face—Birdie glad that she didn't have some pickle puss robot mother clawing at her back. The kind of mother Eunice had grown up with.

But afraid of her? *Oh Birdie, why?*

CHAPTER 10

WHEN Robin woke again, it was because Dorothy was shaking her. Her eyelids flew open.

"What's wrong?"

"We have to go now, dear."

"Go where?"

"You'll see."

She helped her off with her pajamas, then into a silly-looking blouse and pink corduroy pants with elastic waist—though the clothes fit, Robin had never seen them before.

"Tell me, what's wrong?"

"If I tell you, Robin, will you promise me not to get upset or frightened?"

Robin nodded.

"Somehow Eunice found out you were staying here."

Robin drew in her breath. "How?"

"I don't know, she didn't say. She called to say she was coming to pick you up and take you back with her. Now, if we hurry, I'm sure we'll be out of here before she shows up."

"The police . . . we should call the police."

"That's foolish. Now, I'm certainly not frightened of Eunice, Robin, and rest assured, I'd never allow her to force you back. But there's no need for either of us to have to deal with another of her emotional outbursts tonight."

"But where will we go?"

Dorothy sighed. "Oh, and here I wanted to keep it a secret, to surprise you when we got there . . . I have a lovely little country cottage, Robin—I know you'll like it. And it'll be just the perfect spot for you to get some rest."

"I don't want to go. I want to stay and wait for Daddy."

"Pish-posh. We'll be back here by the time Daddy gets home tomorrow."

Silence.

Dorothy stood up and backed up toward the doorway.

"Maybe you don't care about your peace of mind, but I care about mine. If you want to stay here and handle Eunice yourself tonight, then you do it. I intend to go to the country and have a very pleasant time of it."

Dorothy was already putting her arms into her coat sleeves when Robin reached her.

"No, don't leave me!" she cried, grabbing her around the waist. "Don't leave me alone!"

Dorothy crouched down and put her arms around Robin.

"Oh, my dear Robin, why must you always make things so very difficult, when there's really no need?"

"We'll be back tomorrow?" Robin asked.

"Of course. In time for Daddy."

"What about Mollie, my appointment?"

"We'll call her from the cottage and make a new one. Surely your visit with her can wait another day. In fact, the rest might do you even more good than the doctor."

When they got to Dorothy's station wagon, Robin climbed into the passenger seat, and Dorothy stood by while she buckled her seat belt. As they pulled away from the apartment house courtyard, Robin studied the strange pink corduroy jacket she was wearing—white quilted lambs sewn on each arm—then forced her attention out the front window to see if she could spot Eunice's silver sports car on the road. Finally, relieved that they had missed her, she laid her head back on the seat rest and closed her eyes.

It wasn't until a long time later that she woke, turned, and noticed all the luggage and cardboard boxes stacked neatly in the back of the station wagon.

Oh God . . .

What?

Trouble, trouble, double trouble . . .

Do something . . . Quick, fast, hurry.

My arms won't move, my legs won't move, my mouth won't move. I'm dead, I think I'm dead!

Dorothy, who noticed her confusion immediately, reached out and ran her fingers across Robin's forehead. Her hair and skin were damp and sweaty—and though her eyes looked terrified at the moment, Dorothy knew she was the one who knew how to make the fear go away.

She let her hand drop to her jacket collar, smoothing it down, then briefly taking her eyes off the road, smiled at Robin. Oh dear God, didn't she look sweet in that traveling outfit?

Mollie, who had stopped for groceries, didn't arrive home until after eight. While she put her groceries away she listened to her messages on the machine. Robin's message alarmed her—she sounded so lethargic, so depressed. She tried Dorothy's number once, then again a few minutes later. The line was busy, apparently Dorothy liked to chat.

She took Robin's file into her bedroom, lay down on the

bed, and began to thumb through the papers and notes. An hour later she tried Dorothy's number again. Still busy.

Dammit, she wished she had a number for Marcus. There were things she needed to discuss with him. Had he made contact with Amelia's parents, for instance. And then there were other things . . .

Like Robin's phone message. Despite what Dorothy had told her earlier in the day, Robin sounded anything but fine. So much for the Cotton woman's opinion—she should have insisted on seeing Robin today, even gone over there. She looked at her watch: it was after nine. As sluggish as Robin had sounded on the tape, she'd already be fast asleep. Well, wouldn't she?

She took the telephone directory from the bedside table, found the Academy Agency—the local detective agency that Marcus had originally used—and called it. When she reached the answering service, she asked to get through to the head man.

"I'm sorry, but Mr. Oswald doesn't want us to give out his home number."

"Then could you contact him now and have him call me? Tell him it's important. It has to do with Marcus Garr. A Boston attorney, a client of his."

She gave her name and number, hung up, then sat cross-legged on the bed with the phone in front of her waiting for a callback. *Come on Oswald, come on Oswa—Oz* . . . Suddenly she grabbed Robin's file, scattering the papers over her bed until she got to Robin's 'Feelings' paper . . .

And the plastic Wizard has steel jaws that can crush my bones to powder. The plastic wizard . . . could that be the Wizard of Oz, a slightly displaced association with the name Dorothy? Was Robin trying to say she was afraid of Dorothy Cotton?

• • •

Dorothy saw Robin take a deep breath before she asked, "Why are there so many boxes?"

"Well, dear, I need to get some of these things up to the cottage. I haven't really had the chance lately, what with all the time I've been spending with you and Daddy. But I've been wanting to do some more cleanin' and plumpin' and fussin'," she said, her deep dimple flashing. "Oh, you know how I am."

Robin nodded.

"Maybe you'd like to help me. I certainly could use another pair of strong hands."

"I don't know, we might not have time." She looked down again at the matching jacket and pants she was wearing. "These clothes . . . whose are they?"

"Why, they're yours, of course. Just a few little things I made up special for you."

Robin fell back to sleep soon after, but Dorothy noticed the twitches and jumps, the faces she made—no doubt the bogeymen and spirits and spooks and other such nonsense that tend to fill children's dreams. At a service station, Dorothy bought a can of apple juice from the vending machine. Then, gently shaking Robin awake, she slipped a sedative onto her tongue, following it with a swallow of the juice. Finally she took a colorful patchwork quilt—one she had made herself—from a box in back and spread it over the child. Now Robin was warm and comfortable and relaxed; she'd sleep undisturbed straight through the night.

No fitful sleeping, dear one. No nightmares.

Mary had a little lamb, little lamb, little lamb . . . Mary had a little lamb whose fleece was white as snow. And everywhere that Mary went, Mary went, Mary went, and everywhere that Mary went, her lamb was sure to go.

• • •

Mollie called Dorothy's number again. When she found it still busy, she called the operator and asked that the line be checked.

"Sorry, ma'am," the operator said after a moment. "That number is not in service at this time."

"What exactly does that mean?"

"Well, it could be in need of repair or it could simply be off the hook."

"I see." Mollie hung up. Damn that woman. Just as she went for her jacket, the phone rang.

"This Dr. Striker?"

"Yes, who's this?"

"Craig Oswald."

"Oh, yes. I phoned—"

"Something about Marcus Garr."

"Right. Look, his daughter is a patient of mine. The thing is, I'm trying to get hold of him. He went to San Francisco this morning, but I didn't get a number where I can reach him."

"So where do I come in?"

"I know he asked you to put him in contact with a detective agency out in Los Angeles."

"Okay, if you say so."

"Well, what I want is the name of the agency. I'd like to try to track him down."

"Oh. Well, I don't remember offhand what I told him, but the fact is, I'm only familiar with one agency there. The name is King."

"And where's it located?"

"Right in downtown L.A."

"Thanks much," she said, hanging up and heading for the door. First she'd go check on Robin. Dorothy might have taken the phone off the hook, but there was no way she'd get by with not answering the door. And if Robin were willing to come with her, Mollie was prepared to take her back to her brownstone for the night.

The first thing Marcus did when he arrived at his hotel room in Butte City was to call Georgette Lucas' number. Though Howard Lucas' voice was distant and cold once he realized who Marcus was, he did agree after some pressuring to let Marcus meet with him and his wife first thing the next morning.

Relieved, Marcus ordered a sandwich and a glass of milk from room service, then tried Dorothy's number. Busy. He tried again a couple of minutes later, and again after the food arrived.

Actually he was surprised to learn that Dorothy had friends. She had always seemed so available, as though she had no life apart from him and Robin. But, of course, she must have, and the time she spent with Robin must be time taken from other things. When he got back, he'd have to insist that she spend less time worrying about them.

Finally he checked his address book for Mollie's number and called it. It rang four times, then the answering machine clicked on.

"Mollie, this is Marcus Garr," he said after the beep. "Looks like I'm going to get to see Amelia's parents—both of them—tomorrow morning, Keep your fingers crossed on that. In any event, I ought to be home on schedule. I'll call you to let you know what happened."

He hung up, tried Dorothy's once again. Then, shaking his head, dropped the receiver back in the cradle.

Mollie had been standing for five minutes in the outside lobby leaning against the doorbell of Dorothy's apartment. Still no response. She checked her watch, it was after eleven-thirty. But even if Dorothy had been asleep, she couldn't be after all this constant ringing. Finally she picked a first-floor apartment number and pressed a button at random. Within seconds the buzzer sounded, unlocking the front door.

A young man in bare feet met her in the hallway. "Yeah?" he said. "You the one rang my place?"

"Yes. I'm looking for the manager. Would you by any chance know where—"

He blew out a stream of air between nearly closed lips, then went back inside his apartment and slammed the door.

She took the elevator to apartment twenty-two, rapped on the door, then waited. She rapped louder. She was literally banging by the time the short, pale blond woman next door stuck her head out.

"What's going on here?" she asked. "It's the middle of the night. Where do you think you are, in a slum?"

"I'm sorry, really. I'm looking for Dorothy Cotton. Have you seen her?"

"Who?"

"Dorothy Cotton, the woman who lives here."

"Sorry, I wouldn't know her if I stepped on her."

"Oh. How long have you lived here?"

"Twelve years, why?"

A pause, then, "Could you direct me to the management?"

She threw up her hands. "So now you change your mind, you want the super?"

Mollie nodded.

"First floor, apartment six."

Mollie took the stairs up to the Garr apartment and knocked. Convinced that no one was inside, she headed back downstairs to apartment six and knocked.

A giant of a man with a crewcut opened the door.

"What d'ya want?"

She took out her card from her purse and handed it to him. He looked at it, handed it back. "Okay, so what does this mean?"

"It means I'm a doctor. I have a young patient upstairs in apartment twenty-two. I need to see her."

"Oh yeah? Lemme see . . . the Cotton lady's apartment?"

"Right. I've knocked on the door, in fact I've banged on the door. There's no answer."

He scratched his large square head. "So what? Maybe they went out for a while."

His point was well taken, but though it was always possible, it was surely unlikely with Robin feeling the way she'd been feeling when she left the message. Mollie took a deep breath, knowing she was about to stretch her story.

"The girl—my patient, that is—she's far too sick to be out of bed. I can't imagine Mrs. Cotton would take her out at this hour. All I want is to look inside, make sure everything is okay. That's all."

"Hey, I can't open an apartment just like that."

"Not just like that, sir. I said there's a sick young girl to consider. If you'd like to check out my credentials . . . Or, if you'd feel more comfortable, I could contact the police first. I'm sure I could get us some kind of order—" She dropped it there.

And he picked it right up. He pulled a heavy set of keys from a hook near his door and led the way upstairs.

"Christ, I didn't even know the Cotton lady had a kid." He hunted for the right key. "Not that I know so much about any of the tenants here. I handle the complaints, and if the tenants behave themselves, I mind my own business."

Mollie decided not to explain. Finding the right key, he opened the door and stepped back as she entered. The living room light was on. Mollie looked around at the sparsely decorated room. The only personal touch was a couple of plastic novelties on the shelves of the dining-room credenza. The telephone receiver was off the hook; she went over to it and placed it back on.

"I'll just check the bedrooms," she said, already heading down the hallway. Mollie peeked inside both bedrooms . . . sparse decor like the living room, both beds made up—on one bed was a pair of pajamas and a robe neatly folded. Likely Robin's.

Why had she assumed Dorothy would be the fussy kind, with a hundred and one knickknacks on her walls, shelves, and tables? And what about all those music boxes Robin had mentioned? She looked at the glass-topped dresser and the three shelves holding a single box of tissues and a half-dozen magazines, then turned to the super.

"Is this all her own furniture?"

"None of these apartments come furnished, if that's what you're getting at."

She looked back at the dresser and shelves. She must keep the music boxes inside the dresser or end tables . . .

"Looks like they went out," the super said.

"I guess so."

"I thought you said the kid was too sick."

Mollie shrugged. "Maybe Mrs. Cotton took her to another doctor."

"Christ, I should of never let you in here." He hurried her out and locked the door after them. "How'd you get inside the building anyhow?"

"Oh, the outside door. Someone must have left it open."

The super was bending over, examining the front door spring as she left. She hurried to the car, got inside, then looked back at the building. Where would Dorothy have taken Robin at this hour?

When she got back to her apartment, she rewound the tape to Robin's message and listened to it again. Then Marcus' message came on. Mollie grabbed for a pen, but he had left no number, no name of hotel.

Damn, damn, damn! It was like a house of cards—one moved, and all the rest were suddenly off balance. So what did she do now, try to track Marcus down or just wait? Wait while Robin was who knows where? And with a woman who apparently terrified her.

When Dorothy pulled into the narrow deserted roadway leading to the cottage, Robin was still sleeping soundly. Although they weren't that far from town, only ten miles or so, it was the beauty and solitude of the surrounding mountains that Dorothy liked so much. It would also be a good place for Robin, a place where—emotionally and physically—she could mend and thrive and adjust to being part of a real family.

Dorothy left her sleeping in the car while she carried the boxes and baggage inside, except for the one covered box that she put out on the back porch. She had taken from the Boston apartment only what she knew she needed—the sewing machine, antiques, bric-a-brac, and timeworn treasures that make a house a home.

The furniture here was even nicer and cozier than in Boston. And the basement shelves and freezer held enough canned goods, preserves and frozen food to last them for months. As far as Robin's wardrobe was concerned, nothing was needed, she had a closet full of lovely girl's clothing Dorothy had designed and sewn herself.

She went outside, unbuckled Robin's seat belt and sat her up. Then, with one arm around her back and another under her thighs, Dorothy lifted her and carried her inside the cottage.

To her bedroom . . . She sat the child on the bed, took off her new traveling outfit, then slipped a cotton nightie over her head.

"Where are we?" Robin asked with her eyes still closed.

Dorothy laid her down, kissed her forehead, then covered her, tucking the sheets and blankets snugly around her. She almost wished she could tell her now—or, even better, show her—but with the sedatives still in her system, the child was way too groggy to grasp anything so complex.

Before turning off the lights and leaving the room, she placed the red diary on top of the dresser, where Robin could easily spot it. She smiled. Amelia had gone through all kinds of silly machinations trying to keep her diary hidden, so that Dorothy would have to hunt it out in a new place each night.

And Dorothy had never once considered reading Amelia's diary to be prying. She had always believed it was a mother's right as well as her duty to be aware of what her child was thinking.

CHAPTER 11

SOMETIME after midnight, Mollie managed to get through to a staff member of the King agency. But the only thing he knew was that Woody Bagen was handling the Garr case. Woody was somewhere in the San Francisco area meeting with his client—if she could just sit tight until tomorrow morning when Woody checked in, her message for Mr. Garr would be passed on.

At 12:45 Mollie tried phoning Dorothy one last time, let it ring for five minutes. Could Dorothy have taken Robin to a friend's house overnight and informed Marcus? If so, surely Robin would have mentioned it in her telephone message. Could Robin be physically sick enough to be taken to a hospital emergency room? Could Dorothy have—?

God, she was getting crazy, she had to shut down her imagination and get some sleep.

By tomorrow morning all this theorizing would be history, anyway. Robin's appointment was at nine. She'd either show up or she'd phone to tell Mollie why not . . .

• • •

It felt like morning. For the first few minutes Robin didn't move, and then she began to remember last night, bits and pieces of the long car ride to Dorothy's cottage. She pushed herself up onto her elbows and looked around. The room was totally pink and white—from the pink and white wallpaper with nursery-rhyme characters painted on it to the ruffled pink see-through curtains to the shiny white furniture to the pink and white Cinderella doll lamp on the high dresser to the braided pink and white area rug with fringe on the shiny wood floor.

A little girl's room. Why would Dorothy have a little girl's room? Robin's throat felt dry. She swallowed hard, trying to wet it, then stood up slowly, not sure if her legs were going to do their job. She grabbed one of the bedposts, then walked past the desk to the window. It must be a back window—all she could see was a long yard that led to some woods.

She passed the closet, but looked away when she saw girls' clothing hanging from the bar and a black foot locker on the floor. Finally she went to the dresser, looked at the lamp and then at the diary—the red diary with the gold leaf emblem in the right-hand corner. She stared at the diary for a long moment, then lowered her eyes and took a deep shuddering breath.

Finally she went back to the bed and lay down on her stomach, resting her head on the pillow, gripping it with her fists. She'd probably end up sleeping on the drive home to Boston just like on the way up here. She had to be home in time to see Daddy, she had to call Mollie and make another appointment, she even had to work on that dumb science paper for school. It wasn't due for another three weeks, but still she knew she had to get started on it.

She couldn't see Calvin, but so what—she was too busy

to hang out with him anyway. There was so much to do, so much . . . Should she go and wake Dorothy now to tell her it was time to leave, or would it be smarter and politer to wait till Dorothy got up on her own?

And why couldn't she stop her legs from jumping?

Want to talk?

Not now.

Why not?

Too scared, way too scared . . .

Then when?

I don't know, see me later . . .

Ring around the rosie, a pocket full of posies . . .

Quit it!

Marcus arrived at the Lucas house at eight in the morning. Howard Lucas, who looked to be in his mid-forties, had a short stubby beard and thick wire-rim glasses. He introduced Marcus to his wife, Georgette, whose plumpness and good skin made her age difficult to judge.

"I don't know how to begin," Marcus said sitting across from them. "Apologies and condolences are so inadequate."

Howard took a picture from his wallet. As he leaned forward to pass it over, Marcus could smell last night's whiskey. Or was it this morning's?

"This is Amelia," he said. "Taken last year."

Marcus looked at the picture and nodded, then passed it back.

"A lovely-looking girl," he said finally. "Apparently she and Robin were great friends."

Silence.

"Look, what happened this summer was a tragedy. For everyone involved."

"Your girl's alive."

Marcus nodded. "Yes, and I thank God for that, but right now she's not doing very well. She's guilt-ridden to the point that it's taking over her entire life. She doesn't eat, she has nightmares . . . I don't expect her to ever forget Amelia or what happened at camp, but life goes on. Don't you think?"

"It's a good theory, but maybe you're better at living by theories than me." Howard gestured to Georgette. "Ask her, this has played hell on our marriage."

Marcus nodded. "My wife and I separated not long ago. I guess it was a little late in coming—Robin might not have had the vodka if it weren't for my wife."

Howard rubbed his hands together. "Amelia never touched alcohol or drugs or anything like that before she met your girl. She'd still be alive today . . ." He stopped, then sighed. "Mr. Garr, just what is it you want from me?"

"Robin needs to know the accident wasn't her fault, that it *was* an accident. She needs to be able to start putting her life back together. She's dropped a lot of weight, she's scared, nervous all the time . . . I have her seeing a therapist. The therapist thought that maybe if you talked to her . . . well, it might help."

Howard shook his head. "I couldn't do that. I wouldn't know what to say. I'm sorry, but I guess the truth is, I do blame her. I don't want her hurt or anything, I'm not the kind of man who wants revenge on a twelve-year-old kid. But to come right out and say, 'Hey kid, not to worry, it's not your fault . . .'" He shrugged. "No, I couldn't do that. It'd be a lie."

Georgette looked at Howard. "And why should you do it? If you lifted some of that damn guilt off the kid, you'd have to lug it around yourself."

"Be quiet," Howard said. "This doesn't concern you."

"The hell it doesn't. I'm sick of you walking around like

some kind of bereaved saint while you bury your head in a whiskey bottle. Tell the man the truth, you saw your kid—what . . . once, twice a year, tops? Add that to support payments and some fancy Christmas and birthday presents, and you pretty much have it all.''

''That's a lie! I called as often as I could. I answered her letters. Did everything I could to be a good father to her.''

''Except the most important thing—get her away from that nut she was living with.''

''What choice did I have? There's no court in the country that was going to choose me over Dorie, and they would have been right.'' Howard looked at Marcus, who was following the argument as best be could. ''Dorie was the perfect mother—at least, she did all the things a mother is supposed to do.''

Marcus looked at Georgette. ''You're not Amelia's natural mother?''

''No, I'm the wicked stepmother. The perfect mother he's talking about is a real basket case.''

''You don't know that for a fact, you're just saying it because you don't like her,'' Howard said. ''She knew a lot about kids, a lot more than you did. Admit it.''

''You're right, I didn't like her, and yes, she did know more about bringing up kids than I do. But I know that when a kid is scared shitless of her mother like Amelia was, there's something the hell wrong there. Christ, you lived with the woman for a few years and she drove *you* crazy, didn't she?''

''That was different.'' He looked at Marcus and sighed. ''She was a woman who would suffocate a man. Her way was the only right way and everything had to be done her way. Real obsessive about the house and keeping it looking right. But you couldn't ask for a mother who gave more love and attention to her kid. Now, Georgette can say what she wants out of anger, but that's the honest-to-God truth.''

''Tell the man why she didn't let Amelia come and visit you here,'' Georgette said. ''Why it was you who had to fly down there on those few times you *did* see her.''

Marcus looked at Howard, who shrugged.

''Dorie didn't think Georgette was a good influence on Amelia. Swearing, unrefined, loud, that kind of thing. I by no means agreed with all her judgment calls, but she was acting in what she thought were Amelia's best interests.''

''What you mean is in *her* best—''

''Look,'' Marcus said, raising his hands, ''I think I'm getting into the middle of something that's really none of my business. What I need to know is, will you at least think about talking to my daughter?''

''Sorry, I'd like to help her, but in all good conscience, I can't.''

''Mr. Lucas, she's only a kid, she was experimenting with the alcohol the same as your Amelia. Last spring was the first time she ever touched the stuff. *She* could have been the one who—''

''But she wasn't, was she?''

''If Amelia were here now, wouldn't she—''

''Stop it,'' Howard said, standing up. ''Enough!''

Marcus got to his feet. ''Can you at least give me the address of Amelia's mother?''

''You're going to ask her to do this?''

Marcus nodded.

Howard wrote an address in Connecticut on a piece of paper and handed it to Marcus.

''She does worship kids, so maybe you'll have something going for you there. But when I was back east making arrangements for the funeral . . . Well, let's just say Amelia's death left her in more than one piece.''

Marcus headed for Woody's car, still parked across the street. Maybe he was just spinning his wheels, but what other alternative did he have but to contact Dorie Lucas?

Robin, still lying awake on the bed, sat up the moment Dorothy came in.

"I think we should go now," Robin said.

Dorothy looked at her as though she were studying her, then leaned over and pressed her lips to Robin's forehead.

"Oh, dear. It feels like you have a fever, Robin."

Robin shook her head. "I'm okay. Honest."

"No, you're not," Dorothy said, letting her eyes move slowly over Robin's shaking body. "You've got a chill." She pulled the cover up around Robin, then went to the closet. "Let me get you something extra to warm you up." She pulled a pink knitted afghan on the shelf, folded it over her arm and came back to the bed.

Robin stared at the crocheted rosebuds on the afghan and shook her head.

"No, don't . . . I don't need that!"

"Nonsense, dear. Of course you do."

"I want to go home—"

"I'm afraid the trip home will have to wait until you're better."

"But I *am* better. I—"

"Stop that childish whining, Robin. Stop it this instant."

Robin stopped and swallowed hard.

"Just look at yourself," she said, pointing to Robin's shaking hands. Robin quickly tucked her hands beneath the blanket. "Now you know how I feel about lying, don't you?"

Silence.

"I'm talking to you, Robin. Please answer me."

Robin nodded finally.

"Then you admit you do feel ill?"

As much as Robin hated to admit it, even to herself, Dorothy was right. She did feel sick—very sick. She nodded again.

"Well, then, the first thing on the agenda has to be getting you well."

"When . . . ?" Robin said, the rest of the question getting lost somewhere deep in her throat. Which didn't matter since Dorothy answered the lost question anyway.

"You'll go home when you're well and not one minute sooner. Why, Daddy would have my head if I took you outdoors while you're feeling this way! And with a fever, no less."

Before she went to fix breakfast, Dorothy spread the afghan over Robin. Robin stared down at it.

The rosebuds, Robin, you know those rosebuds.

No, I don't either.

Sure you do.

Liar, liar, set your hair on fire. Eunice would never buy me a blanket with rosebuds. Never. Eunice likes big squares and stripes and wild designs, never flowers.

Yeah, what's so bad about flowers?

Nothing, I suppose, but Eunice says flowers are for touching and smelling . . .

And for tattoos on butts?

Yeah, right. Besides she'd never pick lousy ol' faded pink. She likes purple . . .

No way, it's you who like purple.

Okay, so I like purple. But she always bought me purple, so what's the big deal difference?

No difference. But what about the little pink rosebuds?

I told you, I don't know anything about those dumb rosebuds!

• • •

It was eleven o'clock Eastern time—after Marcus hung up from talking to his secretary Shari in Boston—that Woody Bagen passed on Mollie's message to him.

"What's going on out there?" Marcus asked when Mollie picked up. "I was told it was important."

"I'm worried about Robin, Marcus. She had an appointment to meet with me at nine o'clock this morning, she's more than two hours late."

"Maybe something came up. Did you try to contact Dorothy?"

"The last time I spoke to Dorothy was about four-fifteen yesterday afternoon. At the time, she said Robin was resting but felt much better."

"Well, that's a relief."

"The thing is, about eight o'clock last night I picked up a message from Robin on my answering machine. She sounded depressed, tired, said she wasn't feeling good. I tried to reach her, kept getting a busy signal, finally drove over to the apartment. By that time it was after eleven . . ."

"Go on."

"Well, I rang the doorbell, no answer. Finally I convinced the super to let me inside Dorothy's apartment to make sure nothing was wrong."

"And?"

"There was no one there, Marcus."

"Did you try upstairs? Maybe Robin wanted to—"

"Yes, no one was in your place either. I thought maybe Dorothy had taken Robin out shopping or to a movie, but Robin's message sounded so sleepy and sick . . ."

"Well, Dorothy did give her a sedative the night before, right after the snake incident. She felt it was warranted—and I didn't see the harm in it myself. Still . . ."

"Marcus, do you think she could have taken Robin someplace for the night? I mean, does she have family or close friends up around this area?''

''Not that I know of. The only family she's ever mentioned is a sister, died very young . . . But wait—when I first met her, she talked about a country cottage she and her late husband owned. She didn't say where it was, but it could be in the area. She might have decided to take Robin there to cheer her up.''

''Without telling you?''

''I wouldn't think so. But then she had no way to reach me. When I left, I didn't even have an itinerary. And by the time I tried to call, the line was busy.''

''Oh, yes, the telephone. Not busy, Marcus, off the hook.''

A few moments of silence, then, ''Look, Mollie, I agree, it's all very peculiar, but Dorothy is one of the most responsible people I know. Particularly with a child. I wouldn't have left Robin with her if I didn't know that.''

Another long silence, then Mollie said, ''There is one more thing. Last night I was looking through a paper Robin wrote for me on her feelings. In it she refers to a plastic wizard, someone or something she was deathly afraid of. Neither Robin or I could figure out the symbolism, but last night I thought of the Wizard of Oz. Dorothy could be—''

''Hold it right there. For one thing, I can't believe that a person—any person, child included—could be afraid of someone without knowing it. For another, there's no way in hell Robin could be scared of Dorothy. Sure, the Welcome Lady—that's what she calls her sometimes—may not be her favorite person, someone she'd choose for a friend, but Dorothy Cotton as an object of fear is just ludicrous, Mollie.

For Christ's sake, at worst, the woman is a lonely misfit who wants only to feel needed.''

None of which meant Marcus wasn't worried—or for that matter, pissed. Dorothy had no business taking Robin off somewhere—anywhere—without first clearing it with him. It would never happen again, he'd see to it. When he got home, he'd sit down with Dorothy and, being as tactful as he knew how, he'd set the woman straight.

Dorothy sponged Robin down, changed her into a clean nightie, persuaded her to eat some of her breakfast, take her vitamin, and brush her teeth. Finally—unable to contain her excitement any longer—she brought in a small gift-wrapped box, sat down on the bed and handed it to Robin.

"It's for you," she said, smiling. "Go on, open it."

Robin looked at the box, then slowly untied the red ribbon.

"You're such a slowpoke, Robin. Come on, go a little faster."

Robin pulled off the paper, then the lid. Inside was a red diary with a gold leaf emblem on the cover. Robin looked over to the dresser.

"That's right, exactly like that one." Dorothy took a pen from her dress pocket and handed it to Robin. "And like that one, you'll want it filled up with delightful, mischievous, secret thoughts. Don't think I don't know that every girl has those. When I was a girl I had a diary too, though I called it a journal. And it was my very best friend all through school."

The child said nothing.

Dorothy took the diary from her hands and placed it on the bedside table, along with the pen and one tiny key. The other key she slipped into her pocket.

"It'll be right here waiting when you're ready, Robin.

Now I'm going to wish with all my might that you'll begin your first entry today—and I hope I won't be disappointed.''

"What about Mollie?" Robin said.

"What about her?"

"Can I call her?"

"That would be fine if I had a telephone. But I don't.''

"But you said we'd call.''

"Oh, no, I've never had a phone here so I couldn't have said any such thing. It would be a shame to spoil the lovely quiet and privacy we have here with a telephone.''

"But you said—''

"No, you're mistaken, dear. In any event, you needn't concern yourself over Dr. Striker. I'm sure she has enough patients to keep her busy.''

Dorothy mopped the floor and dusted the furniture in the bedroom, then headed to the door.

"Once you're feeling better, Robin, we'll do lots of fun things. You'll see. Oh, I'll want you to share in the chores—taking on responsibility is an important part of growing and mending. But a job is only hard when you dislike it, so we must see that you learn to enjoy those responsibilities. And oh, yes, before I forget . . .'' She turned and faced Robin, with her palm pressed against the doorjamb. "Amelia always called me Mama. I would like you to do the same.''

She walked over, kissed Robin on the forehead, then left.

She said it!

   She didn't say it!

   You heard her say it.

   That wasn't her, stupid, that was my head saying it. Don't you know I'm crazy?

   Mollie says you're not.

Mollie's wrong.

I know who the Wizard is, do you?

No and I don't want to know either.

Well, I'm gonna tell you anyway.

No, you're not. If I have to, I'll put my hands over my ears and press hard and start singing so loud that I'll drown you out!

CHAPTER 12

Marcus landed at Logan Airport, called Dorothy's number, then his own, then Mollie's.

"Marcus here. I just got in. Heard anything?"

"Nothing, and I've been here all day."

"Look, I'm heading over to the apartment now, I'll call you from there."

"No, I'll meet you there, okay?"

As soon as Marcus' taxi pulled up, he spotted Mollie in jeans and a jacket, waiting in front of the building. Together they went upstairs and banged on the door to Dorothy's apartment, then upstairs to his. Once inside, he picked up the telephone.

"The police?" she asked.

"Eunice," he said. "Somehow, she's got to be involved in this."

"Marcus, I don't think—"

"You rang?" the voice answered.

"Eunice, have you talked to Robin?"

A pause, then, "Sure. Last month, last year, when did you have in mind?"

"I mean, today. Or yesterday for that matter."

"Wait a second, sweetie, why ask me, why not ask your daughter direct?"

"I would if I could, but she's not here. And why do I believe you know where she is?"

Eunice laughed. "So, our little girl has gone and run away on her little ol' Daddy perfect, has she?"

"She didn't run away. I went to San Francisco yesterday. I left her overnight with Dorothy, and—"

"Dor-o-thy?"

"Look, Eunice, get serious or get sober, whatever the hell it takes. If you know where she is—"

"For Christ's sake, why don't you ask Dorothy?"

"Because I just got home, and neither of them is here, that's why."

"Well, maybe she took her shopping. Or maybe to church, she looks the church type."

"Eunice, Robin's therapist is here with me. According to her, Robin and Dorothy haven't been home since early last evening. She's been trying to reach them."

Silence, then, "Marc, are you saying what I think . . . My Birdie's been kidnapped?"

"Not kidnapped. Just missing. Temporarily. I just thought maybe you'd—"

The phone slammed in his ear.

He stood there a moment, then headed for the door. Mollie followed him downstairs again to Dorothy's apartment.

He took a credit card from his wallet, crouched down on the hallway carpet, then slid the card between the door and the jamb. After a few tries, the lock released, and they stepped inside.

He looked around: the fussy knickknacks, the dainty

antique dishes, the plaques and pictures and embroidered pillows, the cuckoo clock, even the little doilies on the sofa and chairs . . . All missing. He took a deep breath.

"What, Marcus?"

"This place looks like a—there were things, antiques, all kinds of bric-a-brac."

"Oh, God. When I went through here last night, I had this feeling . . . Dammit, I should have said something."

Marcus went right to the telephone and grabbed up the receiver. This time, the police . . .

Robin's mind had been racing all day. No matter how hard she tried to shut off her thoughts, she couldn't—one side of her head playing against the other, one side of her head always nosing in its two cents' worth, trying to wear the other side down.

Nosing in its two cents' worth . . . Like the Welcome Lady, yeah, just like the Welcome Lady.

Don't call her that!

Why not?

Because her name's Mama, you heard her, didn't you?

Sure, big deal. What's she gonna do if I don't call her Mama?

You'd better hope you don't find out.

You're just a big wimp, that's all.

I am not!

Are too, are too!

Dorothy walked into the bedroom, and Robin looked up. "Tired, dear?"

A shrug.

Dorothy looked at the diary. "Can I take a peek inside?"

A nod.

Dorothy clicked the gold fastener. "You must be sure to

lock it, Robin. Diaries should be kept locked for safekeeping.'' She flipped through the pages until she reached October twenty-eighth—a blank page. She skimmed through the other pages, flipped back to the twenty-eighth, placed the opened diary on Robin's lap and handed her the pen.

''Come now, Robin, do it for Mama.''

''I don't know what to say.''

''Oh, anything. Any feeling, any idea that comes to mind. You'll see, once you get started—it's fun.''

Robin picked up the pen.

''Well,'' Dorothy said, smiling, ''I guess I know when it's time to make my exit.''

Robin put the pen to the page.

Don't do it! Don't!

But I have to.

You don't have to do anything you don't want to do.

Who says?

Eunice says. She said it a million times, didn't you ever hear her? No one can make you say anything or do anything you don't want to. No one!

Eunice, her eyes red and puffy, showed up at Dorothy's apartment a half hour after the police arrived.

''You ass!'' she shouted at Marcus. ''You left Birdie with that psychotic bitch. Birdie knew what she was, why didn't you?''

''She told you that?''

''She didn't have to. All I had to do was see the way Birdie looked at her.''

Marcus sat there, staring at her.

''Damn you, say something!'' She shoved him, then began beating at him with her fists. Derry, the hefty officer standing near the door, came over and grabbed Eunice from the back. As he pulled her off Marcus, she turned on him, landing one fist in his stomach and another on his eye.

"Ow, dammit!"

"Cuff her if you have to," Landry, the other cop, said, circling behind Eunice.

Derry pulled out the handcuffs, snatched one of Eunice's wildly flinging arms, then fought to get the other one while she screamed and cursed. Mollie rushed over to them.

"Don't . . . don't do that," Mollie said. "Let me talk to her. I'm a doctor."

"Look at her." Derry lost one of her arms and dodged a fist aimed at his groin. "You don't talk to this kind, you lock 'em up until they learn to stay still."

Mollie glanced over at Marcus, who looked as though he had never laid eyes on either of them. She turned back to the officer.

"How would this look in a news story?" she said. "Cuffing a mother, hysterical because her child is missing?"

"Well, I . . ."

He pulled back out of the way while Mollie put her arm around the other woman, drawing her tightly against her.

"Let's go upstairs, Eunice," she whispered in her ear, walking her to the door.

"Hey, wait," Landry called out. "I might need to talk—"

"Upstairs," Mollie said.

Robin sat there, staring at the diary. It must have been for a long time, because the sunlight dimmed and the room got darker. Daddy must be home now, wondering where she was. She wished she could call him, but there was no telephone. Was she well yet? No, probably not . . . and what if she never ever got well, what if—

Suddenly Dorothy was beside her. She picked up the diary, looked through it, then, sighing deeply, set it down on the bedside table.

"Turn over, Robin," she said.

"Why?"

"Just do as I say."

Robin rolled over onto her belly. She could feel the cool air as Dorothy's hands gently lifted her nightgown up around her shoulders. One of Dorothy's hands left her back, then it was there again. Suddenly Robin's body jerked as something sharp pierced her skin. Another jerk; she bit back a scream, then began to cry into her pillow as she heard Dorothy quietly begin to count . . .

When it was over, Dorothy sat her up and studied her bleeding back. She took a tissue from her pocket and wiped Robin's cheeks, her lips pressed tightly together.

"Don't cry, they're only little nicks, and you'll see, they'll heal quickly. Would you like me to fix them for you?"

Oh, God.

"Would you, Robin?"

She nodded.

"Then can you ask me nicely to do it?"

"Fix it, please fix it."

"And if you could just use my name, Robin. I would like that so much."

Robin's eyes locked into Dorothy's eyes. She sucked in air and as she let it out, she whispered, "Mama."

Dorothy was back with the first aid kit before Robin even knew she was gone. Quickly and gently the cuts were cleansed, treated with nonstinging antiseptic, then bandaged, and Dorothy was saying good night and kissing her cheek.

"We'll do the first diary entry tomorrow, how's that?"
Silence.

"Robin?"

Finally she nodded. "Can I have one of those pills?"

"You mean a sedative? Drugs aren't to be used so lightly, dear. They can be habit-forming, as I'm sure you know."

"But last time, yesterday—"

"Sometimes drugs are necessary, and sometimes they're not. And only Mama can make that distinction."

I told you what would happen, big mouth, didn't I?

I didn't think it'd be that bad.

What do you mean it wouldn't be that bad, it was way worse for Amelia, wasn't it?

There, you said it! After all this time, I finally got you to say it!

You're hearing things, I didn't say anything. Besides, I shouldn't be talking to you, I should be trying to think what to do.

I've already been thinking.

So what'd you come up with?

I don't know . . . I'm trying to think what Eunice would do.

Nothing—don't you get it yet? Eunice is just a big bag of wind. If I hadn't been so busy trying to be like her, none of this would have happened. Not even Amelia dying.

Well, at least you're blaming her now.

I am not blaming her. It's my fault, all of it!

Then maybe that's why you're here. To get your punishment.

If I get mine, you'll get yours, too . . . Okay, big mouth, run out of words? Wimping out yourself now?

And if I was?

I'd hate your guts.

Okay, so don't worry, I'm not scared. And I'll figure a way out for us, you'll see.

Robin closed her eyes, her back aching, itching . . . Then, as though a light had flared up in some dark place in her head, it came to her: if she pulled up her nightgown to look at her back, now there would be something to see.

Dorothy lifted the tiny manicure scissors out of the alcohol where they had been soaking, dried them with a soft, clean cloth and slipped them into the snug leather holder. It was the same tool she had always used with Amelia . . . small, sharp, and always available in her pocket. The important thing was to keep it sterile to prevent it from causing an infection.

She had tried to act very matter-of-fact about the punishment so as not to upset Robin any more than was necessary, but the truth was, every time she was forced to dole out discipline, it took a little bit of her insides out along the way. She often felt the pain herself, sometimes for days after the actual wound had healed. But punishments were punishments—necessary and beyond her control.

She simply did what she needed to do.

Robin was nearly asleep when it started again.

Ready to talk about it now?

What?

Amelia.

Uh-uh, too tired. Lay off.

We have to.

I can't. I don't remember, at least not all . . .

What d'ya think I'm here for—to do a shuffle-ball-chain across the ceiling?

Tomorrow—we'll talk about it tomorrow?

Every day matters, and we're running out of time. How do you expect me to figure a way off this funny farm when you're not even willing to face facts?

Okay, okay . . . Go ahead.

We already talked about how super modest Amelia was—how she wouldn't show skin, how she wouldn't wear your bikini. Well, that day, when she ran off to the lockers to put on her dork suit, you ran after her holding the bikini . . .

I told her to stop being such an old lady.

Right. Then she told me to face it, she was just the priss type . . . And you said, no way—you, the great Robin Garr, were gonna show her different. You pulled open the locker room door, then—

Oh, God!

Remember?

Say it!

She had her back to the door, but she jerked around, pressing up against the wall. On her chest she had a raised beauty mark, the same kind of mark that was on the Welcome Lady's forehead. Her face was all red, her arms were wrapped across her chest, and her eyes and my eyes . . .

Go on . . .

We just looked at each other. Then she asked me to never tell and I swore to God I wouldn't. Amelia shut the door and I stood there, fighting to erase that picture—that gross, awful, disgusting picture! There were hundreds . . . hundreds of burns and little scars across her back!

Muffled sobs shook Robin's body as she buried her face

deep in the pillow. She should have asked Amelia about it later, but she never did. She should have told someone, but she never did that either.

Now . . . can I sleep now?
Okay, now.

Though the hysteria had fizzled away as soon as they left Dorothy's apartment, Eunice refused to talk to Mollie once they got upstairs. Instead she went into Robin's bedroom and sat inside with the door closed. When the officers left, Marcus came up, made a phone call, then went into Robin's bedroom to try and talk to Eunice. But after only a few minutes, Eunice came rushing out of the bedroom and left the apartment.

Marcus went over to the parlor window and looked out over the street. He watched Eunice get into her car and drive away, then turned to Mollie.

"The police don't see it as a kidnapping," he said.

"What does that mean?"

"They say the circumstances don't justify it. I left Robin in Dorothy's care, and as far as they're concerned, Dorothy may have simply gone off with her for the weekend. There's clothes still in her dresser and closet, dishes and food in the kitchen cupboards."

"What about what's missing?"

"Not sufficient proof that she's moved out. In any event, they're willing to reconsider if she's not back in forty-eight hours. Then they'll likely call in the FBI."

"What about until then?"

"I just made a call to a fellow I know at headquarters, a Detective Downing. As a favor, he's running a check on the police computer now, trying to get some information on Dorothy. She told me she did volunteer work at Beth Israel. Downing's checking that out, too."

"What about a phone tap?"

"It's not about ransom, that much I'm sure of. In a way I wish it were. I just think Dorothy was lonely, she wanted someone to take care of. Maybe she figured taking Robin . . ." He stopped and took a deep breath. "Dammit, I know so little about her!"

Mollie laid her hand on his arm. "Look, don't waste energy blaming yourself. You thought Dorothy was a positive influence on Robin."

"You didn't?"

"Well, sometimes I wondered, other times I did see her as a mothering figure. It just seemed that her interest in Robin developed so quickly. But then again, look at me—I haven't known Robin all that long and I'm involved beyond the call of duty."

"I've got to do something," he said. "I can't just stand around here until Monday night. Maybe the neighbors . . . Dorothy lived here a couple of years, they ought to know something that could help me track her."

"Last night I talked to the woman who lives next to Dorothy. She's been here twelve years and doesn't know her."

"Maybe you just picked the wrong neighbor. Over a couple of years she must have gotten to know someone."

As they headed out to question the neighbors, Marcus said, "All I keep thinking about is that Wizard business you brought up this morning, Mollie. And the idea that Robin's been hauled off by a woman she's been scared of all along. Then I've got to ask *why*—dammit, why? Did she know something we didn't?"

Dorothy left a dim hall light on for Robin. Without the sedatives to help her tonight, the child's nightmares would be back, likely darker and more terrifying than before. And Dorothy would have to be ready to handle them.

She felt wonderful, more alive than at any time since the day Amelia went off to camp. Dorothy had felt a sense of foreboding about the camp from the very beginning. But Amelia had pleaded and cajoled, and made all kinds of lovely promises, then written that letter to Howard asking for the camp tuition. And Howard, so very much like Marcus Garr, was always unable to put his foot down when it came to his little girl.

Still it was Dorothy's decision, as it always was when it came to Amelia. But for some reason—one of those weak moments that came so rarely—Dorothy had gone against her better judgment and given in. Two full months at Camp Raintree. To think of it: one weak moment, one foolish mistake, and suddenly another child is dead. It was a weakness she swore to God she would never let happen again.

Of course, Robin was a different type of child to begin with. Amelia had come to Dorothy as a newborn, unscathed and beautiful. Robin was coming to her with an overload of sorry baggage to flush away. Fortunately Dorothy was a natural when it came to motherhood, she was the kind of mother who could work miracles with any child. She had proven her aptness for nurturing with her daughter, hadn't she? Why, every adult Amelia had ever come in contact with had told Dorothy they had never seen a sweeter, better behaved, more obedient child.

This time it would be more difficult, more like it was with her baby sister. It would take a little more patience, a little more work, a little more love. And as much as she hated having to even think of it, a lot more discipline. Robin was not simply a volatile, spicy, difficult-to-contain personality, she was a child with blood on her hands.

Robin heard the screaming in her head, then felt Dorothy beside her, forcing her to sit up, then suddenly the stinging slap. Her hand went to her cheek, her eyes opened—the screaming had stopped.

"It's okay, Robin, it's Mama."

Silence.

"Were you having bad dreams?"

More silence.

"Answer me."

"I don't know."

Dorothy sighed. "Don't you see, dear? It's your conscience not letting you rest. You killed Amelia, and the only way to be forgiven for that is to be punished. Over and over again, until you can rest easy."

Robin swallowed hard.

"Robin, dear, do you understand that I must be the one to inflict the punishment? It's not something I want to do or like to do, but I have no choice in the matter—I simply do what I must."

She felt a lump rising in her throat. Growing bigger and bigger . . .

Suddenly Dorothy embraced Robin, cuddling her close.

"Now, I want you to be Mama's brave little girl." She lifted Robin out of bed to the floor and led her into the bathroom. There she slipped off the child's nightgown with one hand and turned on the cold water faucet full force in the shower with the other. She opened the clear plastic curtain and pushed Robin inside the stall, under the icy water, holding one of her hands inside the shower to keep Robin from readjusting the faucets.

Dorothy stood outside the stall, biting down hard on her lips. Robin's screams stopped after a minute or two, and she crouched down on the tile floor, hugging herself. Finally Dorothy turned off the faucet, wrapped a towel around her and lifted her out.

"Come, dear, let me dry you before you get a chill. Look at you, you're trembling."

Robin didn't speak as Dorothy rubbed her dry, treated her cuts, slipped her nightgown back over her head, brushed her hair, then took her back to bed. Finally Dorothy pulled the blankets up around her, kissed her forehead and said, "Goodnight."

Just as Robin was falling off to sleep, she heard her bedroom door open; a moment or so later, she heard it close. Then, as she heard the music box playing, she formed the words in her head . . .

Rock-a-bye baby on the tree top, when the wind blows, the cradle will rock. When the bough breaks, the cradle will fall, and down will come baby, down will come baby, down will come baby—

Hey Robin . . .

Silence.

Come on, say something, aren't you gonna say something?

More silence.

Come on, say anything, any little stupid thing you can think to say.

Ondi, Condi, ish kiddie boom boom. Hi Timmy, hey Timmy, ho Timmy, rum dum. Polly witchie cameo.

Well, at least you haven't lost it all yet. That's part of one of those wacky stories that Eunice made up. But I'm too cold to laugh.

Me too.

Silence.

Pst, hey Robin.

Stop it, I wanna go to sleep . . .

Just one question, I promise just one . . . If I don't ask it, I'll never sleep again.

Okay, what?

Is that what crazy really is?

CHAPTER 13

Marcus tried the super's apartment first, found no one home and went on to the neighbors. As he completed the fifth interview on the first two floors—only one neighbor could even place who Dorothy was—he thought of Robin's friend, Calvin.

He went outside: eleven o'clock on a Saturday night he was bound to find some kids around. He spotted two teens in the alley, leaning against a dumpster, drinking beer.

"Either of you guys know a kid lives around here named Calvin? He'd be twelve or thirteen, eighth grade?"

"Who wants to know?" a boy with glasses asked.

Marcus pulled a twenty from his pocket and held it out. "Me. Look, no hassle, I just need to ask him a few questions."

The kids exchanged looks, then the boy pointed to the building next to Marcus'.

"If it's the kid I think you mean, he lives right there. His old man's a con."

Marcus nodded. "What else—last name, apartment number?"

The boy shrugged. "Don't know the apartment, but the last name's Shepherd."

Marcus handed him the twenty and went to Calvin's building. When he found the name Shepherd listed on the third floor, he rang the bell. A woman's voice came over the intercom.

"I'm Marcus Garr, a neighbor," he said. "I'd like to talk to Calvin Shepherd."

"What do you want with him?"

"Just to ask him a few questions. He's a friend of my daughter, Robin. It's important, she's missing."

There was a long pause, then the buzzer rang and Marcus went inside. He took the elevator to the third floor, and as he got out he saw a skinny woman with bad skin staring at him from her doorway.

"I'm Calvin's mother," she said. "And he's been here all evening, so if you're about to—"

"Hold on. I'm not accusing him of anything. I just need to talk to him."

She nodded, then led him into the kitchen, where Calvin was waiting.

"Calvin, I'm Robin's father. She's missing—can you answer some questions for me?"

"Sure."

"When was the last time you saw her?"

"You mean to talk to her?"

"Whatever."

"Well, I was up to your apartment Thursday right after school. Since then, I didn't see her. Rang your doorbell yesterday afternoon to see if she wanted to come out, but there was no answer."

"Do you know Dorothy Cotton?"

"Her? Yeah, sure, I know her."

"You say it like you don't like her."

"Well, I don't like the way she's always snoopin' around Robin."

"What do you mean snooping?"

"Just that she's always around. She waits outside after school to make sure Robin goes right home."

"Dorothy tells her to go inside?"

"Naw, she don't have to tell her. Just her bein' there, watchin', is enough."

"Maybe Robin goes inside because she wants to."

"Maybe. But it sure don't look like it."

A moment of silence, then, "What else do you know about Dorothy?"

Calvin shrugged. "Not much, it's not like she's been around here that long."

"She's lived here two, three years."

"Uh-uh, no way. I seen her move in myself not so long ago."

Marcus stared at Calvin. "How long ago?"

"She moved in just before you guys did."

"How much before?"

"A week, maybe a little more."

"You're sure of that?"

"Yep. I seen the men carry her stuff in."

"Did you see the moving van?"

"Yeah."

"Was there a name on it?"

"If there was, I couldn't see it from my window. The van was parked more toward the corner."

"Can you describe the van?"

"Not much to describe. It looked like a regular-sized movin' van. It was blue."

"Think. Were there letters, designs, markings? Anything at all?"

Calvin thought for a minute, then shook his head. "Sorry."

"What about the color of the license plates? Front plates, back plates, both?"

He shook his head again.

"Okay, okay. Did you ever see Dorothy anywhere besides walking around outside? I mean at a grocery store, a doctor's office, library, church, a neighbor's house, any place at all?"

"Just walkin' around the neighborhood, that's it. When I saw her, she was usually stickin' close to Robin."

"Ever see her talk to anyone, another neighbor?"

"Never. Oh, yeah, once I seen her tell some little kid to get out of the street."

"When was the last time you saw Dorothy?"

"Yesterday afternoon. She was standing out in the courtyard packin' up her car."

"What kind—"

"Chevy wagon, dark blue. I dunno the model, but I'd say it's an 'eighty-six or 'eighty-seven."

"What about the license number?"

"Sorry, I never looked."

"Think hard, maybe the color of the plate. Was it a Massachusetts plate?"

"I don't know, but . . ."

"What, Calvin?"

"I don't remember the color—I'd say if I did. But yesterday the car was parked face on to me. And I could of sworn there was a front plate on it, so I guess it's not a Massachusetts plate."

"Okay. Bumper stickers? Markings?"

He shook his head.

Marcus took a deep breath. "You said you saw Dorothy packing. What exactly do you mean?"

"Ya' know, packin'. Puttin' cardboard boxes in the back of the station wagon."

"Did you see her drive out of the courtyard?"

"No. I stopped lookin' at about five-thirty, six o'clock. I never looked since . . . Mr. Garr, did Dorothy kidnap Robin?"

Marcus swallowed hard. "It looks that way."

"Jesus, shit, I knew that lady was nuts."

"You did?"

"Sure, anybody could tell that. The way she was all over Robin. And she didn't even hardly know her."

Sure, anybody . . . anybody but him. He took a deep breath, then, "Tell me something, Calvin, you seem like a perceptive kid—"

"What's that mean?"

"It means you sense things about people. So would you say Robin was scared of Dorothy?"

"She said she wasn't, but I didn't believe her."

"What makes you think she was?"

"I dunno, maybe it's that perceptive stuff you said I had . . . But whenever Dorothy was around, Robin was real uptight. And most of the times she let her call the shots. I guess I wouldn't of thought it was so weird if it was anybody but Robin."

"Why's that?"

"Well, Robin's tough, not like most girls. I oughta know, she beat me up. But when she was around Dorothy, she was different. Though she did kind of win that last round with the lady."

"What round?"

"Just that Robin knew it pissed Dorothy off when she'd see me or ask me upstairs to your place, but she did it anyway."

"Did Dorothy say anything to try to stop Robin from bringing you home?"

"You still don't get it, Mr. Garr. Dorothy didn't have to say anything. All she had to do was look at Robin. I could tell, it took a lot of guts for Robin to cross her."

After Marcus thanked Calvin, Mrs. Shepherd, who had remained quiet the entire time, walked Marcus to the door.

"Look, I didn't stick my two cents in before," she said, "but everything my kid said about that lady, I believe it."

"Why? Do you know her?"

"I met her once. She came up here to talk to me about your daughter."

"I don't understand."

"I never told Calvin, but a couple of weeks ago she came up here and had the nerve to tell me to keep my kid away from Robin. I asked her why—I figured, hey, maybe he was causing some trouble. But no, it was nothing like that. She said, and I quote, 'I will not have my Robin hanging around with such a low-caliber boy as your son.' Can you believe it? Not even her own kid, and there she is trying to pass out orders."

When Marcus got back to the apartment, he called Downing.

"So far, our computer picks up nothing on the lady, not even a driver's license."

"Look, what about the volunteer service at Beth Israel?"

"Her name wasn't on their list, but they said to try back tomorrow morning when the department head will be in."

"I've been doing some talking to the neighbors here. It seems Dorothy Cotton's car had two license plates."

"Not much help. Okay, so it's not registered in Massachusetts. But the Commonwealth is about the only state left that uses only one plate. Unless you can get me a license plate number, or at least a part of one . . .''

Mollie walked in as Marcus put down the phone from trying to call Eunice.

''I talked to two neighbors who remember seeing her on the elevator, Marcus. But that's about it. It doesn't make much sense—''

''Actually it does. According to Calvin, that friend of Robin's, Dorothy moved here about seven weeks ago, not long before us.''

Mollie drew in her breath; Marcus went over to the hall closet, opened it and skimmed through the clothes until he came to a flannel-lined jean jacket, then slipped it off the hanger. ''Robin's jacket,'' he said, staring down at it.

''She has others, doesn't she?''

''Yeah. But this is the one she always wears.''

Eunice got two tickets for speeding before she stopped at a dingy bar and ordered two double scotches. She had done one hell of a stinko job of watching out for her Birdie, not that Marc had done much better. And it all started with that hokey camp . . .

Now with enough alcohol pumping in her veins to hold off the panic in her brain, she could zero in on her first major mistake—allowing Marc to force Birdie back to camp for another summer of fun and games. But if Birdie really didn't want to go, why didn't she huff and puff and blow the goddamned house in? Hadn't Eunice tried to teach her to stand her own ground, make her own choices?

Hang it away, Eunice, the issue is moot: now some virgin-faced lunatic alias kind sweet neighbor lady is making all the choices for her. She simply horned right into Birdie's space, whisked her up and carried her away. And for how long—a weekend, a week, a month, a year? Maybe forever.

As Eunice finished off her fourth drink, a guy with dark hair and a mustache sat next to her. He gestured to her nearly empty glass.

"Buy you another one, beautiful lady?"

Silence.

"What're you drinking, scotch?" He hailed the bartender, ordered two scotches, and slid one in front of her. "Come on now, don't be so unfriendly. The name's Carlos, so what's yours?"

"Fuck-up."

He laughed. "So okay, you've got a sense of humor—I like that in a lady. Hey, how come I never seen you around here before? You new to the neighborhood?"

"Fuck off," she said.

Again he laughed. "Hey, what about just plain old fuck, you've heard of that, huh?" He waited, when she said nothing, he said, "What do you say we go over to my place. I live not far from here."

She looked up at him. "Yeah?"

He smiled, took out his wallet and tossed some bills on the counter. As he slipped his wallet back in his pocket, Eunice lifted her drink and poured it down his crotch.

He jumped to his feet, grabbing for a napkin. "Damn you, bitch!" he shouted, but Eunice was already at the door.

She strode out into the middle of the parking lot, threw down her purse, cupped her hands to her mouth and began to scream: "Come out, come out, wherever you are! You hear me, Birdie?

"It's me, Eunice, and no fooling around now, I want you home right this minute!"

For the past forty-five minutes, Dorothy had sat in the straight-backed chair by Robin's bed and watched her toss and turn in her sleep. The nightmares were bad, but not bad enough to wake her. It would take time for the nightmares to go, but she had the patience of Job. And though Robin didn't know how much about patience, Dorothy would teach her.

She reached out and stroked Robin's hair. She had always liked little girls in short, neat hairdos, but most young girls wanted to wear their hair long and fussily arranged to attract the boys. That's what she had expected of Robin, both from Amelia's letters and from what she knew of her. Robin's short hair had come as a surprise.

For that matter, Robin's presence still surprised her. Though Dorothy had prepared for this moment she hadn't believed it would come so soon. Where they would live was never an issue—what better place to settle than where Amelia and Robin had last played together? But still, she had to make that emotional connection with Robin—such things didn't always come easy with a twelve-year-old. But the moment Dorothy met her, she sensed the child's desperate need, and though she wasn't eager to reach out herself, when Dorothy did the reaching Robin had grabbed hold of her hand as though she were sinking.

Which, of course, was exactly what she had been doing. If Dorothy hadn't known Robin's home situation by what had happened at camp, she certainly knew it once she met Eunice. Marcus tried his best, but he was, after all, a man, and a man's best was not good enough. Which made her, Dorothy, the natural choice.

Dorothy leaned over Robin, gently pulled down the back neckline of her nightie and lifted the bandage. The injury was already healing quite nicely. When she secured the bandage again, Robin's arms started to swing out. Dorothy grabbed them and held them down tightly at the child's sides, then waited until the calmness set in again.

Robin, of course, didn't have to be told that Mama was

right there keeping her safe while she slept. Children had a definite sense of those things.

Marcus sat with a cup of lukewarm tea in front of him, lost in thought. The phone hadn't rung, but he didn't expect it would. He had been wrong about Dorothy in many ways, but he still felt certain that she wasn't interested in money. What she was interested in was Robin. He had known that, seen it—so why had it never occurred to him that her interest was abnormal?

But the question that really stuck in his mind was why she lied about how long she had lived in the apartment house. What purpose could the lie serve except to keep him from knowing she'd just moved in herself? He'd gone over it a hundred and one times in his head and could come up with only one answer: she had moved here on purpose, to be near Robin.

But if Dorothy had known Robin before moving here, Robin would have recognized her. Besides, even if it were true, how in hell had this stranger learned that he and Robin would be moving from Andover to Boston?

He looked at Mollie, sitting across from him, deep in her own thoughts.

"You know what stumps me the most?" he said.

"Probably the same thing that stumps me. Was it a coincidence that Dorothy Cotton moved here only days before you? And if it was, why'd she lie to you?"

He nodded. "So I'm not out in left field."

"If you are, so am I. Could the move have been planned, Marcus?"

"It had to be. But why? How?" He reached over, took the phone from the counter and brought it to the table.

"What, Marcus?"

He began to press in numbers. "I don't know why, but I can work on the how."

"Who're you calling?"

"My sec— Shari, Marcus here."

"Marcus, do you know what time it is?"

"I need to ask you some questions."

"They couldn't wait till Monday?"

"This is serious, Shari. Robin is missing."

"Oh, my God, what happened?"

"I don't know exactly, but you might be able to help me find out. Before I moved in here, did anyone ask about my new address?"

A long pause. "No one. Even if someone had, I wouldn't have given the address out unless I had your okay."

Marcus sighed. "Thanks anyway, Shari. I guess—"

"Wait, Marcus."

"What?"

"There was one call—it was a little odd. A woman said she was a lawyer and had heard through the grapevine you'd just rented a nice apartment. She went on about how hard it was to find a suitable apartment in Boston, wound up asking for the name of the broker you went through. I gave it to her."

"That's it?"

"That's it. Should I have kept my mouth shut?"

"Probably. Not that you could have known. Anyway, thanks."

Marcus put down the phone and told Mollie what Shari had said.

"So that's how Dorothy got the address," he finished. "But it still doesn't account for how she knew I was moving to Boston."

"Eunice knew you were moving," Mollie said. "Robin knew. For that matter, you knew. You must have mentioned it to friends, associates. The question is, of all the people who must have known, who could have told Dorothy?''

''And we're back to the biggie: Why? She did mention once that Robin reminded her a little of her baby sister. But the sister died years ago when Dorothy was a child.''

Suddenly Marcus stood up and rushed to the bathroom. He pushed aside the curtains, then threw open the window and took some deep breaths of fresh air. He looked down to the street—a bunch of boys together, one kicked a beer can, which hit a moving car. The car accelerated, squealing as it speeded away, the boys roared.

A Saturday night in Boston . . .

CHAPTER 14

ROBIN had been awake since the sun came up. She sat on
her bed, her eyes moving from the new red diary on her
bedside stand to the old diary on the dresser.

Go on, look.

Uh-uh, don't want to.

Why not?

*You just don't go nosing into other people's diaries,
that's why not. It's uncivilized.*

Not something you would ever do, of course . . . ?

What's that supposed to mean?

You really want to know?

*What I really want is to be on the early-bird special to
Boston, but since I'm not, I might as well listen to you. So
go ahead.*

*Remember how every night at camp before lights-out,
Amelia wrote something in her diary, just like at every
bedtime, she'd whip off a single-paged letter home?*

Yeah. I said she must be super close to her mother.

And she said if she didn't write, she'd be in trouble.

Ol' Mama wanted to know everything, every single little

199

thing she did. And if Mama suspected that she wasn't telling everything, she might whisk her right out of camp. Maybe even do worse. Well, remember the night Amelia ground her teeth so loud, you couldn't sleep? You reached over to jab her awake, but instead knocked the diary from where she'd hid it underneath her pillow. You rolled off your cot, down on the floor to pick up the diary. Any of this ring a bell?

Yeah. There were loose pages, I wondered how they'd fallen out . . . Had she torn them out? I checked the date at the top of the first sheet, then opened the diary to put them back. But there was already an entry for that same date . . .

So you read the loose paper for July second, your first day at camp.

That was the real one. The diary pages were just hokey made-up stuff for Amelia's mother.

Right. Just for Mama. But then—

"Rise and shine!"

Robin jumped, then watched Dorothy carry in a full breakfast tray adorned by a yellow rose in a white vase.

"I hope you're hungry, dear." She set the tray on Robin's lap. "I made blueberry pancakes."

Robin hated blueberries, but she nodded.

"I'm going to count one, two, three . . . And by that time I hope to hear a nice morning greeting."

Don't do it . . .

Shut up! Are you retarded? Don't you see I have to?

Robin took a deep shuddering breath, and, before Dorothy reached three, said, "Good morning, Mama." As she swallowed her vitamin with her orange juice, she was already trying to think of something acceptable to write in her diary.

• • •

Marcus, who had fallen asleep on the parlor chair, woke with a start at six A.M. He looked over at Mollie, curled up asleep on the sofa with the blanket he'd thrown over her, left the apartment quietly and headed downstairs.

He banged on the door several minutes before the super finally opened it. The big man scratched his head, then said, "Apartment thirty-two, Garr. Right?"

"Right. Listen, I need some information on one of the tenants. Dorothy Cotton."

He looked at his watch. "Hey, Mr. Garr, it's like dawn. Couldn't this of waited?"

"She's a suspect in a crime."

A sigh, then, "Okay, what d'ya want to know?"

"First off, when did she move here?"

"I don't remember the date, but it was maybe a week before you."

"She made out an application ahead of time?"

"Sure, those are the rules. Everybody does."

"Good. I need to see it."

"Hey, I can't just let you see that. That stuff's personal."

"Friday night my daughter disappeared. I have reason to believe she's with Mrs. Cotton."

"Jesus. You just find that out?"

"Last night. I tried to reach you then."

"I was out. Hey, this got anything to do with that lady doctor who had me open Mrs. Cotton's apartment the other night?"

"It does. So will you show me the application?"

"Shit, I hope I don't get into trouble for this." The man led him into a small room off the living room, opened a drawer and went through files until he came up with one labeled Cotton.

Marcus opened it. The address on the application read: 17

Palm Terrace, Orlando, Florida. Three out-of-state residents were given as references. There was a copy of a similar form from Hook Realty, the same agent Marcus had gone through.

"Can you tell me anything else about her?"

"Hey, I mind my own business. I seen her to nod at two, three times in the hallways, that's it. Oh, she did call here the other day, I think from your place. Wanted my maintenance guys up there to get rid of a snake."

"I know about that."

"Funny, the whole damn thing—snake, box and all—disappeared. My guy had it in the basement, was gonna dump it when he got the chance. Probably some kid took it, but—"

"Look, can we get back to Mrs. Cotton?"

He shrugged. "Sure."

"What about when she moved in, did she say anything about her past? Why she was making the move here, her likes, dislikes? Anything at all."

"Let's see . . . I know she said her husband had died, but that's about it. Except she had some definite ideas about which apartment she took. We had two others available at the time—a first floor and then another one on the top floor."

"Did she say she knew anyone else in the building? Or even the neighborhood?"

He shook his head.

"What about the former address and the references here. Did you follow through on them?"

"Sure I did. You saying I don't do my job?"

By three o'clock in the afternoon when he made his last phone call, Marcus knew the super hadn't done his job at all. The former address, like the three names given as references on the application, were nonexistent. Which didn't surprise him. The department head at Beth Israel Hospital had never heard of Dorothy Cotton. His real estate broker at Hook Agency said that when Dorothy contacted him, she'd given Marcus' name as her referral and asked to see an apartment in Marcus' building. Or at least in the same neighborhood.

Eunice didn't wake from her drunk until midafternoon when the first thought that shot to her brain was Birdie. Her eyes opened. Her mouth was dry, her stomach was knotted and her brain felt swollen and blocked as though it had been dumped in a load of sand. God, did any of it make sense? No, nothing, not since camp and the drowning and Birdie's leap to Never–Never Land. What was it—a horror story, all to end with Birdie zippered into some godawful plastic bag?

Did disaster come in threes or sixes or some odd number she hadn't even reached yet, or was all this muck connected somehow? She got out of bed, then went into Birdie's bedroom and walked around, looking at the things she had left behind.

On a shelf in the big walk-in closet was her duffel bag. Eunice pulled it down, sat on the carpet and emptied out the contents: a Camp Raintree rule and procedure book with a map on the back cover, a pencil-drawn picture of a girl with tiny vertical lines on her back, a piece of paper that looked like the beginning of a letter with the salutation and address scratched out, and half a bottle of vodka. She uncapped the bottle and took a few long swallows to sweep away the sand in her brain.

She picked up the picture of the girl and studied it. *Who are you? Are you the girl who makes my Birdie's skin itch so bad she wants to shred it?* She dragged Birdie's foot locker from the closet and raised the lid. A tangle of summer clothing was still inside; she took everything out, piece by piece. This wasn't what she wanted to see—where were the keepsakes? The memories? Wait a minute! They must be in that box.

The camp director had written months ago asking her to pick up or have shipped a large box of Birdie's personal effects. Eunice, of course, hadn't gotten around to it. Besides, if Birdie had left the box there in the first place, she must not have wanted to face the memories, right?

So Birdie had really made the decision—and hadn't she usually done pretty well at decision-making? But maybe this one was a dud, made by a scared, grieving kid crying out for help. Help? Guidance? Not the kinds of things Eunice won awards for.

Damn you to hell, bitch! Dissect that free-choice act you promoted for Birdie all these years, and what do you come up with? Just another excuse for you to lie low and do your own thing. Eunice curled up on the carpet with her arms hugging herself and her eyes closed, rocking back and forth. *If you're there, Birdie, say something because I'm right here and I'm listening with all my might . . .*

Later that afternoon, Dorothy put her lips to Robin's forehead, then stood up and smiled. She went over to the closet, opened the sliding doors, flung her arm out in a grand gesture to display the girl's clothes inside.

"Come on over and take your pick," she said. "I think it's time you got dressed."

Robin walked to the closet, her eyes avoiding the foot locker on the floor.

"Isn't there any jeans?" she said.

"I'm afraid not. There's an entire wardrobe here. Surely you can find something you like."

"Why is everything pink?"

"Not *everything* is, Robin. Besides, what's wrong with pink?"

"I don't like it."

"Choose something, anyway. You know I don't want to have to punish you, dear."

Robin reached into the closet and pulled out a pair of pink cotton twill pants and a white blouse.

"A very nice choice. Now, why don't you put them on?" She went to the dresser, took out some underwear and socks, laid them on a chair and headed for the door.

"It's three o'clock, you have five minutes to dress, make your bed, and high-tail it out to the kitchen. And if you're quick as a bunny, I just might have a surprise in store for you, young lady."

Suddenly it dawned on Robin that she was well—why else would she be allowed to get dressed? And the surprise, what else could it be but to let Robin go home? She got into the clothes, made up her bed and raced into the kitchen, nearly colliding with Dorothy in the process.

"What—"

"Oh, I'm sorry, I didn't mean . . . Can we go home now?"

"What are you talking about?"

"You said you had a surprise."

"And I do." Dorothy waved an arm toward the counter, where a bunch of ingredients were lined up in perfect rows. "Robin, you're about to bake your first cookies. Remember my funny little baking calendar? Well, Sunday is cookie day."

"No!" she shouted. "I don't want to bake, I want to go home! You said I could, once I was better . . . And I am!"

"Don't raise your voice to me, Robin."

"But you promised! You—"

"Robin."

"I want to go home! Now!"

Dorothy reached out, but Robin bolted for the front door. She got only as far as the oak tree in the front yard before she felt the powerful arm scissor her neck from behind, then drag her down to the ground. She fought and kicked and screamed, none of which helped one bit. Dorothy flipped Robin over onto her belly, dug her knee deeply into the small of her back, then, twisting her arms behind her, dragged her back into the house.

Marcus, with Mollie in tow, was looking through mug shots at the Boston police department. He doubted that Dorothy Cotton had a criminal record, but he couldn't afford to rule the possibility out. Besides, what the hell else could he do? He had found out only one thing for certain: there was nothing coincidental about his meeting with Dorothy Cotton. He and Robin had been handpicked, and her worming her way into the family had all been part of some plan.

He and Mollie got back to the apartment at six, Marcus having recognized Dorothy in none of the thousands of mug shots he'd gone through in the past few hours. Though they had yet to eat a meal that day, the McDonald's takeout in front of them was barely touched. Marcus tried phoning Eunice for the fifth time: still no answer. Where the hell could she be?

Mollie looked at her watch. "Marcus, I have an appointment with a patient's parents, so I need to leave soon. Let's talk it through one more time. It might help to trigger something."

"I don't know what to say. Downing's pulling blank after blank on the computer. It's like Dorothy Cotton never existed."

"Okay, let's start there. How is that possible?"

"An alias," Marcus said.

"Then you think she might be a professional?"

"Professionals have records. And even if she is, why me? Why go through all those machinations just to get me?"

"Have you ever prosecuted cases, Marcus?"

"In the early days. That's where I learned to pick locks."

"Could she be holding a grudge because of—"

"Not a chance. I haven't prosecuted in years, and the little criminal law I do now is hardly big league. And though I've made more than a few litigants mad in my civil practice, no one mad enough to pull a thing like this."

The phone rang and Marcus grabbed it.

"It's Shari. Any news?"

"No."

A sigh. "Well, listen, I didn't want to bother you, I would have told you last night when you called, but I was half asleep, then you threw me with the news about Robin. I would have called you back, but—"

"Shari, what *is* it?"

"When you called from San Francisco, you asked me to verify a Fairfield, Connecticut, address and phone number for a Dorie Lucas. I did, and the number is no longer in service. I checked with the phone company, tried to see if they had a new listing, but I didn't come up with anything. Do you want me to keep on it Monday?"

Marcus sighed. "Forget it, Shari. It's no longer a priority."

He put down the phone and looked at Mollie.

"I forgot to tell you, Howard Lucas refused to talk to Robin. The wife—it turned out—was the girl's stepmother. He did give me an address in Connecticut . . ." Marcus was pacing around the room now, his hands in his pockets, his fingers jingling change, his eyes on the floor. "You know, to reach his ex-wife, to reach Amelia's mother . . ." he went on almost as if he were talking to himself. "Turns

out she's no longer there. Moved, I guess she's
moved . . ."

"What is it, Marcus?"

He stopped in his tracks.

"Dorie Lucas, Mollie. Amelia's mother's name is Dorie."

Dumb, dumb, dumb.

Shut up.

*I'd have thought you'd come up with something better
than that. What did you think, she was just gonna say, 'okay,
fine, buckle up your seatbelt and let's go'? What did you
expect?*

Nothing, I expected just what I got, a big fat zero!

*Okay, let's not get too down about this. Remember, by
now Daddy is out there looking for you. He's sure to get to
you soon.*

Uh-uh, he won't.

Why not?

Robin's palms were pressed tightly against her temples.
Any minute her brains would explode and shoot out of her
head.

She buried her head under the pillow, trying to freeze out
the voice in her head. *You might have told Daddy, or at least
Mollie. I mean, it was obvious from the mark on her
forehead, right? God, are you a mule or what? Oh well,
we'll just have to figure where to go from here. Put on our
thinking caps—remember Miss Chansky used to say that?
What a zitz she was. Better rest now . . . better rest, better
rest . . .*

*Three blind mice, three blind mice, see how they run?
They all run after the farmer's wife, she cut off their tail
with a carving knife. Did you ever see such a sight in your
life . . .*

Cookies? Why do you suppose I smell cookies?
Because it's Sunday.
What if the whole house blew up right this minute? Do you think—
Yup.

It was eleven o'clock that night when Dorothy, having tidied the kitchen, bagged the two dozen cookies, tiptoed into Robin's room, unlocked the diary and read the first entry.

Dear Diary, today I thought I wanted to go home, but on second thought maybe it's not so bad here. I sure wish Daddy was here with us, I bet he'd like it.

Not exactly what she had hoped for, but it was a first step. Eventually Robin would get the hang of it, perhaps seek inspiration from Amelia's diary. But in the meantime, what had happened that afternoon still had to be handled.

Dorothy wished she could let the incident go unpunished, but she well knew that unless destructive behavior was pointed out and stopped, it would only occur over and over again. And in the long run, Robin would be the one to suffer most. Just as Dorothy's baby sister had suffered so many years ago.

Then there was the matter of the gratitude. Robin relied on Dorothy's guidance and help in just about every facet of her life, and it was important that the child start to show some appreciation. Not all mothers were so unselfish: Robin, like Dorothy, knew that from bitter experience. Certainly it wasn't asking too much to expect a little recognition for her good deeds. And though Robin was surely not the only youngster who had ever neglected to thank a loving mother, Robin was no longer just any child—she was Dorothy's child.

Once Dorothy locked up the diary and set it back on the

nightstand, she went out to the back porch. She looked at the covered box for a few moments, drew a deep breath of the cool air into her lungs, then carried it into Robin's bedroom and set it down in the center of the pink area rug. She removed the cover, turned on a dim night-light, and left, locking the door behind her. The water snake, surely awakened by the sudden movement, would be slithering around the bottom of the box: Robin's punishment, waiting for her when she awoke with her nightmares.

She went into her bedroom, feeling a knot begin to squeeze at her stomach. This time, despite the crying and screaming and pleading, Dorothy would not be able to ease her pain.

CHAPTER 15

Mollie hated having to leave Marcus to search for Robin alone, but she had patients to see. Marcus had promised her he'd keep in touch by telephone—at the moment he was trying to reach Georgette Lucas, to confirm Dorie Lucas' maiden name.

If he was right about the identity of Amelia's mother— and the moment he said it, it had made perfect sense to him and Mollie—then he would drive down to Connecticut tonight. He had already contacted Downing, asking him to line up a connection for him with the Fairfield police.

As Mollie stepped into the shower, implications of it all hit her with the force of the hot water. Not only had Robin been scared of Dorothy all along—without consciously knowing she was scared—but on some level she had even sensed the reason for her own fear. Amelia's mother, come to pick up a replacement for her dead daughter or to seek some kind of bizarre revenge—or both. Had Robin been right about her friend's bogeyman as well? If so, the identity of the bogeyman was no longer in doubt.

And now? Had the trauma of being held captive rattled

Robin's subconscious, spilling out its dark secrets while she was alone and vulnerable? What was she thinking, feeling? Robin was one of the gutsiest twelve-year-olds Mollie had ever met, but what she must be going through now was enough to break an adult—even a strong adult. Of course, you never knew how much you could take, not until you were put to the test . . .

Well, you're being put to the test now, Robin. And you've got a load of inner ammunition. Oh, please, honey, use it.

It took Marcus at least two minutes after he heard Georgette say the name "Dorothy Cotton Lucas" to gather his wits enough to ask her a few more questions—but none of the answers were immediately helpful.

Then he called Eunice's number again. He let it ring twenty-five times before he gave up. Maybe she was smashed, and if so, maybe that was good. Or, at least, better than going through what he was going through.

The worst of it was knowing he'd been the one to push Robin into Dorothy's arms, so to speak. A nice, reliable woman who seemed to know a lot about kids, always available, always willing to help. Of course, the shrink had sensed that the nice reliable woman was neither nice nor reliable. Okay, so maybe the shrink's senses were geared to spot the flaws, but what accounted for the druggie and the lush spotting them too?

And the father? Where the fuck was he? Around, at least, as a comic presence, falling over his own feet so as not to upset his daughter for fear she'd freak out. Even Eunice had more faith in Robin than that. Face it, the father had been doing what he did best: setting up the game rules, then taking a comfortable seat in the grandstand so he could count up the plays and errors. Hadn't he had years of practice with Eunice?

He jerked the steering wheel, veering to the left to avoid a raccoon. The raccoon raced safely across the turnpike, and Marcus' thoughts raced back to his conversation with the super, to the part about the missing snake. Then further back . . .

Ashes, ashes, all fall down . . .

Eunice had been lying on the floor of the bedroom next to the duffel bag for hours. Still rocking her body back and forth, still thinking. She'd heard the telephone ring again and again, but hadn't moved from the spot, hadn't dared to break her concentration. Somehow, some way, all the stuff that had happened since last summer was related. Oh God, she wasn't wrong about that, she could feel it in her bones.

And maybe, just maybe, somewhere in Birdie's box of goodies—or maybe even at the camp itself—there was a clue.

It was nearly two A.M. when Robin jerked awake from a nightmare. She bolted up in bed, clapped a hand over her mouth to smother the scream. She looked at the diary on the nightstand, then rested her head on her knees, taking one deep breath after another.

At first she thought the faint rustling sound was coming from outdoors. Then she heard it again, lifted her head—and saw the box. Slowly she lowered her feet to the floor, walked over to the box, leaned down, looked in.

She ran screaming to the door, tried the doorknob. Locked! She banged at the door with her fists.

"Open the door!" she yelled. "Dorothy! Dorothy, do you hear me? Wake up, please wake up!"

No answer.

A short pause, then, "Mama, help! I need you! Help me!"

No answer.

Robin didn't stop the pounding or pleading until her voice was hoarse. Finally, shaking and sweaty, she sank down to the floor, her eyes fixed on the box.

It's probably more scared of you than you are of it.

Wanna make a bet?

Well, it won't come out of the box.

Oh, yeah? Remember that time Eunice found a garter snake in the backyard and put it in a big aquarium in the kitchen? Well, that one crawled out.

Yeah, I remember. I bet Eunice wouldn't be scared of this snake either.

So that's Eunice, not me. Besides, I don't want to hear about her.

Why not?

Just because.

Betcha I know why.

Robin kept her eyes fixed on the box.

Want me to tell you?

I don't suppose you'll shut up till you do. So go ahead, get it over with.

Well, if you talked about Eunice, then you'd have to remember you blamed her for sending that snake the other day. Now, if you go and take a good look you'll see it's the very same snake—

I'm not about to go eyeball to eyeball with a snake. Anyway, I can see for myself it's the same box.

So can you see then for yourself who made all those telephone calls?

Maybe. But why would she?

To scare you.

How would she know about me being so scared of snakes?

Amelia's diary, how else? She wrote about that day you freaked out over a snake that was fifty yards away.

Why was I so sure it was Eunice?

Hey, give me a break, I'm good but I'm not the shrink. You'll have to ask Mollie those things.

Suppose I never see Mollie again?

Then I guess you'll just have to figure it out on your own.

From the moment of Robin's first scream, Dorothy had been wide awake, pressing her face into her pillow where she could shed her own tears and silence her own wracking sobs. Now the screams had finally stopped, and if Dorothy knew her children as well as she thought she did, Robin was crouched in a corner, her eyes fixed on the box. And while she kept watch over the dreaded snake, she was learning some hard but very important lessons . . .

Oh, if only she could run right in to Robin, hold her safe from danger, or, at least, imagined danger—she would never expose Robin to any real harm. But of course she couldn't go to Robin. Despite the pain Robin's punishment cost her, she couldn't give in. A good mother needed to pass down to her child all those good qualities she herself possessed. And not until the child was perfect could she dare to rest easy.

By tomorrow, Robin would have a greater appreciation of the growing strength of their bond. Dorothy reached over for another tissue to wipe away her tears.

Mollie's phone rang and she picked it up.

"Would she hurt her, Mollie?"

"Would who— Oh . . . Would Dorothy hurt Robin." She sighed. "How can I answer that, Marcus? Except for a couple of quick conversations, I don't even know the lady."

"Yes, but you know about her. And you're a psychologist, you study these kinds of things."

"Well . . ." Should she tell Marcus what Robin had said about Amelia's fear? Better not. "Dorothy appears to be obsessive, compulsive," she said finally. "And she's narcissistic."

"In love with herself? I never saw her that way."

"Not quite in love with herself, no. Narcissists are looking for an acceptance they've never had. They actually have very low self-esteem."

"Okay. But you're still not answering my original question."

"I can't, Marcus."

"It wasn't Eunice who sent Robin the snake."

"I know. At least, I finally guessed."

"So would a person who sent a snake to a kid be likely to—"

"Stop right there. I think the snake was primarily a scare tactic. It not only drove Robin further away from Eunice, it also drew Robin closer to Dorothy, the one person she could rely on to keep her safe. I think Dorothy wants to mother Robin, not hurt her."

"But a person who would do something like that . . . Can she be trusted not to cross the line?"

"Marcus, I don't know."

After Mollie hung up, she sat back in her chair trying to piece together a pathology for Dorothy from the few clues Robin had given her. "She's always trying to get me to be the perfect little homemaker just like *she* is . . . she tells me about those nursery rhymes because she wants me to like what *she* likes." Definitely narcissistic. Not that the behavior was rare—it wasn't. Most mothers, to a greater or lesser extent, use their children to satisfy their own unfulfilled needs.

Bad enough. But what about when you add that to manipulative, obsessive, compulsive behavior in a desperate woman who had likely lost part of her own self when she lost Amelia?

First, Eunice tried to call Marc at his apartment, but there was no answer. Next she raced into the kitchen, opened the junk drawer, pulled it out of its tracks and emptied the contents onto the kitchen table. From the pile she picked out an all-purpose jackknife, a flashlight, batteries, several packs of matches, a bottle of aspirins and a handful of thick candles. From the cabinets, she took some canned goods and two bottles of wine.

She looked at the wine, thought about taking a nip, then, considering the long drive ahead of her, slipped the unopened bottles into her canvas bag and swallowed a couple of aspirins instead. From her bedroom she took two heavy blankets—though it had been a mild fall in Massachusetts, it would likely be colder in Maine.

She went back into Birdie's bedroom, found the camp procedure book with map and tucked it into her purse, put on a down parka and hauled her bag of supplies outdoors. It was two o'clock in the morning when she tossed the bag into the trunk of the Z and headed north.

Not once had Eunice actually toured Camp Raintree. She had left it to Marc to check the place out, make the arrangements, then deliver Birdie each summer. Well, it was time good ol' mom checked it out for herself, took a look at the place where her kid spent so much good ol' summertime. Went through the memorabilia she had socked away. And faced down those memories that Birdie couldn't face down herself.

Somehow she was going to discover just what kind of

horror had taken up residence in her Birdie's head. Because once she found that out, she'd be able to find Birdie.

Making only one pit stop, Marcus arrived at the Fairfield police department at two A.M. Now he sat across from Detective Curtis, the fiftyish man with a weatherworn face who had raided the computer files for information on Dorothy Lucas.

None of it gave them a clue as to where she had gone once she sold her one-family house in late August. But a 1987 blue Chevy Impala wagon, license number WRI–670, was still registered in her name. And though this wasn't as yet an on-the-books investigation, Curtis had somehow managed to get an all-points bulletin put out on the car.

Now Curtis was looking over a printout from probate court records.

"According to this, she was divorced from Howard M. Lucas nine years ago and received sole custody of their three-year-old child, Amelia.

"Lucas got the usual 'reasonable visitation.' At the time he was an engineer at a Pratt & Whitney plant in Bridgeport, making nearly sixty grand. He got socked with a combined child support and alimony order for twenty-five thou. A sizable chunk of his income, but I see no complaint or contempt orders here, so he must have paid it. He also signed over the house—whose mortgage was nearly paid off—and gave her a lump sum settlement of twenty thousand."

Marcus nodded. "So if she was careful with expenses, she didn't have to work."

"Right. Apparently she never worked prior to the marriage, either. So what else is new—the judge really stuck it to poor Howard. Might be worthwhile to check with him, see where he's sending his alimony payments."

"When I called Georgette, the second wife, to confirm Dorothy's name," Marcus said, "she told me Howard hasn't heard from Dorothy since the funeral. Besides, he's been out of work. I asked about Dorothy's family, too, but Georgette didn't know anything about them. She did say she expected Howard to call her early tomorrow, and she'd ask him then. I told her I'd check back with her."

Marcus paused for a long moment, trying to think. "We need to have Downing in Boston check out where Dorothy kept her money," he said finally. "What with her savings and the money from the sale of the house, she must have quite a bit. Before she left Boston, she may have had it transferred to another bank."

Curtis made a notation on his pad. "I'll check it out."

"So what do we do now?"

"Well, keep trying to locate her family. Between your feelers and the resources here, maybe by tomorrow we'll have something definite. Other than that, I'd say good old-fashioned legwork. The best way to find out about a homemaker is to talk to other homemakers. You know, former friends, neighbors, mothers of other kids . . ."

"I don't know," Marcus said, "Dorothy's not what you'd call an open person."

"Trust me, she doesn't have to be. Most of these homemakers can run off a life history of every other woman in the area."

"Okay, where do I start?"

Curtis looked at his watch. "Look, it's going on three. What I did when I heard you were coming is book you a room in the local Ramada, just around the corner. Tomorrow's night duty again for me, I go on at five. So how about I pick you up in the morning at nine, and we go off to the lady's old neighborhood for some legwork."

"Look, I really appreciate—"

"Hey, forget it, whatever I can do. I don't know Downing myself, but he knows a buddy of mine on the New Haven force."

When Marcus got to the motel room, he tried calling Eunice. After a dozen rings, he hung up the phone. Where the hell could she have gone?

Robin slept on and off, backed up against the door. From time to time she woke with a start, her eyes going immediately to the box. Now, with daylight starting to come through the window, she was fully awake. She licked her lips and ran her hands through her damp hair, pushing it away from her face.

Go ahead, go look at it.

Uh-uh, I can't.

Yes you can, too. At least go look to see if it's still there.

Oh, God, you think it got out?

I didn't say that, but it wouldn't hurt to make sure.

If I have to look at that ugly thing again, I'll die.

It probably thinks you're just as ugly.

You got that line from Eunice.

Well, she's right, isn't she? Who's to say the snake thinks you're so hot-looking?

Well, I don't force it to look into my face, do I?

What are you gonna do, sit here against the door for the rest of your life?

I can wait here for Dorothy . . .

You mean Mama? Make her day—let her know that you needed her to unglue you from this spot. Maybe you need her to help you go pee, too?

Shut up, will you?

Hey, I got an idea.

I said—

No, really, I've got an idea. Just listen.

Like I have a choice? Okay, go ahead, motor mouth.

Suppose I'm Eunice.

Well, you're not, so that ends that.

Come on, just suppose. You're Eunice, so you go over to the snake, look right in its puny ugly face. You know she wouldn't be scared, she'd probably pick it up and pat its flat head—

There's no way!

I'm not saying do that, I'm just saying go over there and look.

It took three whole minutes for Robin to stand up. She took small steps, but each step moved her closer to the box. When she finally got close enough to see the snake, she jerked back. Then, "Hey there, sweetie, open up and give out a big hello."

Excellent! You even sounded—

Shut up!

With her eyes squinting and her face contorted, Robin watched the snake. Gradually her facial muscles eased up, but she continued to watch the snake as it slithered and curled and uncurled at the bottom of the tin box. Not until she heard noise coming from the other room—Dorothy's room—did she once look away.

Go back quick!

Why?

No time for explanations, just do it.

Robin tiptoed back, then lowered herself onto the floor with her spine pressed against the door, listening for Dorothy's footsteps. Okay, so she'd watched the snake for maybe five whole minutes, and without freaking out. So she even felt kind of good about it. But *no way* could she even imagine picking that ugly thing up.

CHAPTER 16

Having driven seventy m.p.h. most of the way, Eunice reached the deserted campgrounds in the hills of Bangor, Maine, at six A.M. As soon as she got out of the car, she felt her senses sharpening. The vibrant colors of crisp fallen leaves drifted among the cabins, the profound quiet broken only by the faint rustling of blowing leaves, crackling branches and the movement of little animal feet.

She slung the burlap bag over her shoulder and walked past two bare flagpoles and a baseball field with peeling green bleachers to the mess hall. She peered through the windows at the high-ceilinged wood-beamed structure with dozens of long red wooden tables and benches and, behind them, a large kitchen area.

Next door was an even larger structure, half auditorium. Working her way around the building, she was able to spot an infirmary, an arts-and-crafts room, a canteen with a jukebox, four Ping-Pong tables and a couple of video games, and what looked to be a storage room.

She used a heavy, jagged rock to break the flimsy lock on the door, then went through two dozen or so boxes of sports equipment and medical supplies trying to find Birdie's box. Not there. She walked outside and looked around. That's when she spotted the dumpster.

After several tries at climbing up the sides, she went to the area overlooking the lake and dragged back a wooden lifeguard chair. Setting it beside the dumpster, she climbed into it, then into the dumpster—letting go the edges and sliding down into a rough cushion of plastic bags and boxes. She stood up, lost her balance, tumbled backward, then stood up again and began to sort through the trash. She was about midway through when she found the wet sealed box that had *Robin Garr* written across it.

She flung the box over the side, then piled cardboard boxes against the dumpster until she was able to climb up and grab hold of the top rim. She boosted herself up, one leg over the edge and onto the lifeguard chair, then the other leg.

Once on the ground with Birdie's box, she tore it open and dumped the contents. A couple of odd-shaped rocks, a Raintree banner, a snapshot of Birdie and Amelia standing at the water's edge with their arms entwined, two pine cones, a torn piece of bark from a tree, a blue camp T-shirt, a bird's nest, a cardboard sign that said No Campers Allowed. A small book of nursery rhymes with a white leather-bound cover inscribed "To my very best friend in the whole world." Another drawing of a girl with lines on her back. A blank sealed envelope . . .

She tore open the envelope and pulled out the paper inside.

Dear Eunice,
I did something so sneaky that even you might be shocked to know I did it. And now I'm being punished for my sneakiness by knowing a secret that is too awful

*to even talk about. But now that I know it, what do I
do? Tell and maybe make things even worse for her
than they are now? That could happen, you know. Or
not tell and go on worrying like this . . .*

*She could be hurt, couldn't she? She maybe even
could die, and whose fault would it be then? Eunice,
when you're sober you can do things nobody else in the
whole world can do. Remember the time you faced off
those two mean-looking guys who were beating up on
that lady? Remember the time you dove into the
porpoise tank at the zoo and fished out that little kid?*

*Well, do you think you can save her, too? Could you
maybe—*

It ended there. Eunice wiped away tears from her eyes.
Save who? It had to be Amelia. She picked up Robin's
drawing and studied it. *So you're Amelia, huh? What
happened to your back, sweetie, who did it to you? Please
forgive Birdie for not sending the note off to me—she would
have, but she figured when I got it, I'd be drunk. Know
something? She was likely right. And guess she's been mad
at me ever since.*

*So how about it, do I get another chance? This time it's
Birdie who's in trouble. Come on, Amelia, tell me where she
is.*

Dorothy found it hard to open the bedroom door with
Robin's body pressed so tightly against it, but with a little
gentle persuasion, she convinced Robin to move aside.
Finally she squeezed through, got down on her knees, and
took the child into her arms. Once she got Robin back into
bed, she took the box with the snake and returned it to the
back porch. Hopefully there would be no need to use it

again. Finally she came back inside, sat on the bed beside Robin and hugged her.

"With that terrible thing to keep you company, I'll bet you didn't sleep a wink."

Robin nodded.

"I only want what's best for you, dear. And I know in time you'll see that. It's not easy to be a parent, at least not a parent who takes the job as seriously as I do . . . Now, enough thoughts about snakes and nasty scary things. Tell me what you'd like for breakfast."

Robin shrugged.

"No, no, I insist. Today it's your pick."

"Waffles, then."

Dorothy went off to prepare breakfast, Robin closed her eyes.

Say it. Now.

Say what?

You know. Why she's here and why you're here and—

We both know all that.

Say it anyway.

And if I do, what difference will it make?

I'm not sure, but I think some.

What do you do, stay up nights thinking up these dumb things? Remember, you're not a head doctor and you're not my boss, you're just a zero, something I made up to keep me company . . . Hey, you still there?

Afraid I'm gonna take off on you? Relax, I'm not—no matter what you do or don't do.

What's this, the old guilt trip? Okay, okay, I'll say it. She came to take me as a replacement for Amelia.

How'd she know where to find you?

I had the address from Amelia, so I wrote her a letter. Just to say I was sorry.

And you told her you and Daddy were moving?

Uh-huh.

Why'd you do that when you knew what she's like? When you knew what she'd done to Amelia?

But I didn't know.

Yes, you did too know! Did too—

Suddenly Robin turned over, burying her face in her pillow, sobbing. Even when Dorothy brought in the breakfast tray, she couldn't bring herself to look at her or stop crying.

Not until Dorothy slipped away, leaving her alone to rest, did she finally stop, wipe her eyes, sit up and look at Amelia's diary on top of the dresser. She tiptoed over, took the diary, went back to the bed. Her fingers automatically flipped through to the fifteenth page, January 15; a shudder wrenched her body as she saw the entry and remembered reading it before.

Dear Diary . . .

Early that morning Marcus called Georgette, but she hadn't heard from Howard. He then called the King agency in Los Angeles, told them what had happened and asked them to get word to Howard to contact Marcus immediately through Detective Curtis at the Fairfield police department.

Curtis picked up Marcus as promised at nine o'clock sharp and filled him in on his progress. Dorothy Cotton Lucas had originally come from New London, a seaside town in Southeast Connecticut; they were now trying to locate her parents and two siblings. The all-points bulletin on the license plate number had turned up nothing.

As for Downing, a check on Boston banks had turned up an account at the Shawmut for Dorothy Lucas opened on September 1 with a deposit of three thousand dollars. A check had been drawn by her on Thursday evening, October

26, for the balance which, by then, was down to fifteen hundred.

"That still doesn't explain where the money from the sale of the house went," Marcus said.

"No. While she was living here, she dealt with Connecticut Bank and Trust. I've got a call out to them now."

Curtis drove to a large tract of houses, pointing out a neat gray clapboard cape where Dorothy had lived with her daughter. He pulled over to the curb and handed Marcus a list of house numbers.

"You're a lawyer, I don't suppose I need to tell you how to question people. So let's just get down to it. What do you say we meet back here at say about eleven?"

Marcus' first house was not as neat as Dorothy's had been: the grass and shrubbery in the yard needed attention and a screen door hung loose. A woman with curly red hair came to the door, a toddler on her hip. When Marcus explained who he was and why he needed to talk to her, she introduced herself as Greta Brady and invited him in.

"I sure felt sorry for Dorie when I heard about the drowning—I mean, what mother wouldn't?" Greta sat the toddler into a playpen, then quickly moved around the room, picking up toys and papers from the carpet and tossing them into a laundry basket. "But I won't lie and say I liked the woman."

"Could you be more specific?"

"Well, I have two others," she said, "a boy, seven, and a girl, Wendy, who was in Amelia's class. A few years back, Dorie led a Brownie troop in the area. Wendy wanted to join, but Dorie gave me a hard time—she didn't want Wendy in her troop."

"Why not?"

"Well, Wendy's not perfect—she's had her share of staying after school, poor grades, that type of thing—but she's not a bad girl, I mean she doesn't steal or cheat or get into fights. In any event, Dorie looked at it like Wendy wasn't good enough to be in her troop, to associate with her daughter, and I—well, I opened my big mouth. And I finally got Wendy into the Brownie troop. But Dorie harassed her, disciplining her for the least little thing: not having bobby pins in her beanie, not wearing her Brownie belt, wearing the wrong color socks . . . Finally Wendy dropped out on her own.''

"I see. Tell me, would you have any idea where Dorie might have moved when she sold her house?"

"Last I heard, she was heading to Boston, but I could be wrong.''

"Actually, you're not. It's just that when she took off with my daughter, well, I thought she might have come back to Connecticut.''

"I couldn't tell you. But if she did, it isn't because she has friends around her. The truth is, not one of the neighbors liked her. She was strange, she liked to collect things—antiques, music boxes . . . Not that people don't do that, but with her it was, well, peculiar. And though Amelia was a nice, well-behaved child, she wasn't really popular with the other children. I think that was mainly Dorie's doing, though. She didn't like Amelia associating with any other kids unless she was right there to watch. And you know kids—beyond a certain age, the last human they want hanging over them is mommy dearest.''

"Did she abuse Amelia?''

"Funny you should ask that. Out of all the neighbors, I'm apparently the only one who thought so. I mean, it wasn't that the girl had bruises, marks, anything obvious like that, and all anyone ever saw was Dorie's calm demeanor and loving concern. But Amelia was afraid of her. Whenever she did get the chance to be alone with another kid, she would try like hell to fit in, but the minute Dorothy was within earshot she became a totally different personality—stiff, prim, uptight, fussy.''

Almost like Dorothy herself.

Dear Diary,
I know Mama does what she does to make me good, so I'm not mad at her at all. I'm only very mad at myself for being bad and making her need to go through such terrible pain when she punishes me. I'm sorry I was late coming home from school. I didn't mean to make her worried and anxious. But honest to God, hope to die, I won't do it again . . . ever.

Whenever I think about today—and I'll force myself to think of it often so I'll remember this lesson—I'll know how much Mama must love me to put up with all the bad and thoughtless things I do. I know how hurtful it is to her when my actions force her to discipline me. Please forgive me, Mama . . . I love you.

Punishment: six hours tied to the hot water heater in the cellar.

One hour off for good behavior. (no crying)

Tears were slipping down Robin's cheeks again. She kept on sweeping them away with her nightshirt sleeve. There were many diary entries just like that one, except for different crimes and different punishments. Robin knew, because that night at camp after accidentally reading the July 2nd entry, she had stayed up the rest of the night and read through the whole diary.

The pages that didn't describe punishments were almost as painful to read. They always were started ''Dear Diary,'' but the words were always written for Mama. And though Robin knew that Dorothy snuck into Amelia's bedroom to read her diary, she also knew it was all part of a game they played. Amelia knew her mother read it, and her mother knew that she knew.

Oh, God, Amelia. I wimped out on you for sure. I just shoved it all away somewhere in my head and was going to go on my merry way and pretend like I didn't know a thing. If you hadn't drowned, you would have had to go back to *that*. To her . . . And it would have been all my fault.

Okay, enough!

What?

No more time left for crying and feeling sorry . . . Maybe you couldn't save Amelia. Anyway, she's dead—she doesn't need saving any more, and you sure do.

Yeah . . . but how?

Haven't figured that out yet?

You mean, run away? Forget it, bean head, I tried that yesterday.

Give me a break. Do you call that a try? Oh, sure, maybe for a kindergartner, it is.

Robin looked at the window in her bedroom, then through it to the thick woods beyond. She took a deep breath . . .

Tonight?

Maybe you want to vacation here a few more days?

Marcus got intercepted by Curtis on the way to the fourth house.

"Anything yet?" Curtis asked.

"The more I hear, the more worried I get. Nobody's been helpful, though—at least nobody's said anything so far that would give us her whereabouts."

"Well, the computer just picked up some information on her family from some kind of medical form Amelia filled out in school. Apparently Dorothy's folks and one sister are dead, but there's an older brother, Justin, lives with his wife and two teenage kids in New London. We have the address and telephone number. So far no answer, but we'll keep trying.''

"How long a drive to New London?" Marcus asked.

"If you don't hit traffic, less than ninety minutes."

"Give me the address. I'll stick around for more interviews, then leave this afternoon—later in the day there's more likelihood of finding him home."

"Okay. I'll stick around here as long as I can. Once I go on duty, I'll put in an official report of the kidnapping."

Dorothy was surprised by the extent of Robin's remorse when she had gone in with the breakfast tray. At first she had tried to calm the child, but she finally decided that the crying jag was a healthy sign—Robin was feeling so much remorse for what she had done that this would be a lesson never forgotten. So she had left Robin to her shame, knowing that one missed breakfast could always be made up for with a nourishing lunch.

If Robin was calm enough after lunch, Dorothy wanted to start on those baking lessons: Monday was cake day. Suddenly she felt euphoric—it was all working out just as she had known it would. Oh, there would be occasional setbacks, those little snags that occur at different stages of growth.

Goodness, even her Amelia had those . . .

Eunice sat there going over and over Birdie's treasures, each time returning to the snapshot of her and Amelia. She knew she had never seen this thin, pale girl with the heavy-lidded blue eyes before or even heard Birdie describe her, but she still looked awfully familiar. Maybe that was just how Eunice had pictured Amelia. But that book of nursery rhymes stuck out too. Was Eunice so out of touch with kids, or wasn't it a strange gift from a girl of that age?

It was a couple of hours before she decided to move on and see the rest of the camp. The more she saw, the more she found out, the better the shot she had at finding the connection. She tossed Birdie's mementos into her burlap bag, pulled out one of the bottles of wine, held it a few moments in her hand, then shoved it back inside—she would hold out till later. She stood up, heaved the bag over her shoulder and headed for Cabin B—Birdie's cabin last summer.

Again using a rock to break the lock, Eunice explored the cabin, walking through the locker room, the bathroom and the sleeping area, only able to guess which of the fourteen bunks might have been Birdie's bunk.

Finally she headed back outside and down the slippery slope covered with pine needles to the water. Using her hand as a sun visor, she studied the shore carefully until she spotted the small patch of sand across the lake. According to the camp director's accident report, that was the beach where Birdie and Amelia had gone swimming.

CHAPTER 17

AFTER several abortive attempts, Eunice found a winding path through the woods that came out at the site of the accident. She dumped Birdie's mementos into a pile, then sat down, took off her sneakers and dug her bare feet into the cold sand, staring at a spot about sixty feet out near where a huge boulder jutted up from the water.

"All right, Birdie, I'm here, I'm listening. Say something."

She stood up and turned around, slowly backing up toward the water and studying the area. Though it would soon be dark, she could still see beyond the bare trees to the occasional distant rooftop.

A sudden chill hit her. She hunted through her burlap bag, pulled out one of the wine bottles, uncorked it, and took her first satisfying drink of the day. About to take the second one, she stopped, lowered the bottle and heaved it as far as she could into the lake. She took the second wine bottle and sent that one flying into the woods.

Okay, there, I gave it to you—it's what you want, dammit, isn't it? Until I find you, Birdie, I swear on my life I won't

235

take another drop of it. But you've gotta help me out, too. You've got to tell me the rest of what happened. All of it.

Eunice sat down in the sand and began to go through Birdie's things again. As she did, she could feel the nerve endings beneath her skin come alive.

Robin, wearing one of Amelia's hand-sewn dresses and a bibbed apron, stood alongside Dorothy measuring out the ingredients for the Monday cake-bake.

"Now, don't forget to sift," Dorothy said. "We want our cake to rise nice and high."

Robin dumped the cup of flour into the sifter, then shook it over the bowl.

Where will I run?

To the nearest house you can find, that's where. And you can't afford to be dumb about it this time—it might be our only chance.

I'll wait until after Dorothy comes sneaking in to read the diary. . . .

Robin looked up at Dorothy, busy melting squares of chocolate in a double boiler.

"I'll have a lot to put in my diary tonight," she said.

Dorothy turned to her with a big smile. "Oh?"

"Well for one thing, I learned how to bake. I never baked anything before. There's a bunch of other stuff I need to write, too. You know, things I feel inside."

Dorothy's dimple deepened in her cheek.

"I'm so pleased, Robin. I'd ask you more about it, but as I've said, I'm well aware of those certain special secrets between a girl and her diary."

Robin nodded. *Patty cake, patty cake, baker's man, bake me a cake as fast as you can!*

• • •

When Marcus arrived at the address on Ocean Avenue in New London it was nearly five o'clock. No one home. Ten minutes later Grace Cotton, a short, stout woman with salt-and-pepper hair, finally pulled into the driveway. As she got out of the car, carrying a bundle of groceries, Marcus explained who he was and what he wanted.

She led him through the side door into a kitchen and started unpacking her groceries.

"Justin should be home any minute," she said. "Please have a seat."

"Maybe you can tell me something about—"

"Mr. Garr, I'm sorry to disappoint you, but the truth is I don't know Dorie very well."

"When did you meet?"

"Well, I married Justin eighteen years ago, but if I've seen Dorie five times in those years it's a lot. And Amelia, rest her soul, I saw twice—the christening and the funeral."

"There was a rift between Dorie and her brother?"

"No, it's more that Justin's family was never very close. His folks have been dead for quite a few years now, but even before that there was never much family spirit. Though Justin never said so—he hates to talk about his childhood—I always got the impression that when his baby sister died, well, that was the end of any closeness that might have been."

"Is there a big age gap between Dorie and Justin?"

"Three years. Justin's the oldest, then Dorie, then Amelia. Dorie's daughter was, of course, named after the little sister who died. I believe Dorie was thirteen then, so Justin must have been—"

The side door opened and a slight man with a thin, angular face walked in. Grace explained Marcus' situation, then left them alone to talk.

"My sister's the last person on earth to kidnap a child. For God's sake, she loves children, she was a wonderful mother. She practically lived for that little girl of hers."

"Let's get this straight—I'm not asking if she took my daughter, I'm telling you she took her. And not being able to accept Amelia's death was likely the reason she did it. Besides, according to your wife, you had practically no contact with your sister, so what makes you so sure she was such a good mother?"

He sat down. "You're right, I guess I couldn't know. I could only imagine."

"Can you fill me in on her background?"

"There's not much to tell. She married, she had Amelia, she divorced soon after. Personally, I think she only married Howard so she could have a child. Like I said, she's always loved children."

"Her love of kids—would you say it's been even stronger in the years since your sister died?"

He looked up. "How'd you know about her?"

"Your wife. And Dorie mentioned her once."

He shrugged. "Naturally little Amelia's death hit the family hard. And Dorie more so than anyone."

"Why's that?"

"Well, she was very close to her."

"Listen, Mr. Cotton, I'm not here to make small talk. I need some answers, real answers that will give me some understanding as to how Dorie thinks. And I don't have time to sit here and pull them out of you one by one."

Justin stared at Marcus for a few moments, then his features suddenly seemed to crumple.

"Okay. You're right, I didn't see Dorie much at all with her own daughter, but I do remember how she was with our sister. Like a real little mother to her, always teaching her, playing with her, reading her stories and nursery rhymes.

Amelia was a hellion, but that didn't faze Dorie. In fact, Dorie was the only one she'd listen to.''

"What happened to Amelia?"

He lowered his head, closed his eyes for a moment, then looked up.

"Look, I'm going to tell you something I never told a living soul."

Marcus waited.

"My folks were well into their forties by the time the baby was born. She was a beautiful little girl, dark-haired, bright eyes, full of the devil. In our household Mom was the one in charge--Dad was a big quiet guy who only got mean or angry when Mom didn't get what she wanted. Of course, there was never a time Mom didn't want something. She was like a soft-voiced drill sergeant, and her kids were her ready-made platoon. It wasn't unusual for her to walk into your bedroom in the middle of the night and rip it apart because she saw a shirt or pair of pants on the floor.

"You either did it and you did it Mom's way—or else. Disappoint her and she'd either complain to Dad, who'd dole out the beating, or worse yet, she'd give you the silent treatment for days on end—pass you right by without so much as a glance. Like you suddenly ceased to exist. It was the damnedest thing—you actually found yourself going to look in mirrors to be sure you hadn't become invisible. Me, being a boy, I got out from under, stayed out of the house as much as I could."

"And Dorie?"

"Well, she was just amazing. She figured out early on how to please Mom, helped with the cooking, kept her room spotless, as well as the rest of the house. She did what she was told and always with a smile. And then of course when the baby was born—Dorie was only five years old, practically a baby herself—she mothered that little kid like it was her own. And to hear Mom tell it, Dorie was the greatest thing around since sliced bread.''

"And?"

"Well, like I said, Amelia was full of the devil and gutsy as all get-out. She would do some little thing, make a mess—whatever—and Mom, having no use for kids who didn't follow her path, would make her disappointment known to Dad. Funny thing was, her silent treatments were totally lost on the baby—Amelia didn't give a hoot if Mom ever talked to her, she looked to Dorie for any mothering she got. But as little as she was, Dad wouldn't hesitate to take a strap to Amelia. Dorie always jumped in the middle, tried to take the beating herself.

"As Dorie got older, she took to punishing Amelia herself—maybe having her sit in a corner for ten, fifteen minutes, that sort of thing. Trying to teach her what to do and not do so she wouldn't end up being black and blue.''

He sighed, "That's what happened this time. We had gone on a picnic at a park, it was Sunday. I had wanted to go to a ball game—the last thing a boy of sixteen wants is to spend his Sunday on a family outing. But this time Mom insisted so that meant Dad insisted.

"Dad had parked the car up on the grass—there weren't any empty spaces in the parking lot. Later on in the afternoon, Dorie caught Amelia drawing on the back car window with a marker. So she sent her over to a bush not far from the car and told her to sit there and not move. Then Dorie ran down to the duck pond to wet a towel and wipe off the window before the folks spotted it.

"Meanwhile, Mom noticed an empty space in the parking lot. She got in the car, backed it up. Didn't even see Amelia sitting there. Need I say more?"

"She was killed?" Marcus said.

"In a coma for twelve days first. And when you said how

Dorie couldn't accept her daughter's death, well, you should have seen her with our sister. As far as she was concerned, Mom killed Amelia for drawing on the car window. You couldn't convince her any different. She even went so far as to tell the police that, but of course, they didn't buy it.''

"So she felt guilty herself?''

"I'm not a psychiatrist, but I'd say so. And the way she saw it, since I was right there and she wasn't, I should have been the one to stop her from running Amelia down.'' He shrugged. "I did hear the scolding she gave Amelia, but I didn't have a clue as to where she'd sent her. The bottom line was, no one knew Amelia was sitting there—no one, that is, except Dorie.

"After that, she was different, I guess it twisted something inside her. For years after, we'd have to go hunt her up at the park site . . . She'd be sitting, staring at that goddamned bush where she left Amelia.''

Marcus asked the other questions he had come to ask, but apparently Justin hadn't been overstating the case when he said Dorothy had never forgiven him. Though both Justin and his wife had gone to Amelia's funeral, Dorothy hadn't even spoken to them. And neither of them had any idea where she might be now.

He remembered back when Dorothy had said Robin reminded her of her baby sister. In what way? Looks, personality? Or maybe in some way that related to punishment and death?

It was the last house on the block, and though Curtis was tempted to skip it, he decided to finish what he'd started. A very old, very thin woman answered his knock. He had launched into his explanation for calling when she opened the storm door and let him in.

"You needn't go through all that, officer. You don't

canvas an entire neighborhood with a story like this one and not have the word spread around.''

"Then maybe you've been able to think of something that might help me?''

"Well, I've thought all day, but I truly doubt I can be of much help. I'm not much different than the younger women in the neighborhood, I didn't know Dorie well. Of course when I did pass her on the street, she was always cordial. And her daughter was always just as polite and pleasant as could be.''

"When did you last see her?''

"Let's see . . . That would be when she was getting her car packed up to go to that camp in Maine.''

"You mean, where her girl drowned?''

"That's right.''

"This was to get the body, was it?''

"No, it was after the funeral, I'd say mid- to late August. It was her third time up there, as I recall. She was suffering a lot, not able to let it go. It's a terrible thing to lose a loved one, let alone a child. At any age I've seen it happen, and it doesn't make a bit of difference how old the child is—the young are supposed to bury the old, not the other way around.''

"Her third time up there? You're sure of that?''

"Oh, quite sure.''

"Did you attend the funeral?''

"Yes. Despite what the neighbors thought of Dorie, just about all of them did attend. Out of respect, you know.''

"And where was the burial?''

"Now that I couldn't tell you. There was a wake, then a lovely service with eulogy at the Larchmont Chapel, but no one was invited to the burial site itself.''

"Larchmont Chapel . . . whereabouts is that?''

"Next town over. Bridgeport.''

Curtis hurried back to his car, he was already more than thirty minutes late for his shift. Marcus Garr might already be heading back. He'd put in the official report, then get in touch with this Larchmont Chapel. It wouldn't hurt to find out where this kid was buried.

After dinner and their dessert of warm chocolate cake, Dorothy brought out some long white plastic knitting needles and pink yarn in a cardboard tube and started Robin working on a winter scarf. She cast the first stitches onto one of the needles, then took Robin's hands in her own.

"First you lift off the stitch, then wrap the new yarn around the lower needle. Then, pressing down with the tip of the needle, you pull the stitch through. Simple."

Though the lesson seemed endless—Robin kept tangling the yarn and dropping stitches—Dorothy didn't once lose her patience. Finally she took the knitting and tucked it all back inside the tube.

"Well, I think that's enough for tonight. Would you like me to help you with your bath, Robin?"

Robin stood up. "I can do it myself."

Dorothy got her two clean towels from the bathroom linen closet, then laid out a fresh nightie, pink furry slippers, a bathrobe.

"Now you be sure to call if you need me. And don't forget to scrub good, because I intend to conduct inspection."

Robin didn't call her, but as soon as she stepped out of the tub, Dorothy was there. Robin grabbed for a towel and wrapped it around herself.

"Put the towel down, dear, so I can see."

Robin held the towel.

"For goodness sakes, Robin, there's no need to be bashful, after all, we're both girls. Why, I always inspected

Amelia—she never made such a fuss." Dorothy reached forward to take the towel away, and Robin stepped back.

"No!"

"Oh, Robin, I thought we were doing so well, and now this? You know what this will mean, dear."

Do it, do it, do it, do it!

I can't!

Close your eyes, drop the towel, then count to twenty.

Robin closed her eyes and let the towel fall to the floor.

"Turn around, dear," Dorothy said. "Slowly, so I won't miss any spots."

Four, five, six . . .

Dorothy stepped forward, touching her elbows, in back of her ears, under her arms . . .

Fourteen, fifteen, sixteen . . .

And then Dorothy was wrapping the towel back around Robin.

"See now, that wasn't so bad, was it? Now dry yourself and get into your warm nightie."

She went out and shut the door. Robin stood there staring at it, wishing she could jump back into the tub and wash away the memory of Dorothy's fingerprints walking all over her skin. Instead she climbed into the nightgown and robe, then went into the bedroom where Dorothy was waiting.

"I was thinking that maybe tomorrow we'd get out in the fresh air, take a nice long walk together. There's something very special I'd like to show you."

Silence.

"That is, providing I hear some enthusiasm for this little outing," Dorothy said.

Robin looked at her, took a deep breath and put her arms around Dorothy.

"I'd like that, Mama," she said in a little-girl voice.

Dorothy returned the hug, grasping Robin so tightly that

she couldn't wiggle free. When Dorothy did finally allow her to draw away, Robin saw that Dorothy's blue eyes were moist.

Eunice sat in the sand with the two blankets hooded over her head and wrapped around her body.

Why would Dorothy want to take Birdie? She was a sick, lonely lady, but so what—the streets were full of lonely sickies who didn't go around snatching twelve-year-old kids. Besides, why Birdie?

Okay—fine, Eunice. Why *not* Birdie?

From the moment that cardboard-faced crazy came into the picture, she'd taken over the whole operation, suckering Marc into thinking she was just what Birdie needed. Had Dorothy planned it that way? A goddamned intrigue, plotted and executed by someone as tight-assed as Dorothy Cotton? Give it up, Eunice.

She took two candles from the canvas bag, lit them and stood them in the sand. Then she picked up the snapshot again and stared at the picture of Amelia. Dammit, she reminds me of somebody, I've seen her somewhere.

Who is she, Birdie, who the hell is she?

Robin thought out the words very carefully before she wrote them in her diary:

Dear Diary,
I'm sorry for my temper tantrum yesterday and for all the other bad things I do. I'm going to try to behave better, I really am. While I was sitting all alone and so scared in the room with the snake, I had lots of time to think about Mama. And that's when I realized she was punishing me for my own good. The way I see it now, she didn't really have much choice.

*I guess she knows all the right things to do, and I
don't. But I hope she won't give up on me, because I'd
be a pretty sad case without her around to teach me
right from wrong. Oh, yeah, when I baked my first cake
today, it was fun. So was learning how to knit. Maybe
I can surprise Mama, and when I'm done with the scarf
wrap it up with fancy paper and ribbon and give it to
her as a gift.*

Robin was curled up snug under the blankets when
Dorothy came in, unlocked the diary and read the first entry
by the night light. Robin had made amazing progress—she
had surely sneaked a look at Amelia's diary.

The fact was, these were still Robin's own words, and
even if she didn't quite believe them herself yet, after
thinking and writing them enough times she would come to
believe them. Repetition was all part of the learning process.

She refastened the diary, set it back on the nightstand, and
headed for her bedroom. Maybe one of these days Robin
would hide the diary the way Amelia had—making Dorothy
hunt around the bedroom every night until she found it.

She and Amelia were always playing secret, fun games,
and the best part of all was that neither of them ever had to
explain the rules of the games to the other—they knew
instinctively. Amelia was that connected to Dorothy.

And someday Robin would be too.

Robin had taken the pink and white sweatsuit and pink
cotton jacket from the closet and quickly dressed. For the
first time, she looked at Amelia's foot locker. She stooped
down, opened it, then took out the Camp Raintree flashlight
she knew would be inside; ever so carefully she raised the
window, then the screen, climbed over the sill and dropped
to the ground.

She looked around, her eyes straining to adjust to the darkness. She could go out front and run along the deserted paved road she had seen yesterday, but if Dorothy discovered her missing she would follow her in the car. Better to go through the woods. If she went far enough, she'd have to come out somewhere.

She made her way quietly through the backyard and into the woods, turned on the flashlight and began to run.

CHAPTER 18

I⊤ was after eight o'clock by the time Curtis got hold of the director of the Larchmont Chapel, apparently the only one with authority to go into the files.

"You know, this is my second request for information on this same child—some fellow from Boston wanted to know. Can't remember the name now, but—"

"Marcus Garr?"

"Yeah, that's it."

"Okay. Just read me what you've got."

"Let's see . . . There's an address in Los Angeles, 2694 Remington Road—that's for the parents. Then a notation here says Raintree, that's in Bangor, Maine. The Garr fellow reminded me that Bangor was where the girl drowned, where we picked up the body."

"Where was the girl buried?"

"That I don't know."

"Christ, isn't it in your records?"

"It would be if we had done the burying. But since it's not here, the family must have taken care of that themselves.

Sometimes people want to do the burial out of state, whatever.''

''Who was the body released to?''

''Sorry, not here, and I grant you it should be. But I'd lay you money it was the guardian of the deceased. There's no way we'd release the body to just anyone—we've been in business fifty years now, and we run a proper operation.''

Curtis hung up the telephone, wondering if his next call should be to the Bangor police.

Marcus tried Eunice's number when he stopped for gas. Still no answer. He called Mollie and filled her in on his conversation with Dorothy's brother.

''The thing that hit me is Dorothy going back over and over to the spot where her sister was killed. I can still hear him saying it. Listen, Mollie, do you suppose . . .''

''I know what you're about to ask, and yes, it's possible. People often go back to the scene of the death when they can't let go.''

''One more thing, Mollie—if history repeats itself with child abuse the way they say it does, then it's a pretty good bet that Dorothy's an abuser, am I right?''

A pause, then, ''Well, I was thinking about Robin's obsession with her back, how I kept saying I was missing something. It finally dawned on me that the feeling was probably brought on by something she actually saw, something too painful to remember. So to answer your question, yes—my best guess would be that Amelia had some telltale signs of abuse that Robin saw.''

When Marcus got off the phone with Mollie, he called Curtis and told him about his visit with Justin Cotton.

''Christ, it fits,'' Curtis said. ''I just found out Amelia Lucas' body wasn't buried by the chapel that did the funeral. The body was picked up—supposedly by her guardian, who I assume would be her mother—and taken away for burial elsewhere.''

"You think maybe up near the camp?"

"I don't know, I was just about to— Hold on, I've got a call.'' When Curtis came back, he said, "That was the Connecticut Bank and Trust. Seems Dorie Lucas withdrew thirty thousand in savings on August twentieth. She also passed papers on her house that same day, netted a hundred and fifty thousand dollars from that. The bad news is, three days in advance she made a request to be paid in cash, so there's no checks to trace.''

"Damn.''

"How far are you from here, Marcus?''

"I hit some bad traffic earlier, but at this point I'd say ten minutes, tops.''

"Okay, let me see, it's near nine now. Why don't I give Bangor police a call, see what I can find out about bank accounts, purchases of property, cemeteries. In the meantime, you should know the FBI's been notified. I suspect you'll be hearing from them tonight, tomorrow morning at the latest.''

Dorothy's thoughts turned again and again to Robin's heartwarming diary entry. Not just the regret so appropriately expressed but her plan to give the knitted scarf to her Mama as a gift. It was something she wouldn't have expected of Robin, not after the long years during which her insensitivity and selfishness had been allowed to go unpunished. And though Dorothy expected her labors on Robin's behalf to bear fruit eventually, she hadn't expected such a quick flowering.

So even though she had been in Robin's bedroom less than an hour before, Dorothy felt one of those urges impossible for any mother to ignore—she needed to go and take one last peek at Robin before she could sleep.

Dorothy stood up and gasped as a warmth swept through her body—an intense rush that no man on earth could possibly give her. Was there anything, anything at all as precious and pure and innocent as a little girl asleep?

Robin had run what seemed like a long way before she stopped to rest. At first she thought she might have come to the end of the woods when she saw the clearing, but then she noticed the big white shiny stones and realized she had come to a cemetery. She backed up a little.

Come on now, give me a break. Since when have you been scared of cemeteries?

I never visited one alone in the middle of the night before.

Big deal. What's gonna happen at night that can't happen in the day? They're all just corpses, right?

Yeah, I suppose.

So what do you think this is, Night of the Living Dead? Rest here a while—it's as good a place as any.

Then what?

Then try to find a road. Where there's a cemetery, there's a road for people to drive into. Right?

Hey, good idea. You know, you may not be so dumb after all.

Robin sat on the cold base of one of the gravestones and rested her head against the tall white plaque. She shined her flashlight around—it was only a small cemetery, maybe a hundred graves in all. What caught her eye was the pinkish glow circling several gravestones off to her right. Could that be some kind of fence?

A pink fence?

Curtis had just put down the telephone when Marcus burst into his office.

"Well?" Marcus said.

"They'll get right on it, but don't get your hopes up. It could be a few hours before they locate the right bank—assuming the lady has an account in one of them—then get someone in to open up the registry records, assuming she's bought property in the area. They're also going to check out the local cemeteries."

"How far is the airport from here?"

"An hour. Hey, look, this is still pure speculation, Marcus. I don't know if you ought to go running down there just yet. And then there's the FBI to consider."

"What about local airports, can I hire a plane?"

Curtis sighed and handed him the Yellow Pages.

Robin had been staring only a couple of minutes when she stood up and made her way to the small gathering of gravestones. A family plot? One large center stone, three smaller ones surrounding it. The weird part was the huge shiny pink-painted boulders circling the plot and setting it off like some kind of Do Not Enter barricade.

She swallowed hard, then stepped onto one of the two-foot-high boulders, then down inside the circle of gravestones. She shone the flashlight beam onto one of the inscriptions:

1964–1972
Here lies my first loving daughter,
Amelia Cotton

Cotton could that—? No, her name wasn't really Cotton, it was Lucas.

Robin beamed the light on the next small stone:

1978–1990
Here lies my second loving daughter,
Amelia Lucas

Ohmygosh! Amelia *here?*

She took three deep breaths, then her heart drumming against her chest, stepped over to the last small stone. Biting down hard on her lip, she directed the beam of light and read the inscription:

1978–
Here lies my third loving daughter, Amelia Garr.

The scream was out of her throat before she could stop it. She dropped the flashlight, dived to retrieve it—and ran smack into the large center gravestone. Her eyes only inches from the inscription, she read:

1959–
Here lies Mama,
Dorothy Cotton Lucas

Forgetting the flashlight, Robin got up, tripped as she crossed the boulders, then got up again and ran, her legs going so fast she could no longer feel her feet hit ground.

When she heard the screams, Eunice had just made the connection—Amelia's pale, slightly pinched, pretty looks in the snapshot reminded her of *Do-ro-thy!*

And she had damned well heard something, she was sure of it. She cupped her hands over her mouth and screamed back: "BIRDIE! IT'S ME, EUNICE. ANSWER, DAM-MIT!"

She knelt on the ground, rummaged through the burlap bag and shoved the jackknife, matches and a couple of candles into her coat pocket.

Then put on her sneakers, picked up her flashlight and headed in the direction of the scream.

• • •

Though the Bangor police hadn't gotten back to them, both Curtis and Marcus had been on the telephone with three airline services, trying to get a private plane to fly out that night to Bangor.

Curtis looked up. "Marcus, I've got a guy here who can take you to Massachusetts, land you in a small airport in Burlington. That's the best he can do."

"How long a drive to the airport?"

"Ten minutes, and he'll leave as soon as you get there. A forty-minute flight time."

"Tell him I'll take it."

"What about—"

Marcus picked up another line and called Shari in Boston. It rang six times before she finally answered.

"Marcus here. Don't talk, just listen." He looked at his watch. "I'm in Connecticut now, I'll be arriving at Burlington Airport about ten-thirty. I need a flight to Bangor, Maine, waiting for me when I get there. Call the guys we've used before. If you can't get them, call Judge Weitzman, tell him to pull strings if he has to, but it's urgent. Any questions?"

"I have it, Marcus."

Dorothy had been driving slowly down the long mountainous road for fifteen minutes before she pulled over to the shoulder. Robin could never have covered such a long distance in so short a time.

She swung the car around and headed back up the mountain until she came to the road leading to the cemetery. She turned in and, despite the bumpiness of the gravel beneath the car tires, picked up speed. If Robin wasn't at the cemetery, Dorothy could always drive farther down to the Camp Raintree road and wait for her there . . .

• • •

Run, Robin, run.
  My grave.
  Faster, go faster.
  My grave.
  Don't stop, don't—
  What?
  A motor, something . . .
  Hearing things.
  Am not—look.
  Headlights—a car!
  Wait, maybe—
  Can't let it miss me.
  But—
She raised both arms in the air above her head and ran to the center of the road.

CHAPTER 19

MARCUS, now on the plane alone with his thoughts, kept replaying Mollie's latest theory: it was Amelia's abuse that Robin's conscious mind had been tuning out all along. Bruises, burns, cuts, what, where, and dammit, hadn't anyone seen it, reported it? And what about now, would Dorothy hurt Robin? No, not intentionally, but in the name of discipline? Or to protect Robin from herself? Wasn't that what she'd been doing when she punished her little sister?

Obsessions, compulsions—most people managed to deal with those quirks without letting them get too out of hand, right? The "step on a crack, break your mother's back" nonsense—hadn't just about every kid gone through that one? Well, how strong were Dorothy's compulsions, how far would they push her?

He suddenly remembered something. It was something so unimportant that he felt he ought to be laughing, but instead a shudder shook him. Had Dorothy rearranged his kitchen cabinets because she had no choice?

• • •

The horror and shock of running directly into Dorothy's arms had made Robin's throat so tight it was impossible to scream. In her head she counted the slaps Dorothy's hand made on her face. Twelve in all, and she hadn't felt one of them.

Dorothy pulled a length of clothesline from her pocket, wrapped and tied her wrists together, then her ankles. Finally her strong arms lifted Robin into the back of the station wagon.

Before long Robin felt those arms lift her again and carry her back to the pink and white bedroom. Dorothy laid her onto the bed, released her wrists, undressed her down to her underwear—then, suddenly, with the length of rope still tied to each wrist, she yanked her arms upward, leaving no slack, tying Robin's wrists, then her ankles to the four white bedposts. Robin began to cry.

"It seems to me you should have thought of the consequences earlier," Dorothy said. "That's your major failing, Robin, you don't think things through, you simply act. Just like my first little Amelia. And thanks to your destructive influence, my second Amelia fell into that same dangerous habit. And both of them are now dead because of it. Doesn't that make you pause to wonder about your actions?"

"I'm sorry," Robin whispered.

"Words are meaningless, Robin. You must *feel* sorrow to know what it truly is. It's a deep, bleeding, pulsating wound that makes your insides constrict and shudder. And before I'm through with you, you will know the feeling well."

"How long . . ." Robin dipped her head toward the ropes, but Dorothy left the room without even tossing a cover over her. She shivered, already cold; her arm and leg muscles already aching from the tension of the rope stretching her limbs.

• • •

The bedroom door opened. Was Dorothy coming back to give her something to eat? A blanket, a lecture, a bullet, a—

Wiggling on the edge of the thick stick Dorothy carried was the snake! She walked over to the bed and held it just above Robin's stomach.

"No!" Robin screamed. "Please don't—oh, please don't!"

"Hush, Robin. I want you to listen carefully because I will only say this once."

Robin caught her breath, looked up at Dorothy, then again at the snake . . .

"Though this snake is not poisonous, it surely does bite. And it's very likely to bite if a person moves or makes loud noises to scare it.

"So if you lie here and take your punishment like a good girl, you're apt to come out of this without a mark on your body. On the other hand, if you scream or cry or thrash about, this punishment will be even harder on you. In which case, Mama will have a lot of doctoring to do in the morning. So you see, it's all up to you. It might help to keep in mind that snakes are simply another of God's creatures. Just like you and I are, Robin."

Every muscle in Robin's body went rigid as Dorothy laid the snake on her stomach. She could feel its thick leathery skin slowly move across her own skin. She watched Dorothy place straight-backed chairs against the bed frame, barricading the snake.

Leaving the night light on, Dorothy headed out of the room.

"Goodnight, dear."

It seemed to Eunice that she walked for hours, but actually it was only fifty minutes before she came to a tall chain-link fence. She slipped the flashlight into her jacket pocket, then grabbed the top bar with both hands. She dug the toe of her sneaker into one of the fence grates, pushing herself upward: her toe slipped out of the hole, both feet sliding down to the ground. She tried again, this time maneuvering her body to the top bar, then swinging both legs over the fence and tumbling into a pile of leaves on the other side.

She stood up, got out her flashlight and beamed it in all directions: woods, woods, and more woods. But the scream had come from up here, she was certain. And hadn't she seen a rooftop when she looked this way earlier in the day? She started to walk again, her steps quickening as she went . . .

I'm coming, Birdie. Hang in there, I'm coming!

When the plane touched down briefly in Burlington, Marcus called Curtis.

"Did Bangor police—"

"Nothing yet. You make your flight connection?"

"The plane's fueling now."

"Okay. Bangor police will be waiting to meet you, apparently the field where you're landing is about fifteen miles out. How long you figure it'll take you to get there?"

"The pilot says an hour."

"I'll notify them right away. By the time you get there, they may have something concrete."

"Then you don't think I'm on a wild-goose chase?"

"I think you have to follow your instincts. If it were my kid, I'd be right where you are now."

Eunice . . . Eunice, where are you?
I'm right here.
I don't want you, I want Eunice.
Gee, thanks. What's wrong with me?

Can you get this snake off me?

No, but—

*But nothing. Eunice can. She's the only one who can.
Even Daddy would have to use a stick to pick it up.*

Well, who knows, maybe she'll come.

*Oh yeah, sure. Her, Santa Claus, the Easter Bunny, the
Tooth Fairy, and Sting, all riding up in the same van.*

Remember, whatever Eunice wants, Eunice gets.

*Yeah, I remember. Why do we always think that about
her?*

*Because she used to go around the house singing it so
much, she brainwashed us into believing it.*

That's funny.

Then why aren't you laughing?

*The same reason I'm not crying. You know, I don't know
how much longer I can lie here and not scream. I can feel—*

*Don't think about it, don't talk about it. Just keep your
eyes closed and sing to yourself so it's real loud inside.
Come on, I'll even sing along with you.*

I've got a wicked bad voice.

You don't suppose mine's much better, do you?

Uh-uh . . . Okay, what do we sing?

Whatever Eunice wants, Eunice gets . . .

Eunice didn't stop until she reached the cemetery. And she
wouldn't have stopped there if, when she shone the flashlight around the cemetery, she hadn't spotted the pink
glow . . .

She went toward it, stopping when she came to the
boulder barricade. *What is this, some kind of private club?*
Finally she leaned forward, directed the beam of light, and
read the inscription on the center gravestone: *Dorothy
Cotton Lucas.*

She stepped over the barricade, stooped down and picked

a flashlight from the ground: a blue and silver flashlight marked with the Camp Raintree insignia. Aha! She pocketed it, turned and read the inscriptions on the gravestones surrounding the larger one.

When she came to the one for Amelia Garr, she froze . . .

This was the ninth time Dorothy had wound up the silver sixteenth-century music box since leaving Robin's bedroom, yet still she hadn't been able to repress the pain tearing at her insides. Well, she would keep replaying the tune—twelve times, twenty-four times, thirty-six times, or all night if that's what was necessary to get her through Robin's dreadful punishment.

Was tonight an omen? Robin having taken the route through the cemetery rather than the logical route along the roadway? Had Robin sensed Amelia's presence, and had she needed to go to her? And if so, did that mean that Robin now knew about the family plot?

If so, she also knew that it was Dorothy's intention to change her name to Amelia. She had wanted to wait a little longer, talk it over with her so that the child could get used to the idea. In fact, she had planned on their outing tomorrow to show Robin the family gravestones.

Now, no matter what Robin was suffering or what temporary anger she might be feeling toward Dorothy, at least she knew deep down where it counted that her Mama loved her and had every intention of taking care of her. Not just in this world, but in the next world as well.

So you see, Robin, there's nothing you could do—absolutely nothing, no matter how sinful or selfish—that would convince Mama to abandon you to the others who would only hurt you.

Yes, dear, mothers are like that.

• • •

After leaving the cemetery Eunice had quickened her pace, but it was nearly forty minutes before she saw the speck of light filter through the trees. As she got closer, she saw that the light was coming from a house—one of those rooftops she had spotted earlier. She stood at the edge of the woods long enough to catch her breath, then quietly entered the yard, stalking the back of the house.

She peeked in the first window . . . the kitchen. A dim light above the stove was lit. The next window was the bathroom, and in the next there was a night light. Standing on tiptoe, nose pressed to the windowpane, she looked inside, but the small light was not bright enough to really see anything. Finally, she lifted her flashlight and shined it in . . .

Holy shit, was that a snake crawling . . . on top of somebody?

A uniformed police officer who introduced himself as Officer Phillips met Marcus at the airstrip, waited until he got into the back of the patrol car, then read from a sheet of paper.

"According to the registry of deeds, a Dorothy Lucas bought the property at Five-eleven Route Ninety-two on August thirtieth of this year. So what do we do now?"

"We go," Marcus said. "And fast."

Phillips pulled out onto the road and pushed the accelerator to the floor.

"This is a kidnapping?" he said.

"Yes. My daughter."

"That right? I never worked on one of those."

"Maybe you ought to radio in for some backup."

"I would, but my radio's bummed out. I had to use a pay phone to get the report from the registry. We could stop at the station first if you want, it's less than three miles out of the way.''

"You do carry a gun, right?" Marcus asked.

"Sure thing." Phillips put his hand to his waist.

"Forget it, then," Marcus said. "No stops. Just get us to that address."

When Robin saw the beam of light strike the wall, then the bed, she knew someone was standing at the window, looking in . . . Her first instinct was to scream, but she swallowed it down hard, waiting.

It was less than a minute after the light landed on her face that she heard the screen slide up, then the window. Trying to avoid sharp movement, Robin slowly turned her head— and she saw Eunice's face, Eunice's shoulders, Eunice's leg, her other leg, then suddenly Eunice was standing in the room!

She ran over to the bed, picked up the snake with both hands and heaved it through the open window. Then, taking her jackknife from her pocket, she sawed through the clothesline, releasing Robin's hands and feet. Robin flew into her arms, and Eunice planted kisses all over her face and neck, making their tears run together.

"Let's get out of here," Eunice finally whispered into her ear.

Eunice got a jacket from the closet, then a pair of pants, shirt and sneakers. She hurried back to Robin.

"Looks like a January pink sale in there." She helped Robin quickly into the clothes, then together they headed toward the window.

"Just what do you think you're doing?" Dorothy said as she snapped on the overhead light. The stainless-steel butcher knife clenched in her fist was pointed at Eunice.

• • •

Marcus had been chewing his lip and tapping his hand against the back of the front seat.

"Hey, take it easy, we're almost there."

"How much longer?"

"Four miles, five at the most."

"Dammit, something's wrong."

"Like I say, it won't be long—"

"Now. Something's wrong *now*!"

"Come to Mama, Robin," Dorothy said.

Eunice pushed Robin closer to the window with one hand, lifted one of the straight-backed chairs with the other.

"Birdie, climb through the goddamned window. And run like your backside's on fire!"

"No," Robin cried. "I'm waiting for you!"

Dorothy took a step toward Eunice. And another. Eunice swung the chair and threw it at her; Dorothy reeled, stumbled against the wall and regained her balance just as Eunice brought another chair down on her shoulder.

Dorothy was now doubled over, panting.

"The window, Birdie—come on!" Eunice swept her up onto the windowsill.

"Watch out, Eunice!"

Eunice turned in time to see Dorothy rush her with the knife. Eunice jerked away: the knife grazed her shoulder, but Eunice swung out, smashing her in the face twice, then grabbed for the knife.

They struggled, wrestling with the knife until Eunice stumbled over a chair, falling on the floor, stomach down with Dorothy on top of her, holding the knife.

Robin, now off the windowsill, picked up one of the chairs and cracked it across Dorothy's head, but not before the knife cut into Eunice's leg.

Both Eunice and Dorothy were now on the floor. Robin rushed to the bathroom to find something to tie off Eunice's wound. Just as she turned away from the linen closet, Dorothy's arm came around her. In her hand, she held the knife. She reached into the medicine cabinet with her other hand, took the bottle of sedatives and slipped it into her pocket.

"Come with me, dear. It's time."

When the squad car pulled up at the house, the station wagon was in the driveway. Phillips ran around the back, Marcus took the front door. He tried the doorknob—it was locked—and started banging.

Finally he went to the front parlor window, threw a rock through it, cleared the glass out of the way and climbed inside.

"Anyone here?" he shouted.

Nothing.

He ran through the living room and down the hall, finally coming to a bedroom. That's when he saw the trail of blood.

They walked quickly through the woods. In step, Dorothy beside Robin.

"Oh dear, it's so chilly. Amelia, look at you, you should have put on warmer clothing. Dear me, what could have been going through my mind, not paying attention to what you were wearing? I swear, you girls are all alike, like three little piggies in a blanket. If Mama didn't watch you closely, you'd run around in short pants right through the winter. And Mama would be having to nurse all her little girls back to health."

Robin didn't know which she hated most, the feel of the blade touching her throat or the feel of Dorothy's arm around her shoulder.

"But I think this late-night visit is important, dear. Sometimes we have to take risks we wouldn't normally take. It's very much like the sedatives, Amelia. Drugs are risky—dangerous, even—yet sometimes their use is justified. And visiting the cemetery in the chilly night air is risky, but then you'll be able to be with your sisters."

In her free hand, Dorothy held a flashlight. She beamed the light straight ahead, picking out the pink ring . . .

Ring around the rosy, a pocket full of posies . . .

Marcus followed the spots of blood down the hallway, through the kitchen and out onto the back porch.

Phillips called out to him from the backyard.

"I've got a lady here who was trying to get away into the woods. She the one you're looking for?"

"Get your paws off me, you dickless son of a bitch!"

"Eunice!"

He found her kneeling on the ground, fighting to get free of Phillips' grip.

"Leave her alone!" Marcus yelled.

He knelt down beside her, got out of his coat, tore free a part of the coat lining and tied a tourniquet around her leg.

"Jesus, Eunice, what happened?"

"She's got Birdie, Marc."

"I know. Where are they?"

Eunice pointed into the woods. "There's a cemetery about a mile down. She has a knife."

Marcus looked at Phillips. "Is there an easier way there, maybe a road?"

He shrugged. "Hey, I haven't lived here that long. But we could get in the car, try some roads."

"No, we'll stick with what we know. Look, you get her back to the house, I'll get a head start and—"

"No way." Eunice grabbed onto the branch of a tree and hoisted herself up. "I'm going."

"You'll never be able to walk—"

"Then you'll help me. Come on."

Marcus grabbed one arm; Phillips grabbed the other. They headed into the woods.

Dorothy had lifted Robin over the boulders. Now they were sitting on the ground together, facing the tombstones, Robin in Dorothy's lap, the knife blade tight against her throat.

"I know this comes as something of a surprise to you, Amelia, but there was just no need to frighten you in advance. And now that I'm telling you, I don't want you to be the least bit afraid—Mama's going to be right there with you, all the way. Surely you don't think I'd let you take such a long journey alone, do you?"

With the fingers of one hand she combed Robin's hair away from her face.

"No, of course I wouldn't do that—once you reach the girls, you tell them I'm on my way. And it won't hurt, not at all. You must understand, Amelia, this isn't a punishment. And once this is done, there will be no more punishments. Mama will be watching over you and your sisters and no one will ever, ever be able to hurt any of you again."

Ashes, ashes, all fall down.

"The thing is, dear, it's getting harder and harder to take care of all you girls, having to run back and forth like this. And there are wicked people around who would surely like to break up our family. But they'd have to wake up pretty early in the morning to be able to put something over on your Mama. But then you know that, dear, don't you? Why, from the very beginning you saw that I was the only one strong enough to protect you."

• • •

Despite Eunice's bad leg, they made good time. Marcus spotted Dorothy and Robin in the pink circle from fifty yards away. He knocked Phillips' lantern so that the beam pointed down.

"Look," Phillips said, "I don't like the look of this, I think we ought to go get some backup."

"Fuck that, there's no time." Marcus pointed to the gun. "What's the story, do you know how to use that thing?"

Phillips took it out. "Hey, yeah, but I'm no marksman. It's dark as hell out here. Besides, I'm not gonna get a clear shot at her with the kid right there."

"I've got an idea," Eunice said.

Dorothy, satisfied that Amelia understood what she was going to do, lifted her off her lap and stood up next to her.

"Now, Amelia, I want you to take off your jacket and shirt, and lie down right on your nice smooth white stone. It'll be like taking a long nap. No more nightmares, no more being scared, no one to ever bother or hurt you again. Just the four of us, one happy family."

Amelia just stood there. Dorothy shook her head, then helped her out of her jacket.

"Now, why are you trembling, dear? Didn't Mama tell you not to be afraid?"

Suddenly a voice—a sweet, smooth, little girl's voice— came from the woods.

Mama! Help me, I'm lost!

Dorothy jerked to attention.

It's me, Mama, A-me-lia.

Dorothy glanced at the child in front of her.

"Amelia? Which Amelia?"

Which one do you think?

"Where are you, dear?"

I'll tell if you promise you won't get mad.

"Ah-hah. Now I know, it's my little dickens, my little imp. Now you tell me this instant, where are you?"

I know I shouldn't of done it, but I left our circle, Mama. I went into the woods, then I got lost. And I can't find my way back.

Dorothy took a wide step over the boulders.

"Oh, dear, dear me, always my little mischief-maker—what is Mama going to do with her Amelia?" She took a step toward the bushes, then another. "Haven't I told you—"

Then something hit her hard.

Marcus had been huddled between two trees, a good twenty feet from Eunice. Now he lunged out at Dorothy and brought her to the ground. He grabbed her hand and twisted it until she dropped the knife. He lifted the knife and tossed it into a bush. Phillips ran over, took her, and Marcus stood up.

Then with tears running down his cheeks, he looked at Robin standing silently in the circle. *God, dear God.* He rushed over and scooped her up into his arms. She wrapped her arms tightly around him.

"Daddy? Eunice?"

He turned with her so she could see Eunice limping toward them, laughing and crying and singing out, "Birdie!" all at the same time.

The three of them had already started back when Phillips finally cornered Dorothy inside the pink ring . . . He pried her hands from the gravestones and snapped the cuffs on her wrists.

EPILOGUE

It was December twentieth . . . a light snow was dusting the streets of Boston. Robin, who had arrived at Mollie's office ten minutes late for her appointment, got out of her purple ski parka, knitted hat and gloves and settled into her seat across from Mollie.

Mollie held out a plate of Christmas cookies.

"You made these?" Robin said.

"Well, me and that guy, Duncan Hines."

"Want a quote from the Dorothy Cotton rule book?"

"Okay, I'm ready—hit me with it."

First Robin stood up and took on a stiff Dorothy pose: "My dear, packaged goods are for the inept and lazy—the bozos and baboons of the universe."

Laughing, Mollie leaned forward. "Come on now, did she really say that?"

"Just the first part. The last of it is a Robin Garr original."

Twenty minutes into the session, Robin said, "If all that horrible stuff happened to Dorothy, why would she go do those same things to Amelia? And then me?"

"Because to her sick way of thinking, it was a way to protect you. If she could only make you perfect—at least, perfect as she saw it—then no one would dare harm you."

"But she *was* harming me. She must have known I hated it, must have hated what was done to her."

"That's the point, Robin—it's all she knew. A lot of abused children grow up and do it to their own children because it was done to them. By the people they most loved and trusted."

"I still don't get why I forgot it all—I mean, I really didn't remember seeing Amelia's back or reading the diary or any of it."

"Forgetting is often a way of escaping something too painful to remember. I'd say your escape mechanism most likely switched on the night Amelia drowned."

"Why then?"

"I think I know, but I'd rather you tell me."

Robin thought about it, then suddenly as if she had finally hit upon a lost scrap of information, she looked up at Mollie. "I don't get it, how could you even know?"

"Because it's a natural response, Robin. Now it's just a matter of your admitting it."

Robin bit down hard on her lip and her eyes became moist.

"Because way deep inside, I thought that maybe Amelia was better off dead. Then the moment I thought such an awful thing, I felt so guilty I wanted to die."

At the end of their session, Mollie walked Robin to the door and stood watching her bundle up.

"All set for Christmas?"

"Yup. Just picked up your present yesterday, it was on special order. Wait'll you see it, you'll bust."

Mollie smiled. "I hear Eunice will be spending Christmas day with you and your Dad."

Robin smiled. "Who told you, Daddy?"

"Actually, it was Eunice. She breezed in the other day after her visit with you."

"She tell you about her drinking—or I should say, her not drinking? Aside for one glass of wine on November twelfth, she hasn't touched booze since that night in Maine. Daddy asked her if she joined A.A. but the only thing she admits to is yoga."

"She's quite a ticket, your mother. It's easy to see where you get your chutzpah."

"What's that?"

"Spunk, spirit, backbone, arrogance, boldness. A lot of real neat things."

"Then you do think Daddy will go back with her?"

"Look, I know it's what you want, Robin, and I'd love to see it happen too. But who knows, maybe we're both just a couple of hopeless romantics. In any case, it's not up to us, it's up to Eunice and your Dad—alcoholics can often stop drinking, but most of them can't stay stopped—at least, not without help. And we don't know that Eunice is getting any help."

"Well, New Year's is coming up, I don't suppose it can hurt to make it my wish."

"I think you've got that wrong—it's supposed to be resolutions, not wishes."

"Who makes up those rules?"

"No one person in particular, it's just tradition."

Robin worked her fingers into her gloves, then as if she had settled an issue, shook her head.

"I say, hang tradition, Mollie. This year, I'm going to go with a wish." She threw her arms around Mollie, hugged her, then with a wide grin on her face, hurried outdoors.

443

New York Times bestselling author of
BLINDSIGHT

The Chilling National
Bestsellers . . .

ROBIN COOK

___MORTAL FEAR   0-425-11388-4/$5.99
A world-class biologist stumbles upon a miraculous
discovery, and the ultimate experiment in terror begins . . .

___OUTBREAK   0-425-10687-X/$5.99
Fear reaches epidemic proportions when a devastating
virus sweeps the country, killing all in its path. "His most
harrowing medical horror story." – The New York Times

___MUTATION   0-425-11965-3/$5.99
On the forefront of surrogate parenting and genetic
research, comes a novel of spine-chilling terror.   A
brilliant doctor's dream son is changing – becoming more
and more the doctor's worst nightmare . . .